IMPERFECT
SPIRAL

IMPERFECT SPIRAL

Debbie Levy

SCHOLASTIC INC.

ISBN 978-0-545-62992-8

12 11 10 9 8 7 6 5 4 3 2   13 14 15 16 17 18/0

Printed in the U.S.A.   40

First Scholastic printing, October 2013

For Rick Hoffman,
my husband, friend, and partner
in countless games of catch

IMPERFECT
SPIRAL

1

SOMETHING LIKE SLEEP

The morning after, I take refuge in my bed.

Each time I surface into consciousness, I will myself back down into sleep, or something like sleep. I don't think or dream about anything, unless a big, black canvas of nothingness counts. I feel my mother come into my room twice, once putting her hand on my forehead as if to feel for a fever.

"I'm not sick," I mumble.

"I know," she says. "I just wanted to touch your forehead."

Sometime later I feel another presence in my room; not my mother, though.

"Danielle."

It's Adrian. "What are you doing here?" I squint. "Don't you work on Saturdays?"

"I slept over," he says. "Thought I'd spend some quality time with my sister."

"Oh."

"Anyway," he says as I turn over to burrow, once again, into my bed and avoid whatever this day has to bring, "I'm not going to have quality time or quantity time with you if you sleep all day. It's one fifteen. Get up and I'll make you my award-winning salami omelet."

"I'll get up," I say into my pillow, "if you *don't* make me your award-winning salami omelet."

"That works, too," Adrian says. "See you downstairs."

When I flop into a kitchen chair fifteen minutes later, my washed hair dripping down the back of my T-shirt, Adrian puts a plate in front of me.

"But," I say.

"My award-winning cheese omelet. No salami."

Mom and Dad appear as I take the first bite.

"How're you feeling this morning, Danny?" Dad asks.

Empty. But I don't want to say that out loud.

"Numb," I say. Numb is true, too.

"Understandable," he says.

I chew and swallow, chew and swallow. Mom and Dad sit down at the table with me.

"Want to talk?" Dad asks.

"How about later?" I counter.

"Later is fine," he says.

Adrian finishes drying the omelet pan and sits, too.

"Someone's already started one of those roadside memorials," he says. "Stuffed animals. Flowers."

"You know, in some places they're not allowed," Mom says.

"You mean like certain streets?" Adrian asks.

"No, I mean some cities and towns, also some states, have laws against them," Mom says. "Or at least regulate them. On the theory that they're distracting to motorists, or an improper use of property."

"How about here?" Adrian asks.

"No, I don't think we have any rules about them," Mom says. "It's easy enough to check."

"I get the sense you think these rules are a good idea?" Adrian says.

"No," Mom says. "I was just—saying."

"But you don't like them," Adrian says. "The roadside memorials, I mean. Not the rules. You do like the rules, I gather."

This is how things begin between Adrian and Mom. I don't know whether Mom is oblivious to the fact that her always-opinionated, never-neutral statements push Adrian's buttons. I don't know whether Adrian knows that Mom usually doesn't mean anything by it. That is, she does mean what she says, but she doesn't mean anything personal by it. Opinions course through her veins. It's who she is.

"I don't really have an opinion about it," Mom says. "I shouldn't have said anything." This is her disappointed voice, the voice that I know drives Adrian crazy.

But he's been able to let it go since he moved out last

February. He still seems compelled to call Mom out on things she says that push his buttons—so he can't just let her make her observation about roadside memorials without challenging her—but he doesn't have the need any longer to follow up with a full-blown argument. She, too, shrinks back these days from voicing her strongly opinionated dissertations on—everything. At least at home.

I eat; the talk shifts to nothing in particular, which is good. It's as though we're strangers sitting at the same table in one of those family-style restaurants. We feel the need to make conversation, because that is what polite people do, but we are careful to keep the conversation safe. Nothing to ignite sparks between Adrian and Mom. Nothing to upset me.

We aren't always like this. Adrian and Mom do rile each other up all the time, but they forge ahead in explosive conversational territory anyway. I am not always such a delicate flower in need of protection from the elements. But we aren't always having breakfast on mornings like this.

So: It's a beautiful day outside. Not too hot. We all agree on that, even me, although I haven't been outside. People always say you have to leave town in August if you don't want to stifle to death—today is August 1—but really, August just gets a bad rap. We all agree on that, too. August can be, and often is, really nice, not the heat-and-humidity hellhole people always say it is. August needs better publicity. Yes, it could use a good ad campaign. But then more people would stick around in August instead of heading off to the beach, and part of the charm of

August here in the suburbs of Washington, D.C., is that there is less traffic, shorter lines at movie theaters, more chances to get into the trendy restaurants. So we all agree to keep the considerable charms of August our little secret.

And that is that conversation.

The day oozes by. I sleep more. Adrian hangs around, which he is doing for me, which I appreciate. There is dinner, which he cooks. There is sleep, which I lunge into gratefully. And then there is another morning, which dawns despite my urgent request to the universe that the earth just stop in its tracks for a while.

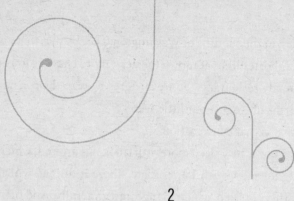

2

MORE OF A BLUR

This much is vivid and clear: my hands cradling Humphrey's head. I'm trying to make him comfortable, to cushion him from the unforgiving asphalt. He isn't crying or anything; he's very still, but I can feel him breathing.

The larger scene is more of a blur. Police. Neighbors. Ambulances. Fire trucks. A blanket to keep Humphrey warm—this is all before the flashing lights. Mrs. McGillicudy brings it out from her house. I want to tell her that Humphrey isn't cold; it's warm out and we've been running around, but I don't say anything. After tucking the blanket around Humphrey's legs, she squats beside me in the street. She says nothing; neither do I. At one point, she puts her arm around me.

The Stashowers are next on the scene, I believe.

"Oh my God. Oh my God," Mrs. Stashower cries.

"Who is it?" Mr. Stashower asks.

"It's Humphrey," I say. "Humphrey T. Danker."

"It's the little Danker boy," Mrs. McGillicudy says, and I realize that I didn't actually answer the question out loud.

"Oh my God," Mrs. Stashower repeats.

"Has anyone called 911?" her husband asks.

"Before I came out," Mrs. McGillicudy says.

"Stay there," Mr. Stashower yells. Stay there? Where else would I go? But he has his back to me. He isn't telling *me* to stay there. People must be gathered on the side of the street. "You kids stay there. Stay out of the street."

I hear car horns honking. We're holding up traffic. "Should we—move Humphrey?" I ask Mrs. McGillicudy. This time words do come out of my mouth.

"No, no," she says. "Whoever's honking doesn't know what's going on. They'll just have to wait."

Next, Mrs. Raskin appears. "Where are Tom and Clarice?" she asks.

"I'm babysitting," I say in a whisper. "They're out." Mrs. McGillicudy transmits this to Mrs. Raskin.

"Where are they?" Mrs. Raskin says.

They went to a movie. An early movie and late dinner, or early dinner and late movie, I'm not sure what the order of this Friday evening was. I have their cell phone numbers programmed into my phone, which somehow makes its way from my back pocket to Mrs. Raskin. Or to Mr. Stashower. To someone.

Then the rescue-squad people come. I look next to me and Mrs. McGillicudy is no longer there.

"What do I do—?" I ask the uniformed woman who's taken Mrs. McGillicudy's place.

"You've done a great job," she says. "I'm going to place my hands under yours. When I say 'okay,' that means I've got him and you can remove your hands."

"I don't know if I feel him breathing anymore," I say.

"That can be hard to detect," she says. "But we're going to take good care of him."

She relieves me of my place on the asphalt. Now it's her turn to be Humphrey's cushion.

Another rescue-squad person, a guy, sits on my other side. He looks into my eyes, checks my pulse, does a few other things you see on television shows where people get into car accidents or are found dazed at the scene of a crime. "How're you doing?" he asks. He is, I notice when he holds my hands to wash them with some stuff out of a bottle, unusually good-looking. He can't be more than six or seven years older than me. Maybe eight or nine years. My sense of being on the set of a television drama grows.

"Fine," I say, stupidly. "I mean, I'm not hurt. I didn't get hit by a car."

"No?" he says. "You're sure?"

Am I sure? Can you be unsure of such a thing?

A third rescue person, a woman, materializes. "We're

taking you to the ER so you can get checked out," she says. "Even if you feel fine, you need to be seen by a doctor."

"What about Humphrey?" Panic rises in my throat. "Shouldn't you be taking care of Humphrey?"

"He's got his own team. See?" says the woman. Four people hover over Humphrey, and a stretcher has been pulled alongside him. "We're taking care of you."

Two other paramedics wheel a stretcher over to me. "On three . . . ," one of them says, holding me under my elbows. I want to object, to point out that I walked here on my own two feet to the middle of the street and crouched down next to Humphrey, I wasn't bulldozed here by a car, I didn't even fall down, and if they want me on a stretcher, I can very simply stand up and put myself on a stretcher.

But I find, when I try to raise myself on my own two feet, that it isn't as simple as that. My knees buckle.

As the paramedics ease me onto the stretcher, I hear Mrs. Raskin talking—her voice loud and raspy as usual, matching her name—to Mrs. Stashower.

"They don't answer," she's saying. "They're not answering their cell phones. Who doesn't answer their cell phones when they leave their child with a babysitter? Isn't that the whole point of cell phones—so you can be reached in an emergency?"

"Oh my God," Mrs. Stashower says.

Mrs. McGillicudy appears again as I lie on the stretcher waiting to be lifted into the ambulance. No one answered the door or the phone at my house, she tells me. Were my parents reachable?

"Oh—my cell phone," I remember. "Mrs. Raskin."

While Mrs. McGillicudy goes to find Mrs. Raskin and my phone, my team of rescue workers lifts my stretcher into the ambulance.

"But she's got my phone," I object.

Either I don't say this out loud or I do and no one cares. The hunky guy and the woman climb in the back with me. Before the doors to the ambulance close, I notice, for the first time, the teal blue minivan at the head of the line of cars snaking backward on Quarry Road. It's the car closest to Humphrey, and its position in the lane is sort of skewed. From what I can see in the deepening dusk, the car hasn't suffered a bit of damage.

Humphrey, however, is still lying in the road. I see him vividly and clearly, despite the gathering darkness.

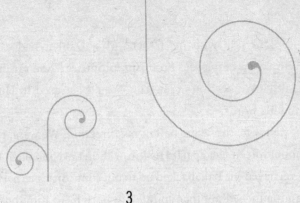

3

A PERFECT SPIRAL

I can throw a perfect spiral. Not only that, I can throw it hard, a spiral with speed. Humphrey was surprised by my football-throwing prowess—I saw it in his perfectly open and transparent face, the fair and transparent face of a blond, surprised in a totally delighted way. This was at the start of our summer together, when Humphrey and I were first getting to know each other.

"You can do that?" he squealed after the ball bounced out of his arms.

"I just did, didn't I?"

"It wasn't an accident?"

"Gimme the ball," I said, "babysitt*ee*."

"If you're the babysitter," he had said on my first day, "then I'm the babysitt*ee*."

"Law talk with his father," Mrs. Danker had explained. "Employer, employee. Promisor, promisee." She ran her hand gently over her son's crew cut. "You'll get used to Humphrey and his words."

Now he threw the ball in my direction. We were, I figured, about fifteen feet apart. His throw didn't even make it halfway. I retrieved the ball, backed up to put some distance between us, and launched another spiral. It was right to him, but the kid didn't have a chance. He really couldn't catch the ball.

"Wow!" Humphrey yelled. "Can you teach me?"

I don't know football. I don't follow the Ravens or Redskins, don't go to high school games, don't follow college play. But I do like to throw and catch a football.

"I don't know if I can teach you, exactly," I told Humphrey. "But I can play catch with you. I can help you practice."

"Oh, come on—teach me how to throw a spiral!"

I tried. I know nothing about the mechanics of passing, but I looked at my hands on the ball and tried to place Humphrey's hands like mine. No way. He had pretty big hands, it seemed to me, for a little kid—*he'll be tall when he grows up*, I thought— but he still couldn't really grip the football.

"Come on, Danielle," Humphrey said after sixteen unsuccessful attempts. "Try something different!"

"Follow me!" I exclaimed, running away from him. "To the spaceship!"

On the edge of the field was a small, kind of sad, toddler playground. It had a swing set, three bumblebees mounted on springs, a climbing gym about as big as a king-size bed, and a roundabout. It was deserted, as it usually was, not only because it was just about dinnertime, but also because there was a much better playground with all the latest equipment a few miles away.

I let Humphrey catch up with me. "To the spaceship!" he screamed. "Hurry, before they get us!"

Humphrey reached the roundabout, which was, as it had been on previous visits to this park, our spaceship.

"Don't leave me behind, Humphrey!" I pleaded. "Don't let them get me!"

When I reached the roundabout, I grabbed hold of one of the handles and spun it around a few times, creating momentum before I jumped on opposite Humphrey.

"Takeoff!" he screamed joyfully.

"Into the atmosphere!"

"Away from the . . . away from the . . ."

"Aliens!" I prompted him.

"Away from the aliens!" Humphrey said.

The roundabout spun for a surprisingly long time.

"Coming in for a landing," I said as we slowed down. "And . . . we're here."

Humphrey jumped off. "A new planet," he said. "It's never been discovered."

"We'll have to name it, then," I said.

Humphrey looked at the bumblebees and bugged out his eyes. Pointing, he screamed, "New aliens!"

"But could they be . . . friendly aliens?" I asked.

"Let's see," Humphrey said. He approached the bumblebees slowly. "I come in peace," he said, stretching out his hands. "Look, Danielle, they want me to ride them."

"That's very friendly," I said.

He climbed on the back of a bumblebee that used to be blue—most of the paint was worn off—and rocked himself to get the springy action going. After about a minute he stopped and got off. "Thanks, Bumble-Boo," Humphrey said. "His name is Bumble-Boo."

"That's a fine name," I said. "And the planet's name is . . ."

"The planet is Thrumble-Boo," Humphrey said.

"Thrumble-Boo?" I said. "Not Crumble-Boo? Maybe it's made up of cookie crumbs. Or Strumble-Boo? Maybe everyone here strums a banjo. Or Dumble-Boo? Maybe it's only for dumb aliens."

Humphrey fixed his serious green-eyed stare on me. "It is not for dumb aliens. There are no banjos or cookie crumbs. It's Thrumble-Boo. It's Thrumble-Boo because of . . . the thrumbles."

After a return spaceship ride to planet Earth, we set out for the walk home. Quarry Road was crammed with cars, slowly making their way in rush hour. I stretched out my free hand—the one not holding the football against my hip—and Humphrey took it.

"Danielle," Humphrey said.

"That's my name, don't wear it out."

"When I told you to try something different before, I meant

you should try something different to teach me how to throw a spiral."

Huh, I thought. And here I'd assumed that after sixteen efforts Humphrey had been ready to move on.

"Sorry, Humpty," I said. "I thought you were tired of that."

"No, Dumpty," said Humphrey. "I'm very persistent."

"You're persistent?" I asked. "Are you also a genius? How do you know the word 'persistent'?"

"I know lots of long *p* words," Humphrey said.

Long *p* words?

"Like what else?" I asked.

He thought. It was one thing to know them, another to remember them.

"Um," he said. "I forget. And anyway, I'm hungry!"

Twenty minutes later, Humphrey was sitting at his kitchen table shoveling SpaghettiOs into his mouth, followed by chasers of chicken tenders and cut-up apple chunks. His favorite meal.

"I remember some of my other long *p* words, Danielle," he said.

"I'm listening."

He swallowed before launching into his lexicon: *Particular. Persnickety. Pugnacious.*

"Wow," I said. "You are one smart boy."

He thanked me and continued.

Predictable. Prognosis. Perculiar.

"*Pe*-culiar," I corrected him.

"*Per*-culiar," he corrected me back. "My dad told me."

I seriously doubted that. I seriously doubted that the esteemed Thomas R. Danker, Esq., a famous lawyer who argues cases in front of the United States Supreme Court, gave his son incorrect instruction on how to pronounce a *p* word.

"It really is *pe*-culiar, Humpty," I said.

"I like *per*-culiar," he said.

I looked at his SpaghettiOs-stained face and smiled.

"I like perculiar, too," I said.

4

WHAT ABOUT HUMPHREY?

After three hours in the emergency room, I'm officially declared uninjured. By this time, my parents are at the hospital. As we emerge from the treatment room to the crowded waiting area, we see Adrian and a bunch of neighbors, including, no surprise, Mrs. Raskin.

"I keep my phone on vibrate, even in the theater," she is saying to Adrian.

"Sometimes you can't feel it vibrating," Adrian says.

"I hold the phone right in my hand," Mrs. Raskin replies. "That way I don't miss a call. And if—"

She breaks off when she sees us.

"They finally answered the phone," she says. "When the movie ended. They're with Humphrey. Unless he's being operated on. At any rate, they're here."

"Any word on him?" my father asks. "Does anyone know how Humphrey's doing?"

"Not yet," says Adrian.

Both sets of the Dankers' next-door neighbors are in the waiting room—the Crenshaws, who brought their three kids along, and the other couple, who don't have kids and whose name I don't know. There's also Mrs. Hermann, whose house is on the corner of Quarry and Franklin, right next to where the accident happened. Mr. Stashower, whose house is on the opposite corner of Quarry and Franklin. Mrs. McGillicudy, who lives on our street. She gives me a hug. So does Adrian, who also slips my phone into my hand.

"I had to pry it away from the crazy bat," he whispers in my ear. "I think she wanted to download your contacts."

I don't really get what he's saying. She what?

"Seriously—are you okay?" he asks.

"I don't know," I say. "Did you see Humphrey's parents?"

"Yeah. They came through the waiting room and went right back to wherever Humphrey's being treated."

"Did you see Humphrey?" I ask.

Adrian gives me a quizzical look. "How could I—"

"I thought maybe when they brought him in. Maybe you saw if he opened his eyes."

"I didn't get here until way after," Adrian says. "Anyway, they don't bring the ambulance patients through the waiting room."

Right. I should know that from those television dramas.

"Why is it so crowded in here?" I ask. Besides the neighbors, there are lots of people milling around.

"Friday night in the ER," Adrian says. "The end of the workweek. The beginning of the weekend. Doctors' offices are closed, and people start doing crazy weekend things."

I see my parents speaking with a policeman, over in a corner.

"You're probably going to have to talk with the cops," Adrian says.

"Right now?"

Couldn't they just talk to Mrs. Raskin or someone? Someone with lots of ideas about what happened out there?

"Well, soon, I bet. They'll want to get to you while your memory is fresh."

Mom and Dad come over. Yes, the police need to interview me. It will be a quick interview tonight. We don't have to go to the police station; they will come to the house. Just a few questions, and if they need more details, they'll follow up tomorrow.

"But what about Humphrey?" I ask.

"I'm sure the doctors are doing everything they can to help him," Mom says. "It's time to get you home."

"Tell us what happened. What time was it when you and Humphrey were walking home?"

"Around seven fifteen. Seven twenty. Maybe seven twenty-five by the time we were on Quarry near Franklin."

"You were playing with the football?"

There are two police officers in our living room, a man and a woman. They're taking turns asking the questions. I'm having a hard time focusing on who's saying what.

"Yes. We were playing with the football."

"So you're tossing the football back and forth while walking home?"

"Oh, no. No. We played with the football at the park. We did that a lot. We were just going home and we dropped the football and it rolled into the street and Humphrey ran after it."

"So when you say *we* dropped the football—"

"*I* dropped the football."

"And then."

"And it bounced into the street. Humphrey ran after it."

"Did you notice the car before it hit him?"

"No. I wasn't looking at the cars. I wasn't expecting Humphrey to run into the street."

"Did you notice if any cars seemed to be speeding, or driving recklessly?"

"No. I didn't notice anything like that."

"Could you describe the car that hit Humphrey?"

"I don't think I can describe it. It's like I sensed Humphrey getting hit more than I saw him getting hit."

"You didn't see the accident."

"I know I must have seen the accident, but what sticks in my mind is sensing that it happened. Sensing the—impact."

Weirdly, I also seem not to have heard the accident, which

may defy the usual laws of nature, or at least physics. But I don't tell the officers this.

"Were you distracted by something else when Humphrey ran into the street?"

"No. But I wasn't expecting him to run into the street, so I was surprised. It all happened so quickly."

"We understand," says the female half of the team. "So about the car that hit Humphrey—can you tell us anything?"

"Not really," I say. "Wasn't it the blue minivan?"

They don't answer my question. I guess *they* get to ask the questions here, not me.

"We're just trying to understand the sequence of events leading up to the accident," the man says. "Whether there was anything going on in terms of speeding, reckless driving, distractions, whatever."

I have no idea.

They take pity on me and say we're done for the night. If I remember anything, I should call them—they give me their cards. And they will probably want to talk to me more, but for now they know I need to settle down and try to get some rest.

The phone rings as soon as Dad closes the door behind the police officers. Mom picks it up in the kitchen, then comes to the living room where I'm still sitting. She settles next to me on the sofa, puts her arm around my shoulders, and squeezes.

"Humphrey didn't make it," she says.

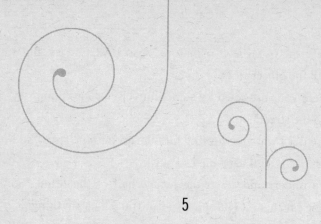

5

A Matter of Habit

Sunday—the morning after the morning after—the earth stubbornly continues to spin, and my buzzing phone forces me to give up fighting the daylight.

> I heard. Quelle tristesse. R u ok? I can't text or
> call as much as I'd like to—you know camp rules.

Becca. *Quelle tristesse* is like saying "How sad," only more so. French really is better at some things than English, and Becca likes to sprinkle French into her speech. And into her texts. She was in super-duper-advanced-AP-plus-plus French last year when we were freshmen. They've already run out of French classes for her to take. She adores French.

This summer Becca's been at camp, the camp I used to go to, and love, as well. She's a CIT. I didn't want to go back as a counselor-in-training and be a babysitter for a whole bunkful of little babysittees. I didn't think I'd be good at it.

It's more than that. It's more than whether I'd be good or bad at being a CIT. CITs have to be leaders—song leaders, cheerleaders, dance leaders, team leaders. Not my thing. So I stayed home for the first summer in six years and was a babysitter for just one little babysittee.

I'm okay. Thanks.

The phone buzzes again:

Vraiment?

That means "really," in case you're not as *française* as Becca and me.

Oui.

I take French, too. I'm not as fluent as Becca, but I can keep up with her in our texts.

Vraiment vraiment?

I hesitate. Then I type:

> I was holding him. He might have died in my
> arms.

> I am so sorry.
> You must be in pain.
> How awful for you.
> Danielle?

Three unanswered texts; she's wondering if I'm still here.

> Yes, thank you. I am. It is.

> Mon amie, it's the wake-up gong. Must go. Talk
> later.

I know that using your cell phone is basically forbidden at camp. I remember that if you're a counselor, you're allowed to have your phone in your possession—which isn't permitted if you're a mere camper—for use when you're off work. I don't know what the rule is for CITs, but I'm sure Becca won't be getting to her phone much.

I wonder if she's already turned it off and put it away. I did want to say one more thing. Quickly, I type:

> He was such a great kid.

I send and wait. No response. She's moved on. Which may be a metaphor, anyway, for where our friendship is going.

Our "friendship." I'm not sure why I feel the need to put quotation marks around that. Becca just called me *"mon amie"*—friend—in her text. We have been friends forever. But sometimes I'm afraid it's becoming more a matter of habit than of feeling, at least on her part.

Becca Sherman and I have known each other since elementary school. She's older than me—almost everyone in my grade at school has always been older than me. I have a late December birthday, and my parents sent me to school with the older kids rather than hold me back a year. Believe me, it was all about height, not brains or maturity. I was taller than nearly everybody my own age, and looked like I belonged with the older kids. I still am taller than nearly everybody my own age; to be precise, now I'm taller than nearly everybody of every age. When people meet me for the first time, they always expect me to be a basketball player.

"No?" an adult will say. "Western's girls could use a center like you. You'd be awesome!"

Adrian, by the way, thinks people over forty should be barred from using the word "awesome."

Or, if it's not that I owe it to society and Western High School to become a basketball player, it's that I owe it to my family:

"You could save your parents a boatload of money in a few years by getting yourself a nice athletic scholarship, heh-heh."

Is it so terrible that I just use my body to move myself around the planet?

Becca and I not only went to regular school together, we also used to go to Sunday religious school together, and then Tuesday–Thursday Hebrew school, before our Bat Mitzvahs. We would demolish the boys in Ping-Pong matches in the synagogue's youth lounge before class. Height, I'm happy to report, is an unsung advantage in table tennis. In class, we used to pass games of hangman back and forth when the Hebrew teacher wasn't looking—Hebrew hangman, since we figured that it would look better, and be more forgivable, if we were caught.

Now, though, our pointless Ping-Pong matches and Hebrew hangmen are history. Becca doesn't do pointless anymore; the two words—*p* words, coincidentally—that describe her these days are "purposeful" and "passionate." She's doing all kinds of school activities. In the fall, she's going to be one of the editors of the school newspaper, a huge deal for a sophomore. And she'll be an officer on the student council. And she'll join a bunch of other clubs and groups, and about two minutes later she'll be their treasurer or vice president.

Becca has tried to get me involved, but I've always declined. She tried to get me to come back to camp as a CIT. I declined. I think this has made her impatient with me. I think she thinks I've become apathetic, and apathy is annoying to Becca. Of all people, she must know it's not apathy. But she can't help herself from pushing and encouraging me; she's just such a go-getter.

"Tall people have a huge advantage when it comes to

leadership," she told me last year. "People just naturally look up to them. No pun intended."

"And you know this how?" I asked. Becca is five two.

"I read it somewhere. Studies have been done."

"Becca—"

"I know, I know," she said. "All I'm saying is I know how good you would be if you came out of your shell. If you could get over your—thing. You'd sweep everyone off their feet, and you'd have more fun."

"I'm having tons of fun already, thank you very much," I said in a prim voice meant to get her to laugh and stop being so earnest. "Tons. Metric tons—the big ones."

It worked. She laughed.

I love Becca, but I don't want to get elected to Student Council or be a student journalist or go out for the French club or be a center on the girls' basketball team. We can't all be leaders and overachievers. Deep down—actually, not so deep, but pretty much right on the surface—I'd still rather be playing Ping-Pong in a basement. Becca and I on the same team, crushing the boys in a meaningless competition before settling into a dozen or so harmless games of hangman while the Hebrew teacher droned on. *That* was a metric ton of fun.

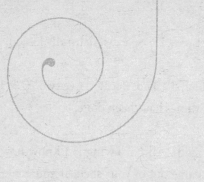

6

THE GROWN-UP ROOM

I'm fully awake after my exchange of texts with Becca. No use fighting it, so I head downstairs. Adrian stayed over again last night—that makes two nights in a row—and he's standing over a frying pan of French toast.

"More quality time, Danny," he says by way of a greeting.

This is our private little joke. Emphasis on *little*. "Quality time" is Dad's thing. "I want us to spend some real quality time as a family"—this weekend, this holiday, this vacation, whatever the occasion happens to be.

"So the difference between 'quality time' and 'quantity time' is what, exactly?" Adrian asked me one Thanksgiving weekend a few years ago. It wasn't a real question, though, because he answered it himself immediately after asking it.

"In 'quality time,' say a Monopoly game, you don't know

when it's going to end, or if it's ever going to end," he said. "Whereas in 'quantity time,' say going to a movie, you know you're committed for about two hours and then everyone goes their own way again. It's like the difference between torture, when your kidnappers black out the windows and take away the clocks so you end up going crazy from losing all track of time and a sense of reality, and a regular jail sentence."

Adrian would opt for quantity time any day. I don't have such strong feelings about it. But I also don't have the head-butting relationship with our parents that Adrian does. I don't feel like everything I do is a disappointment to them. I didn't move out of the house the day after I turned eighteen.

Of course I didn't. I haven't even turned fifteen yet.

Our parents join us in the kitchen.

"What would you think about going over to see the Dankers for a quick condolence call?" Mom asks.

Oh.

"Should I?" I ask.

"I think it would be appropriate," Mom says.

"Have you talked to them yet?" I ask.

"No," Dad says. "We'll come with you, of course."

So an hour later the three of us walk to the Dankers' house. Adrian stays behind. ("I'll go another time," he says, drawing an unconvinced look from Mom.) There are cars parked outside the house. Good, it won't just be the Dankers and the Snyders. When Mom taps on the front door, an unfamiliar woman—a youngish woman, maybe in her late twenties—answers. She leads us into the living room, to the left of the front hall. It's a room I've never been in during the two months this summer that I've been babysitting. Although the Dankers never told me to stay out of it, I always had the sense that it was off-limits to Humphrey, and if it was off-limits to Humphrey, it was off-limits to me. It's the grown-up room.

Mrs. Danker is sitting on a sofa. Another woman I don't know—someone around her age—sits next to her, holding her hand. A friend. Mrs. Crenshaw, the next-door neighbor with three kids, who are not here, is on the big sofa, too. She looks uncomfortable; not physically uncomfortable, but not at ease. She looks strangely glad to see us enter the room.

"Clarice," my mother says to Mrs. Danker. "We're so very sorry." Mom bends down to say this softly, and to take the hand that isn't being held by Mrs. Danker's friend.

"Thank you, Jan," Mrs. Danker says.

Mom straightens up and moves to one of the chairs. Next, my father squats down beside Mrs. Danker.

"So sorry," he says quietly. "What a great kid." Not that Dad has any idea, really, whether Humphrey was a great kid or not.

My turn. Just then Mr. Danker enters the room with the young woman who answered the door and another man. The man looks like Mr. Danker, minus about, I don't know, twenty or thirty years. He has the same rectangular head, with the same kind of hair—like a grown-out crew cut, thick hairs standing at attention, only Mr. Danker's is salt-and-pepper and the younger man's is dark brown.

Dad is getting up from his squat when Mr. Danker walks in. "Tom," Dad says. "My condolences." He pivots to do one of those elbow-grabbing non-hugs men give each other.

Mr. Danker nods.

Mom jumps up when she sees Mr. Danker, and she, too, offers her condolences—as well as a hug. He doesn't say anything to Mom, either, and he stands straight as a general for her hug before he sits next to his wife on the sofa, squeezing Mrs. Crenshaw out of the way. He has to brush against me slightly to get between the coffee table and the sofa. He seems not to notice me.

It's still my turn, though. I scrunch down on my knees. The rug is thick and forgiving.

"I'm sorry," I whisper. "I'm so very sorry."

Mrs. Crenshaw, who is still sitting on the sofa, only now appearing physically as well as psychically uncomfortable, looks at me expectantly. That's when I realize I haven't actually said anything out loud. It seems I've been having this problem since Friday night. I try again.

"I'm so sorry about Humphrey."

Mrs. Danker looks at me blankly at first. I've put on a skirt and blouse for the condolence call; could it be that after all these weeks, she doesn't recognize me without my T-shirt and shorts?

No, of course she knows who I am. "Danielle," she says, and immediately she starts to cry. "Oh, you poor thing. We know it wasn't your fault. Right, Thomas? Humphrey could be so—so . . ."

She trails off.

"Humphrey could be a bit out of control," says Mr. Danker.
No. No, he could not, not really.

"Yes, but," Mrs. Danker says. "What five-year-old has great impulse control . . ."

Again she trails off. Her friend nods and squeezes her hand. Mrs. Crenshaw shakes her head, but I know that she, and the friend, and my father (who is also nodding) all mean to agree with Mrs. Danker's statement.

But not me. No. Humphrey's impulse control was excellent. *Vraiment.*

"Perhaps if we'd focused on that," Mr. Danker says. "On self-control."

"You can't do that, Tom," my mother says. "You can't second-guess."

Mr. Danker looks at her directly for the first time since we walked in. "I can," he says. "It's very hard not to."

Mom's face turns slightly, but noticeably, red.

"We can't help but second-guess," Mrs. Danker says. "What if this? What if that?"

"What if someone had trained him never to run into the street?" Mr. Danker says. "What if we'd trained Humphrey to stay with the adult, or—whomever"—gesturing toward me— "when walking on Quarry Road?"

What if the stupid babysitter had held on to the boy's hand?

"Well, it's understandable," my father says. "Of course it's understandable that you wonder 'what if.'"

After a few more minutes of this agony, we leave. We leave

Mrs. Danker swallowed up by her enormous comfy sofa. We leave Mr. Danker sitting next to her, his straight back and neck resisting the sofa's embrace, his hair relentlessly at attention, a tiny army of soldiers on guard all over his rectangle of a head.

7

THERE WILL BE POLEMICS

"Those were his children from his first marriage," Mom explains to Dad on the walk home. "The son looks just like him, doesn't he? And the daughter—the one who answered the door—she has his face, too. The shape of his head. They both live out of town, isn't that right, Danny?"

I don't know. I don't know about Mr. and Mrs. Danker's lives as *people*. They're just the parents of the boy I babysat. I know that they're older than usual for parents of a five-year-old, and Mr. Danker is even older than older than usual. I guess it doesn't really surprise me that he had a family before Humphrey.

"Was she married before, too?" Dad asks.

"I don't think so," Mom said. "I think she had a career

in—something scientific. They moved here a few years before she got pregnant with Humphrey. Is that about right, Danny?"

I don't know that, either. I know that Mrs. Danker wasn't going out to work on the weekdays when I babysat; she was going for cancer treatments. Breast cancer treatments, and then, usually, a couple of hours of rest at home. Other than the time she spent resting in her bedroom, she didn't act sick. She didn't talk about being sick. She was matter-of-fact about her appointments.

Mom knows all that, too, so I don't bother to bring it up.

"Tom really jumped down your throat, Jan," Dad says to my mother.

"I was only saying that second-guessing is—well, what's the point of it. But I shouldn't have said anything. I don't know him well enough."

To me, it's interesting that someone who is as particular about words as Thomas Danker must be—he used the word "whomever" when a regular person would have said "whoever"—referred to a failure to "train" Humphrey. Didn't he mean to say there was a failure to "teach" Humphrey? You train a puppy. You teach a kid. I suppose you do train a kid to use the potty and graduate from his diaper. But still, it sounded odd to me.

On the other hand, there is the possibility that Mr. Danker was a tad preoccupied and not thinking about using the most appropriate words in the context at hand.

"It's tough," Dad says. "It's the toughest thing."

Mom doesn't say anything to that, but stops walking for a beat so that I can catch up to her. "It was brave and kind of you to make this condolence call," she says, putting her arm around my shoulders.

Wait, you gave me a choice?

"I don't know what good it did," I say.

"It was just the right thing to do," Mom says. "I'm sure the Dankers appreciated it."

I'm sure they neither appreciated nor didn't appreciate my visit. I'm sure that Mr. Danker doesn't know my name. I'm sure that Mrs. Danker is trying very hard not to blame me.

At home, Adrian is on the porch fiddling with his laptop.

"Can you stay over tonight again?" Dad asks.

He can't. Adrian lives in a rented room way farther out in the suburbs—the exurbs—where rents are cheap. He has worked a bunch of jobs—busboy at a steakhouse, detailer at a car wash, hauler of junk for one of those companies that will clean out your basement. Most recently he's signed on as a plumber's apprentice. This is not the dream career path of anyone I know. I can't imagine it's the career path of Adrian's dreams, either. And yet—whenever I see Adrian these days, he seems happier than he's ever been.

He isn't staying for dinner tonight. Sunday nights Adrian still works at the steakhouse. He's kept that job a few nights a week. The plumbing apprenticeship is a Monday-through-Friday daytime gig.

Mom and Dad go inside. I stay on the porch with Adrian.

"How'd it go?" he asks.

"It went."

My phone buzzes. I glance at the text.

So sorry about what happened.

"It's Marissa," I tell Adrian.

"Good old Marissa," Adrian says, smiling. "Marissa and her seven brothers."

"Her five brothers," I correct him.

"I thought maybe she got a couple more since I saw her last."

"She's sorry about what happened," I say.

Adrian nods. "What else is there to say?"

I haven't talked to Marissa in—I have to stop to count—seven months. More than half a year.

"Actually, there's plenty else to say," I tell Adrian.

"O-*kay*," he says, drawing the word out. "Start saying it."

I don't, and he doesn't press except to add, after a minute, "And are you going to answer her?"

I text back:

Thanks, Marissa.

I'm here if you need to talk.

She's a good listener, but seven months is seven months.

Hanging out with my brother just now.

Maybe later.

OK. Take care.

"Hey, Danny-boy," Adrian says. His nickname for me. Sometimes, for variety's sake, Danny-girl. "Look at this."

"I can't see," I say. We're next to each other in rocking chairs; the angle isn't right for looking at his screen.

"This is how messed up people are: there are websites selling roadside memorial signs. You customize them with a photo of—the deceased." He slides the computer onto my lap.

"Shut up," I say in disbelief.

"I know," Adrian says. "See where the ad brags about the sturdy hardware they include so the sign will withstand the elements?"

"Who thinks up this stuff?" I say.

"Definitely not high school dropouts," Adrian says. "Don't blame the dummies."

Adrian is one of the least dumb people I know. I don't fully get why he dropped out with only a few months to go before graduating, except that maybe it was the worst thing he could do to Mom that was legal. It may have been the worst thing he could do to Dad, too, but Adrian would not have been thinking about hurting Dad.

He would not have been thinking about hurting me, either, but that doesn't stop the ache. When Adrian was still here, the house felt full. We hung out, watched television, talked, played music together—he on drums and I on guitar. I went to his hockey games. When he had friends over, they usually played loud video games, followed by crazy bouts of touch football in our backyard, followed by more video games. I could keep up with the best of them in Rock Star. I wasn't bad at Madden NFL. I stayed out of the real football games—they could accidentally kill me. Because Adrian was nice to me, his friends were nice to me, too.

I have not always been as nice to my own friends, I'm afraid. There's the thing with Marissa—our seven months of silence. It began in January. Or, I should say, she probably thinks it began in January.

We'd made plans for her to come over with her guitar. Marissa, who's a grade ahead of me, goes to a small private school; we met when I was ten and she was eleven, in a guitar class at the community hall. After that first class ended, we kept taking classes together, all classical acoustic guitar. There are a lot of great Spanish songs written for two, and Marissa and I could play for hours. We stopped the classes in middle school, but we still played together sometimes.

Unfortunately, just at the moment Marissa arrived that day in January, I had taken the lead in a "Score Duel" match.

"This is historic," I said when she came in.

"And yet fleeting," said Sam, one of Adrian's friends.

"Or the start of a new and enduring Rock Star legend," I countered.

"Marissa, give it one level," Adrian said. "I admire my sister's skills, but I don't think that her lead is going to last."

Only it did last. Really, who *cares* if you win at Rock Star's head-to-head competition, or any other video game—and yet I was obsessed. Marissa was not. Not obsessed and not amused. After about ten minutes, she made a point of not watching the action on the screen, which is what everyone else was doing. Ironically, the only person in the room who paid any attention to her was Adrian.

Ironically, that is, because lately Marissa had been making remarks about Adrian that I did not appreciate.

The remarks weren't insults, at least not outright. More like little questions, but they were questions wrapped around disapproval. *Isn't it too bad Adrian quit hockey? He hasn't applied to college? Why does he talk that way to your parents?*

Marissa has her big family, with her five brothers, and they are all happily following the path that every parent craves. AP classes and sports teams in high school. Awards. College scholarships. Internships.

"Does it bug you what Adrian is doing?" she said last fall after she'd been over for dinner.

"What do you mean?"

"He's pretty negative," she said. "Like when your mother was talking about Thanksgiving plans and doing something as a family and he shut down every single idea she and your dad had."

True, he had. I hadn't thought he was negative, just honest.

No thanks, he didn't want to join them for a movie, a hike, Black Friday shopping, a jazz club.

"I mean, he was rejecting you, too, Danielle," Marissa said.

"That's just Adrian. He's going through some stuff," I said. "But he's the best."

"Well, if you don't think it's hurtful . . ." Marissa just left that hanging there.

"I don't feel hurt," I said. "And I think my parents can take care of themselves."

She didn't say anything to that.

Marissa's parents, I know, wouldn't tolerate Adrian's brand of "honesty." They run a "yes, sir" and "yes, ma'am" household. Our parents do not.

"We may not be everyone's idea of a perfect family," I added. "But we get each other."

"I didn't mean to sound judgmental," Marissa said. "I just thought it might be hard for you. Since you have a decent relationship with your parents."

"Everybody has a decent relationship with everybody," I said. "We're just fine."

"Every family is different," Marissa said.

"Yup," I said.

So maybe I was a little too into my Rock Star game last January precisely because I knew Marissa would disapprove.

"Hey, Danny," Adrian said at one point. "We will concede victory. Go ahead with Marissa."

No way. A conceded victory was not good enough. I wanted to win for real.

After about forty-five minutes, Marissa left. I didn't even pause the game. I know—very, very bad, abominable behavior. I called and texted afterward when I came to my senses. She didn't pick up or respond. I stopped after a week. She had every reason to be angry. But I had reasons of my own, so I wasn't going out of my way to fix things between us.

It was true that even last autumn Adrian had already started to feel caged at home; Marissa's observations about him weren't so wrong. But I didn't need to hear them from her, with her picture-perfect family. Everything Mom and Dad said to Adrian—about school, about hockey, about how he spent his free time, about the daily news, about, really, it could be the weather—grated. Especially Mom, from the moment he set foot in high school: Why aren't you signing up for AP history? So-and-so's mother says he's taking three AP courses this semester. Why isn't the coach starting you in the hockey games? So-and-so starts, and he hasn't been playing as long as you have. Why didn't you try out for the school's jazz band again? Why don't you go after an internship? It's never too early to build your résumé. To get a start on your career. And on and on.

Adrian didn't create noisy scenes. But the more she suggested, the less he did. He stopped playing hockey. He signed up for no AP classes that last, abbreviated semester of high school. His drum set went untouched. Instead, he started to take jobs. He worked after school, nights, weekends.

Some parents would be happy about this. My father seemed kind of awed by Adrian's industriousness. Mom—she wasn't awed. She was annoyed. She knew it was a sort of push-back against her. She didn't seem capable, though, of backing off and seeing what might happen. It didn't occur to her that if she left Adrian alone, he just might stick to the path she thought kids in middle-class families like ours should follow. Higher education and careers. Careers, not jobs.

She never did back off. And Adrian left me last February, marooned at home and in high school.

But he is here now.

"Isn't anything just left alone?" I say. "Just, a terrible thing happened. Let it be. No customized signs ordered off a website. No wondering what if someone had done something different. No police investigations. Just let it be."

I cover my face with my hands so tears don't splash on Adrian's laptop.

"Okay," Adrian says. "It's okay. A terrible thing happened. It happened to you, too. You're allowed to cry."

The thing is, I don't cry. The laptop is in no danger.

"But you know that people will not just let it be," Adrian says. "A kid gets hit by a car on a neighborhood street. It's not the type of thing people can just let be."

"It's not?" I say mournfully. Of course I know he's right.

"No," Adrian responds. "Even in the ER Friday night, there was Mrs. Raskin ranting that she knew something like this was going to happen because there aren't streetlights on Quarry Road."

"But—"

"And Mr. Stashower complaining because there's no crosswalk at Quarry and Franklin."

"But that doesn't have anything to do with anything!" I say.

"And?" Adrian says. "All I'm saying is—there will be polemics."

"*Polemics*?" I say.

"Yeah. People will be huffing and puffing over what could have prevented this accident."

Polemics. Wouldn't Humphrey have liked that word? Well, it isn't quite up to the level of showiness that he favored. Maybe if I turned it into something longer. *Polemicist. Polemicization.*

"And you're going to need to be tough, and not take the huffing and puffing personally," Adrian adds.

"Okay."

"Okay."

I will pertinaciously perambulate around the periphery of the polemical piffle.

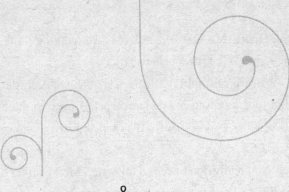

8

GIVE ME TEARS

Humphrey wasn't a linguistic prodigy, although he could recite a prodigious number of words that began with the letter *p*. Those words, Mrs. Danker explained to me at the end of my second week of babysitting, began as a diversion. Humphrey had become obsessed with certain one- and two-syllable *p* words that his parents preferred not to hear over and over again.

"So," Mrs. Danker said, "Tom started this thing where he taught Humphrey these long, sophisticated *p* words, which, he convinced him, were better, because—bigger is better, right? And it worked."

At the start of my third week on the job, I was surprised to find Mr. Danker at home. It was late in the morning, and I'd expected that he would be at his office.

"Hi, Mr. Danker," I said.

"Hello," Mr. Danker said. He called up the stairs. "Clarice, the—she's—the sitter is here."

I heard Humphrey's little feet in his cute little Converse high-tops running on the uncarpeted upstairs hallway floor. Then, softer, padding down the carpeted steps, followed by Mrs. Danker.

"You really don't need to take me," Mrs. Danker said to her husband. "I've been driving myself just fine. It's no big deal."

"I know I don't need to. I want to. It's your birthday, and I'd like to spend time with you."

I wondered: Was Mr. Danker a dad with a thing about quality time, too?

"In the waiting room?" Mrs. Danker said.

"We'll go for a nice lunch afterward," he said.

When Mrs. Danker came home from radiation, she didn't usually eat. It wasn't that radiation made you sick, Mrs. Danker had told me. It wasn't like chemotherapy. It just made her feel a little whipped. After she rested for an hour or so, she usually ate something small and cold. A yogurt. A little container of cottage cheese. She liked cold red plums.

But here was her husband trying to do something special for her birthday. So she smiled and said, "That would be lovely."

Mr. Danker hung behind as Mrs. Danker went out to the car.

"Young lady," he said to me, "would it be asking too much for you to go to the mall with Humphrey and pick out a gift from him for his mother's birthday?" He held out two twenty-dollar bills.

"Yes!" Humphrey said.

"For Mommy," Mr. Danker said. "Only a gift for Mommy. This is not a time for a present for Humphrey."

"I know," Humphrey said, his eyes cast down.

"Humphrey had a bit of trouble last night concealing his disappointment when his mother received gifts at a little birthday get-together we had," Mr. Danker said. "He was under the mistaken impression that he should receive gifts, too."

"Aw, Humphrey," I said. "Weren't you happy for your mommy?"

"Yeah," he mumbled.

"Humphrey, what do we say?" Mr. Danker said. "What do we say to answer in the affirmative?"

Humphrey continued looking at the floor, but he clearly knew the answer. "Yes," he said.

Wow, I thought. *In the affirmative.* I wondered if Mr. Danker preferred "yes, sir," like Marissa's father. But he didn't press Humphrey on that.

"And when you go to your cousin's birthday next weekend, Humphrey, who is the only one who is going to get presents?" Mr. Danker asked.

Humphrey blew out a sigh. "Juliet," he said.

"Don't be bummed, Humphrey," I said. "When it's your birthday, who's going to get all the presents?"

That got him to look up. "I will!" he said.

"That is not precisely the expectation or lesson that I'm trying to reinforce here," Mr. Danker said.

Now my eyes were on the floor, too.

Mr. Danker continued. "Humphrey's aunt brought him a monogrammed handkerchief, just like the kind that I carry. And, Humphrey, what was your reaction?"

Humphrey didn't respond.

"Son?"

Another big, audible sigh. "I said it wasn't a real present. And I cried."

"Yes," Mr. Danker said. "And crying when someone gives you a present is not an appropriate reaction, is it, Humphrey?"

"No," Humphrey said to the floor.

"Now, Humphrey, will you look at me and say good-bye?" Mr. Danker said.

Humphrey looked up. "'Bye, Daddy."

Mr. Danker reached down and ran his hand across Humphrey's crew cut. "We'll see you later."

We took a bus to the mall. I wished I'd asked Mr. Danker what he had in mind for this present. Cologne? Fancy hand cream? Stationery?

A window display at a swimwear boutique caught Humphrey's eye.

"Look!" he said.

Bikinis galore. Oh, sure. Just the thing.

Next, the cheapo toy store with a window full of plastic.

"I think Mommy would like a robot," Humphrey said.

The high-end toy store.

"That train set would be perfect," Humphrey said, his eyes following the cars as they chugged along. "Mommy loves trains."

We drifted into one of the nice department stores. There had to be something. Here were women's—whatevers. I wasn't sure what to call this stuff, and there was so much of it. Lounge-wear? It was all slinky, velour-ish suits. I looked up and saw a sign: ACTIVEWEAR.

"Come on, Humphrey," I said. The round clothing racks of activewear were so close together, and Humphrey was so small, that I couldn't see him. "We're moving on."

No answer. I walked around some of the displays. "Humpty Dumpty?"

I pushed my way through two overflowing displays. A third one quivered. Wait. Unless that rack was alive, it had no business quivering. Unless.

I found Humphrey nestled between two velvet leisure suits. He was holding the purple fabric of the jacket between the index and middle fingers of his right hand, and holding—no, clutching—one of the purple pant legs in his left hand.

"Humphrey!" I exclaimed.

He was absolutely in rapture. "These give me tears," he said.

The pantsuit could not have been uglier. But when I reached out to touch the fabric, I understood. It was a flower petal, only sturdier. But not too sturdy, not rigid—it was a flower petal that draped and flowed. It was beautiful to the touch, and Humphrey, sensitive Humphrey, who, Mrs. Danker had told me, needed the tags cut out of his shirts so they didn't bother his neck, was practically moved to a tearful trance by the softness.

"It is really soft and nice," I said.

"And it's beautiful," he said. "Can we get it?"

Oh. This was really not a good look for Mrs. Danker. She was old, but not so far gone as to be velour-leisure-suit-wearing old.

I looked at the tag. Saved. "It's too expensive, Humphrey," I said. "We can't spend this much on your present for your mom."

"Pl-ea-se?" This was Humphrey's whiny voice. But it was offset by the way he clasped his hands, as if in prayer. "Are you sure?"

I was sure.

"When it's my birthday," he said, "remember to tell my parents about this. I would like it."

"Humphrey," I said, "this isn't for you. It's a pantsuit for a big lady. A big *old* lady."

"I don't have to wear it," he said. "I just want to have it."

We chose a picture frame, stopped in the food court for lunch, and caught the bus back to Quarry Road. Walking back to the Dankers' house, I asked Humphrey when his birthday was.

"December seventeenth," he said.

"Not too far from now," I said encouragingly, thinking that

it must feel like an eternity to him. "Mine is in December, too, the twenty-eighth."

"We're almost birthday twins!" he said.

"We can have our own private party," I said.

"My birthday is the next birthday in our house. Mommy's is today. Daddy's was before. Next is me!"

"Sometimes people don't give you the greatest presents, though," I said.

"Yeah."

"But you also get great presents, too, don't you?"

"Yeah."

"So then," I said, "if you get a present that's disappointing to you, you could say to yourself, 'That's all right. I'm going to get great presents, too.'"

He hesitated. "Yeah. But sometimes the disappointment just pops out."

"Maybe practicing would help. Maybe if we practiced getting the worst, stupidest, crummiest presents in the whole world, you would remember to just say 'thank you' and know you'll end up with great presents, too."

He stopped and looked at me as if I were crazy. "That's silly."

"Just an idea," I said.

"Okay!" Humphrey said.

"Okay," I said. "Humphrey, I'm your aunt Cruella, and I'm giving you this lovely, lovely gift of"—I reached into my purse for a tissue—"this wonderful tissue!"

"Oh!" he said. He looked puzzled.

"So you accept it politely and say, 'Thank you so much, Aunt Cruella,'" I prompted.

"Thank you so much, Aunt Cruella," Humphrey repeated.

"Because you know you're going to get something you really want from someone else," I said.

"Yeah!"

"All right," I said. "I'm your uncle Frankenstein, and I say, 'Hey there, young whippersnapper, here's a gift for you,' and I give you"—I found a ChapStick in my purse—"this. What do you do?"

"Accept it politely and say, 'Thank you, Uncle Frankenstein!'" Humphrey yelled.

We practiced with a crumpled sheet of paper, a piece of thread, a hairbrush. Thank you, thank you, thank you.

"One more, Humphrey. I'm Mr. Mushy Misery, and I am pleased to present you with this gift of"—into my purse again, for another tissue—"a used, but very elegant handkerchief! It's even monogrammed with your very own initials! What do you do, Humphrey?"

He didn't hesitate. "Give it to Daddy."

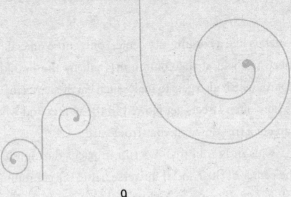

9

A FEW QUESTIONS

The day after the condolence call, Monday, Mom and Dad go to work. Normally I would be due at the Dankers' at eleven fifteen. Now my schedule is wide open. I'm not sure what to do with myself.

We live in a chummy neighborhood called Franklin Grove. It's in the suburbs of Washington, D.C. When we say "downtown," we mean downtown D.C. But when we say "our town," we mean Franklin Grove. It's not technically a town. There's no mayor. Local government is mostly taken care of by the county—Meigs County—which passes laws and has police and courts and all that. But Franklin Grove is very much a community, more than some of the other suburbs. People here tend to know their neighbors, and they also tend to know what's going on around the neighborhood. There's the community hall building, which is like a community center, only more official. There are meetings held at the community hall by the Franklin Grove Board, which also gets to make such earth-shattering decisions as how often streets get plowed in the winter and whether you can cut a tree down in your front yard.

Kids in Franklin Grove run in packs during the summer, the center of their social universe being the community swimming pool. If you're in high school, and good-looking and buff, you might climb the pinnacle of the summer social order and get a job as a lifeguard. If not—maybe, like me, you do babysitting, maybe you work at the mall, maybe you cut lawns, maybe you go to summer school—you show up at the pool whenever you can. You join the swim team. The kids order pizza, play water polo, swim their practices, and otherwise hang out.

Sometimes I had to take Humphrey for swimming lessons. The lessons were in between the prime times for middle and high school kids—after the morning team practices and before the late-afternoon social hours. So it was pretty much me, a bunch of little kids, a few mothers, and the full-time nannies.

I've never been a big fan of the pool. I don't like the way my knees look—to call them knobby would be paying a compliment. The rest of my body would be utterly forgettable, except for the fact that it is so ridiculously long, which of course makes it noticeable, and not in a good way. My dark hair, when it's wet, forms more of a chin-length helmet than a slinky mane. It could be worse. But not a great look.

Anyway. I will not be filling up what remains of this summer with long afternoons at the Franklin Grove Swim Club. Not that I have anything else planned, other than going to some kind of counselor or therapist once a week. My parents "suggested" this yesterday, and by "suggested" I mean they told me I would be going.

"You understand it's not because we think there's anything wrong with you," Mom said. "It's just—after what you've been through—"

"I get it, Mom," I said.

"And I don't want you to think there's any pressure on you to deal with your—to deal with any other issue right now. This is about the trauma of the accident for you."

"I get it, Mom," I repeated.

I take a cup of coffee out to the porch. It doesn't seem possible that Humphrey is gone. I think about him lying in the street. Holding him, so quiet, not like Humphrey at all. That makes it real. Where did he go? I mean, he was laughing and being his usual self, and then—gone? To where? I've never been big on thinking about souls. And we Jews don't tend to spend a lot of time stressing about the afterlife or heaven or whatever. But this line between alive and dead, this on/off switch that was tripped on Friday night—was that it? Live boy. Dead boy. Would anybody else ever have the exact same laugh as he did?

"Humphrey, are you out there? Humphrey T. Danker?" It's quiet. There is no answer, and then the telephone rings.

"Hi, I'm calling for Danielle Snyder?" She makes her statement in the form of a question, as if she's a contestant on *Jeopardy!*—or a girl in high school.

"This is Danielle."

"Hi. This is Diana Tang from the *Observer*?" The *Observer* is the weekly suburban newspaper, which covers a bunch of neighborhoods, not just Franklin Grove. Everyone gets it, since it's delivered for free.

"I wanted to talk to you about the accident last Friday involving you and little Humphrey Danker."

Little Humphrey Danker. Little Humphrey and big, bad me. Stop it. That is not what she said.

Should I talk to a reporter?

"I have just a few questions to start with," Diana Tang presses on in the absence of any response from me. "We want to get your side of the story."

There are sides to the story?

"Um—hello?" she says.

"Yeah, no, I'm here," I say. "I don't think I should be talking to a reporter."

"We don't have to use your name. I mean, we generally don't name minors who are involved in—incidents."

In *incidents*? I thought they didn't name minors who were accused of crimes. When some girls from our school were arrested for breaking into the Halloween store that opened temporarily in the shopping center near school, the story was in the *Observer*, but their names were not. Only—the girls told everyone at school what happened. So much for not naming names. But another time, when a boy was arrested for robbing a frozen yogurt shop, the *Observer* did publish his name. It turned out he hit the guy in the store with a bat, and he had done something like this before at a smoothie shop, so he was charged as an adult. And, apparently, when kids are charged as adults, the *Observer* no longer treats them as kids, and their names are fair game.

I'm not entirely sure I have the ins and outs of the *Observer*'s rules down. And I'm not sure what they have to do with me. I'm not accused of a crime. And when kids aren't accused of crimes, the *Observer* throws their names around right and left—for winning science fairs, scoring goals, earning swimming medals, raising money to fight multiple sclerosis. They don't just print the kids' names; they **boldface** them.

Meanwhile, Diana Tang is waiting on the other end of the line.

"Well . . . what are some of the questions?" I ask.

"So," Diana Tang begins, "were you able to see the cars clearly when you were walking with Humphrey, and do you think the drivers could see you?"

"Um—sure," I say. "There was still some daylight."

"Quarry Road has a lot of trees," Diana Tang says. "So was it still light enough to see at eight o'clock at night?"

"It was closer to seven thirty," I say. "And yes. It was light enough."

"Some people have said streetlights would increase safety

on Quarry Road," Diana Tang says. "Would streetlights have improved your ability to see the oncoming cars, or the drivers' ability to see you and Humphrey?"

"I don't know," I say.

"If Quarry Road had a sidewalk, do you think that could have made the accident less likely?"

What? Does she think we were walking in the middle of the street? Quarry doesn't have a real sidewalk, but people walk on the side of the street. There's a line painted there; you walk on the outside of the line, or in the weedy strip next to that.

"I don't think so," I say. "We were way over on the side, where everyone walks."

"Have you ever felt in danger walking on the side of Quarry Road?"

"No."

"Danielle, did you ever take those babysitting classes offered by the Red Cross?"

"No."

"Hmm. Do you know any kids who have taken the classes?"

"I don't know."

I really shouldn't have answered the phone. I thought maybe it was Adrian or Becca, but they would call my cell, not the house number.

"I have to go," I say to Diana Tang, interrupting her next question.

"I have only a few more questions," she says.

"Sorry." I hang up.

10

PURPOSEFULLY PERAMBULATING

GUILT-RIDDEN TEEN HANGS UP ON REPORTER

NEGLIGENT GIRL IGNORES DANGERS
"Everyone" walks in street, she asserts

TEENAGER TO RED CROSS: DROP DEAD

I could spend the rest of the day imagining nightmare head-lines for a nightmare article. But I don't. School starts in three weeks and since I have nothing better to do, I might as well tackle my summer reading list. Of course, the idea is that you read these books in a leisurely, book-loving way over the twelve weeks of summer vacation. Not that I'm a reliable spokesperson for the high school zeitgeist, but nobody does that. I like to read, but during the summer I want to read what I want to read, which isn't *Brave New World*, *Fahrenheit 451*, or *As I Lay Dying*.

But now I don't want to read what I want to read. So, I figure, I might as well read what I don't want to read. I'll take the bus to the library, check out the books, and add misery on top of my misery by reading about dystopias and death. Why not?

Actually, it feels good to be outside, walking, with a destination. It's only been a few days, but I feel as if I've been curled up for months in the fetal position under my bed. Well, I *have* been curled up in the fetal position, on top of my bed. My legs and arms, even my head, feel stiff. Walking loosens my tight muscles, my rigid jaw, my one-note (NO! NO! NO!) brain.

It feels so good that I decide to walk to the library, which is a little bit farther than the mall. It'll be a very long walk, but that's just what I want. Purposefully perambulating. In a few minutes, I'm on Quarry Road, passing the bus stop. And in a few minutes more, I'm upon the scene of the crime. What was I thinking? All roads lead to this site—I almost never have a reason to go the other direction on Quarry Road. Of course I would end up here.

It looks a mess because of all the roadside memorial paraphernalia that people have strewn about. I count five teddy bears. Six sad little bouquets. (Whose job is it to remove the dead flowers at a roadside memorial?) Three plastic action figures, but not figures corresponding to any hero or villain who's currently popular. Some kids must have dug into their boxes of discarded toys. One heart-shaped pillow. A bunch of cards, already yellowing and curling, and a large sign: WE LOVE YOU, HUMPHREY.

Okay. It's true that Humphrey was too young and too sheltered to be really known by the neighbors or their kids. But my heart turns in on itself at this stuff. Teddy bears? The kid didn't have a single one. Action figures? He wasn't allowed to watch the television shows the figures were based on, and so he didn't know that he was supposed to care about them.

My God, doesn't anyone know that Humphrey's ambition in life was to throw a perfect spiral? That he loved aliens, specifically aliens of the Bumble-Boo persuasion? Or that, in the stuffed animal department, he passed over teddy bears in favor of turtles and frogs? His parents must know this, but I'm assuming they don't have anything to do with this collection of junk.

I keep walking, and soon I'm at the entrance to the park. Our park. I could walk on. I do have a destination. But I'm drawn in.

Here are the Bumble-Boos on the planet of Thrumble-Boo. Here's the spaceship. The playground is deserted, as usual. I cross the field to the scrubby area where a few old picnic tables and an ancient grill have failed to entice anyone to have a cookout for as long as I can remember. I sit up on one of the tabletops and look around. This park is such an ugly duckling. Yet I've always liked it. I don't remember riding on the springy bumblebees—excuse me, Bumble-Boos—but we have photos to prove that I once did, when I was Humphrey's age and younger. I do remember spinning around on the roundabout, with Adrian providing most of the propulsion. I feel protective toward this park. And now, to me, it's more of a memorial to Humphrey than the collection on Quarry Road.

Over on the basketball court a guy is shooting hoops, alone. See, that's another good thing about a run-down park. Not many people come here, so you can get the court to yourself, if that's what you want. Or, like with Humphrey and me, you can make the playground your own private planet with your own private aliens without interference from other, ordinary human beings.

It appears I have spoken too soon. I'm about to have interference.

"Hey." It's the boy from the basketball court. He probably wants to see who's invading his private domain.

"Hey," I say back.

"I've seen you here," he says. "I couldn't tell it was you right away. But I've seen you here. You play catch with that kid."

He saw me? I guess I did notice some guys playing basketball when Humphrey and I were here. But barely. Hey, I was very busy. I was babysitting. Much too attentive to my responsibilities to notice some high school guys sweating on a court all the way across the field, even if one of them was unusually nice-looking.

"He's too young to throw a regular football," he says.

"I didn't know you could be too young to throw a ball," I say.

"I mean, they make smaller footballs for younger kids," he says. "They can get their hands around them better. So they can get the grip right and actually throw the way a football's supposed to be thrown."

"Excuse me," I say. "It's the only football we had."

"Yeah, no. I'm not blaming you. Just saying. It's not like there's anything wrong with using a regulation football."

How relieved I am not to be blamed for using the wrong football. All that's left is forgiveness for walking at dusk, dropping the football, and having no control over the child I'm supposed to protect.

"They sell the youth footballs at the mall," he says. "At that toy store there."

"I won't really be needing one," I say. "Anymore."

He looks at me with deep brown eyes, dark lashes—and then I see my words registering.

"Oh, jeez," he says. "He's the boy. The one who got hit by— that car."

"Right," I say.

"Jeez."

"Yeah."

He doesn't immediately say anything more. From the look on his face—half horrified, half incredibly sympathetic—I sort of expect him to walk away, to go back to the basketball court. He doesn't, though. He leans against the picnic table, hesitates, and then pushes himself up to sit on top, like I am.

"I'm really sorry," he says.

"Thank you."

"So you were his babysitter."

I nod.

"I'm really so sorry."

"Me, too."

"His name was Humphrey, right?"

"Or Humpty," I say.

"Humpty?"

"Sometimes that's what I called him. Or Humpty Dumpty. Short for Humphrey," I say.

"That's quite a name," he says.

"I think it was a family name. Someone in Mr. Danker's family—like his father or grandfather or something. The point is, it wasn't for Humphrey Bogart."

He thinks about this for a moment. "But I wouldn't say Humpty is short for Humphrey," he says. "You know? Humpty. Humphrey. Two syllables, either way."

"I never really thought about it," I say in a voice that I hope is cold. Who asked him to count syllables? "It was a nickname."

"Sorry. That was stupid." He sounds embarrassed. "I didn't mean anything by it."

I wave the apology away.

"Did Humphrey like the Humpty Dumpty nursery rhyme or something?"

"Or something," I say. As if Humphrey would stoop to nursery rhymes. Could this conversation be stupider?

"So you were with him. When he. You know."

"Yup," I say. "I was."

"Jeez."

"Yup."

"Man."

"Yup."

We sit there for a few minutes without talking.

"Do you . . . do you go to Western?" he asks. Smooth transition.

"Yup."

He gives me a kind of look, I assume because I've now said "yup" four times in a row. If he were Thomas R. Danker, he would inform me that this was an inappropriate means of expressing the affirmative. But he's not Thomas R. Danker.

"Do you know . . . ?"

He names a bunch of people I don't know.

"How about . . . ?"

Now come the names of Western's mini-celebrities, including a few hockey players.

"I don't *know-them* know them," I say. "But I know who they are. Partly because my brother used to play hockey, so I used to go to all the games."

"Why'd you stop?"

"Because I was at the end of my sentence."

He laughs. "No, why'd you stop going to hockey games?"

I deflect the question. "You don't go to Western, though, do you?" I ask.

"No. MacArthur. I'll be a junior."

"So you don't even live around here," I say.

65

He laughs again. "I live close enough. Why? Is there a geographic limit on who can use the basketball court?"

"No. Just who can sit on the picnic tables."

"I see," he says.

"Okay."

"I play hockey. Not well, but I play. And not for MacArthur, just for the rec league."

"Good for you."

"Does that give me any more of a right to be on this picnic table?"

He has a snorty laugh, but a good smile, very white teeth set off against skin that I suppose I should call "olive," except I don't like the greenish suggestion that goes with "olive." Anyway, with the dark eyes, it's a pleasing combination. He's tall, too—taller than me.

"We play basketball here, my friends and me, because the court is always open," he says.

"Because it's such a dumpy park," I say.

"I like it," he says.

"Well," I say. "Thanks for the fascinating conversation."

"Nice to meet you, too," he says.

He turns to walk back toward the court; I get up and head toward Quarry Road.

"Hey!" he calls after me.

I turn.

"That was cool of you to try to teach the kid to play football. I shouldn't have said the thing about using the wrong size ball."

"That's okay," I say. "I wasn't teaching him to play football. Just to throw a perfect spiral."

He grimaces. "Oh, man," he says. "*So* much easier with a smaller ball."

"Nice to meet you, too," I say, and continue walking to Quarry Road.

At the library, I find all of the depressing books I'm supposed to read and check them out on my card. On the walk back, I stop at the mall. The high-end toy store doesn't have footballs, not in any size. The cheapo toy store has an entire basket of them—all PeeWee size. I buy two, one for Humphrey, one for me, and when I pass the roadside memorial on Quarry Road again, I stop to clear away some of the stupid stuffed bears and in their place I put his football, approved for league play, featuring the patented Ultimate Grip cover, and aerodynamically designed to spiral in flight.

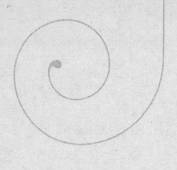

11

Journalism I

TRAGEDY REKINDLES SAFETY DEBATE

by Diana Tang

Observer reporter

A tragic accident on Quarry Road in the Franklin Grove neighborhood has revived an old debate about pedestrian safety along that busy thoroughfare.

On July 31, Humphrey T. Danker was struck by a car when he darted into traffic while walking home from a nearby park with his teenage babysitter. Humphrey, who was five years old, died shortly afterward. The driver of the car that hit Humphrey, Eugene Guzman, has not been cited for a motor vehicle violation or charged with a crime. Police are still investigating the cause of the accident.

"A tragedy along this stretch of road was bound to happen," said Doris Raskin, who lives near the site of the accident. "No streetlights or stoplights. No sidewalk. And the only crosswalk is a long hike from here." The accident occurred near the intersection of Quarry Road and Franklin Avenue, a street that leads into the residential area. The closest crosswalk is three-quarters of a mile away at Quarry and Vance Street, but, as Raskin also pointed out, even that crosswalk lacks a crossing signal.

Area residents have been advocating for improvements to Quarry Road for years, according to another neighbor, Donald Stashower. Stashower was on the scene of last week's accident.

"We almost had tragedy on top of tragedy here," he said. "There was a group of children ready to surge into the street at the intersection of Quarry and Franklin. I had to tell them to stay on the side of the road. Kids don't think anything can happen to them. We need a sidewalk so people can be safe when walking along Quarry Road. A line painted on the side of the road just isn't cutting it."

The accident is also causing some neighbors, as well as people who live elsewhere, to think about how prepared teenagers are to work as caregivers for active young children. The Red Cross offers classes to train middle school and high school students to work as babysitters.

"Our courses emphasize safety," said Chloe Greely, local spokesperson for the organization. "They're free and a great idea for any young person who wants to babysit."

Another neighbor, who asked that her name be withheld, said, "I'm not saying teenagers shouldn't babysit. But they should be prepared to react when things get out of hand."

Britney Schaeffer, 14, is a graduate of the Red Cross babysitting program. "It taught me a lot," said the rising Western High School freshman. "I learned basic life-saving skills, but also things about how little kids behave and how you have to expect the unexpected."

Humphrey Danker's babysitter had not taken the Red Cross classes.

My phone buzzes; a text from Becca.

How r u?

A-OK.

Danny!

I'm fine.

R u seeing the shrink?

Yes. Kind of a waste. But not awful.

Bonne idee. I'm glad you are.

You think I'm crazy?

No! I think it must be really hard for you. You
went through a traumatic experience. So it's
good to talk about it.

I suppose so.

Maybe you'll also talk about that other
problem?

I don't respond. She tries again.

That problem that shall not be named?

Oh, that.
The problem that, if I did not have it, I would have had the

courage it takes to be a CIT. That problem that, if I did not have it, I would have been at camp this summer, Humphrey would have had a different babysitter, and he would not be in the newspaper.

When I was thirteen, I had a Bat Mitzvah, just like most of my Jewish friends. Becca and I shared the Bat Mitzvah, even though her birthday is months earlier than mine. Most kids had shared Bat Mitzvahs and Bar Mitzvahs, because there were so many of us, and not enough Saturday mornings for us to all have singles.

There I was, up on the bimah—the stage—of our synagogue. I had already led the congregation in a few prayers, and just finished a responsive reading. (I say a line/you say a line/I say a line/you say a line, etc.) It was time for the highlight of the morning, in which I would chant from the Torah in Hebrew and then give a little speech sharing my wisdom about the meaning of what I just chanted. As I stepped up to the table on which the Torah lay, rolled open to the section I was to read, it happened.

"It" was not, I am sorry to say, a powerful and uplifting spiritual experience. It was, absolutely, a powerful experience. But it was more crushing than uplifting. As for spiritual, I suppose if by "spiritual" we also mean the Jewish concept of a dybbuk, a spirit that enters your body and controls it and is altogether terrifying, then sure, it was spiritual. I was hit by a huge wave, and it knocked me over, sweeping away my voice, my ability to think, to fully control my hands and feet. It felt absolutely lethal. You could call it panic. I think that's too gentle a word.

I did manage to remain standing, in a frozen sort of way. And when the rabbi pointed to the section I was to chant, I did manage to open my mouth. Some words came out. They were Hebrew words, and they were from my Torah portion, but I stumbled on the ones I said, and totally skipped others. I didn't chant them in the special way I'd been practicing for an entire year. Nor did I say them in a manner that allowed anyone beyond the first two rows of seats to hear them. In short, I totally blew my Bat Mitzvah.

And I wasn't finished. After the Torah reading, it was time for my speech, which I'd also been working on for nearly a year. I was proud of the insights I'd come up with about my Torah portion, which is the part in the Bible where Jacob knows he's dying and he gives this kind of awkward blessing to his son Joseph's two sons. But the wave was way too strong for me, and it swept me off the stage and down the short hallway that connects to the rabbi's study, where I tumbled into a chair and hyperventilated.

My mother soon appeared. I told her I couldn't give my speech. At first she told me I could, but then she took in what a complete wreck I was—shaking and sweating—and she gave it up. After a while I decided that I could make it back out there, but only if I didn't have to sit up on the bimah, and only if I didn't have to utter another word, which is *not* how Bat Mitzvahs are conducted.

Meanwhile, Becca had carried on. She chanted her part of the Torah and she gave her speech. When I came slinking back in and took a seat in the front row, she caught my eye from her place at the Torah table. She was reading something in Hebrew, but here's what I heard: "*Quelle horreur!*"

My mother told everyone that I'd gotten sick. I miraculously recovered in time for my little luncheon party an hour later and for Becca's party that night. In response to the inevitable questions, I rolled my eyes, looked embarrassed, and said something about never eating soft-boiled eggs again. I did tell Becca what really happened. And she really did say: "*Quelle horreur!*"

And so, for two years now, I have been unable to get up in front of people and speak. Yes, I know, other people get panic attacks, too. But I can't believe it's all that many people, because if it were, this country would come to a grinding halt. You cannot know the thumping terror of it, the total loss of control, the willingness to just die rather than keep going through it, unless you've lived through it.

My mother has tried to get me to see a therapist about this. I've refused. Just as I've refused to risk re-creating the experience: I will not give a presentation in class, no matter what this means for my grade. I will not raise my hand to be called on in class. That I have tried. Here's what happens. The seconds after I stick my hand in the air, and before the teacher calls on me, turn into an eternity. During that eternity, my heart beats uncontrollably, my mouth goes into lockdown, my throat closes up—and I pull my hand back to my side. It is not worth it. Weirdly, though, if a teacher ambushes me—that is, if I am called on without having volunteered myself—I can get the words out. It must be the surprise and spontaneity of it. There's no time for the wave to build.

"Being a CIT would be the perfect baby step," Becca said last winter when we talked about going back to camp. "Because you only have to be 'on' in front of little kids who are going to love you no matter what. No pressure."

But it's not about pressure. Pressure is beside the point. It really is like being possessed. And it really is a problem with no name, as Becca says in her text. You have to call it something, so people use words like stage fright, panic attack, social phobia—none of which really covers it. You might as well call it a dybbuk.

%

So:

No, I don't expect to be talking about that particular problem.

What about following your dream?

75

My dream. That would be my half-formed idea of going to law school—so far into the future you can't even see it from here—and then becoming a lawyer who takes cases for people who have been discriminated against. Or who have been treated unfairly by big and powerful interests. Those important, public interest cases, like Erin Brockovich did in the movie. In the movie and in real life, I should say, since she was real.

Maybe I'll be the type of lawyer who doesn't argue cases in court.

Stubborn.

Hey, EB didn't speak in court.

Right. She wasn't the lawyer. But don't you want to be her boss?

To be honest, I'm really not thinking about my future as a lawyer right now. To be more honest, I'm never thinking of my future as a lawyer or anything else as much as Becca is. She has direction and drive. She wants to be a journalist. She wants to end up as a columnist and commentator. So she's already working on her plan. I think the two of us halfway just made up the idea that I want to be a lawyer, so that I wouldn't be left completely in the dust of her ambition.

I did have the fleeting fantasy, when I got the babysitting job with the Dankers, that Mr. Danker and I would have the chance to talk about being a lawyer, that he would see something in me that would cause him to encourage me, that he would invite me to the Supreme Court to watch him argue a case on one of my days off. I later learned that the Supreme Court doesn't hear cases during the summer months. And, of course, Mr. Danker saw nothing in me at all, except a nonentity that he occasionally called *Young Lady*.

Becca seems to give up, for now, on getting my commitment to the goal of becoming Erin Brockovich's boss.

What else r u doing?

Reading an article about how everyone but me takes the Red Cross babysitting class. So they will expect the unexpected and not let little kids run into streets.

Who says?

Some girl in the Observer.

???

An article about the accident.

Zut. Are you in it?

No not really. Although I was interviewed.
The reporter asked a lot of questions.
But I guess I gave the wrong answers
because the only thing the article says
about me is that I didn't take the
R.C. course.

You told her that?

Afraid so.

Everyone does *not* take classes. I haven't.

They're free. Maybe you should.

Anyway, I meant what are you doing in general,
not this minute.

What I'm doing is trying to figure out what
I'm doing.

Je comprends.

And are you teaching the kids French?

Ha. Sure. In our arts and crafts class.

Why not? Monet. Manet. Cezanne.

Ha again. Arts and crafts. Not art history. Plus these kids are 7.

Eager young minds. They'll love your French expletives.

ZUT ALORS!

SACRE BLEU!

I mean ZUT ALORS I have to go.

OK bye.

You still haven't told me how you are.

To be continued.

I scroll up to the top of our text string. And then farther up, where I wrote "He was such a great kid" after Becca had already put her phone away.

I wish she had asked me about Humphrey. I wish anybody

would ask me about Humphrey. Not about me. Not about my emotional state. Not, Ms. Diana Tang, cub reporter, about the sickening sequence of events that everyone in Franklin Grove just calls The Tragedy. Ask me about Humphrey T. Danker, the highly interesting little person I hung out with this summer.

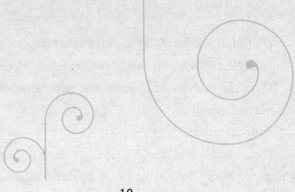

12

Opposite Day

"We're drawing!" Humphrey exclaimed, breathlessly, as soon as he opened the door.

"Oh—goody!" I said. But Humphrey had already turned around to run toward the back of the house. It was Wednesday, my third week of babysitting.

"Come on!" he yelled over his shoulder.

It was raining hard. I left my umbrella outside, propped against the house next to the front door. My sneakers were wet; I slipped them off.

Humphrey and his mother were at the kitchen table, which was covered with pencils, crayons, colored pencils, erasers, rulers, a protractor, and sheets of copy paper. Humphrey was wearing his pajamas. Mrs. Danker was not.

"Do you like to draw?" Humphrey asked me.

"Sure," I said, lowering myself into an empty chair.

"Here," he said, pushing paper and pencils my way. "You can join our marathon."

"Your *marathon*," I said.

"Our marathon is about drawing twenty-six drawings," Humphrey said. "They have to be good drawings. Not just scribble-scrabble."

"Wow, twenty-six pictures," I said.

"*Drawings*, not pictures," Humphrey corrected.

"Got it," I said.

"Humphrey, sweetheart, Mommy has to go now," said Mrs. Danker. "I'll see you a little later, okay?"

"Okay," Humphrey said.

"Danielle, there's a nice watercolor set and painting easel that Humphrey's daddy set up in the basement," Mrs. Danker said. "Maybe Humphrey will want to do some painting after he gets tired of drawing."

"I never get tired of drawing!" Humphrey said.

The completed drawings were spread out on the kitchen table. They were all in pencil and colored pencil; no crayons. Some of them resembled—roughly—architectural or engineering drawings; others looked more like maps with lots of landmarks.

"Wow, Humpty Dumpty," I said. "These look cool. Want to tell me about them?"

"Wait," he murmured, barely audible, not looking up

from the sheet in front of him. "I'm in the middle of a very important . . ." He trailed off, his pencil moving furiously.

After a minute or two, Humphrey sighed heavily. "It's getting harder," he said, still not looking up.

"Want to show me?" I asked.

"No! I want to crumple it up and throw it away. I want to throw them all away!" But he didn't.

"Maybe you just need a break," I said. "Every artist needs a break sometimes."

"I'm not an artist," Humphrey said. "These aren't pictures. They're drawings. They're supposed to be for inventions. Inventions for space exploration."

"Show me."

He was too busy.

"Do the space-cars park outside?" Humphrey said, bending over the papers. "But then how do the people get inside? Or do they drive right into the space station, like into a garage? But then it has to be so giant. That's not how it would be in real life. A space station can't be so huge. But then why'd I draw all these space-cars driving there? There's no room for them. My ideas aren't good! I hate this!"

I had no experience with whining kids. A minute ago, he'd been all happy and excited: *We're drawing! I love this!* Now, five minutes later—*I hate this!*

"But these are amazing, Humphrey," I said.

"No, they're not," he said. "They're stupid." He laid his head down on the table.

"Only if it's Opposite Day," I said. "If you catch my drift."

It was as if you could see the gears turning in Humphrey's head. Opposite Day.

"Look at the sun shining out there!" he said, pointing toward the window.

"It's a beautiful day for playing outdoors," I said.

Pause. Gear shift. Then: "I got dressed as soon as I woke up this morning," Humphrey said.

"And look at me," I countered. "I walked out of my house still in my pajamas."

"I had chicken for breakfast," Humphrey said.

Hmm. "Is that an opposite? I mean, what would be the opposite of that?"

"I had chicken for dinner!" Humphrey said.

"Not—I had cereal for breakfast?"

Click, click went the gears. It was like looking through a kaleidoscope and seeing all the tiny shapes fall into place. Did all little kids have brains that were so—clickable?

Humphrey agreed to get dressed. Afterward, in the kitchen again, he gave me a tour of his drawings. They most certainly were not just pictures, I agreed. They were designs for a wondrous exploration.

"So, is the idea to build a city on the moon," I asked, "or to build a space-station city?"

"Silly, that's not the moon!" Humphrey said. "Do you think that looks like the moon?"

"Uh—yeah, no," I said. Last week we'd agreed that "yeah,

no" was the perfect thing to say when you didn't know what to say.

"It's Thrumble-Boo, silly!" Humphrey said.

The rain didn't let up. After a while, when I could tell Humphrey was running out of steam, I suggested a nap.

"You know I don't take naps," Humphrey said after we climbed the stairs.

"How about breaking into those watercolors your mom mentioned?"

"Too messy," Humphrey said.

"And you're such a neat person?" I said. I gestured around. We were in Humphrey's room, which was, as usual, in a state of confusion.

He explained. He didn't mind the kind of mess his room was in. It was the messy mess of painting he didn't like.

"This is a clean mess," he said. "Painting is a dirty mess." He looked at me. "If *you* catch my *drift*."

"So you're *fastidious*," I said, "but not *fussy*." I waited for Humphrey to say that yes, indeed, he knew the meaning of "fastidious," and, by the way, here are sixteen other interesting *f* words his father had recently mentioned.

"Okay, let's paint," he said.

I was surprised. We went to the basement and painted. Humphrey's paintings were uninspired and unplanned—the opposite of his drawings—just random brushstrokes on the page.

"This is fun," he said. "Look at my beautiful pictures." His voice was listless.

I figured I should encourage him. "It is fun," I said. "I don't even mind the mess, do you?"

"No," he said. "I love it."

"Humphrey?"

"I love it if it's Opposite Day," he said.

We heard the front door open and close.

"Shall we go say hello?" I asked.

He shook his head. "Let's say good-bye." He put down his brush and started toward the stairs.

It was Mr. Danker.

"Are these your shoes?" Mr. Danker said to me.

"Oh—yes." My shoes had been on the hall rug since that morning.

"Let's move them out of the way next time," Mr. Danker said. "I almost tripped on them."

"I'm sorry!" I said. But I couldn't help but wonder—really? He didn't see, he almost tripped on, my chartreuse size eight-and-a-half sneakers?

"Where's Mommy?" Humphrey asked.

"She'll be home shortly. What have you done on this rainy day, Humphrey?"

"Nothing," Humphrey said.

Way to go, Humpty, I thought. *That makes me look just great.*

"Nothing?" his father said. "That's not good. What's all this on the kitchen table?"

"They're just *pictures*," Humphrey said. "They don't mean anything."

Either I've created an Opposite Day Monster, I thought, *or something is strange here.*

"Very well. If they don't mean anything, let's clean them up, shall we? Mommy doesn't need to be cleaning up messes when she comes home."

Zing.

"It's Opposite Day, Daddy," Humphrey said. "Danielle said so. So that means Mommy wants to clean up messes when she comes home. It's her favorite, favorite thing to do. Right, Danielle?"

Yeah, no.

"If that's the case, Opposite Day is over," Mr. Danker said. "Thank you, Danielle. We appreciate your help today."

From the way he said "appreciate," I was pretty sure Opposite Day was still in effect. At least for the duration of his sentence.

13

NO, JUST NO

Humphrey's funeral is today. That doesn't seem like the sort of thing you'd say about a five-year-old.

At the same time, though, it also seems like it's too late for a funeral. It's Thursday; the accident was last Friday. You do the math. Isn't that just a really long time for a person to be—there's no pretty way to say this—lying around dead? We Jews get our dead people in the ground quickly. My grammy Ann died on a Wednesday night—technically, early Thursday morning. Her funeral was Friday morning. I don't know why we do it so fast, but I think it's a good idea. It's bad enough to be dead, isn't it? To be dead and hanging out in the basement of a funeral home, where people drain your bodily fluids and replace them with—what?—in an effort to preserve you—for what?—like some kind of pickled biology lab specimen. . . . I'm sorry, but no. Just no.

I realize it's not as if the alternative is great. To think of Humphrey closed up in a box and put into a huge hole with six feet of dirt piled on top of him—again, no. Just no. Of course, Humphrey would be asking about how much dirt that is, exactly. To be specific, how much does that dirt weigh? As much as a kitchen chair? A living room sofa?

Anyway, at long last, the funeral is at two o'clock, an hour from now. Dad came home from work a few minutes ago. Mom will go to the church directly from her office. I think, but I'm not sure, that Adrian will meet us there, too.

The phone rings.

"Can you get that?" Dad calls from upstairs. "I'm changing."

I can get it. But I choose not to. Ever since I talked to the reporter, I'm kind of not interested in picking up the house phone. Today it's probably that Diana Tang, wanting to ask whether I've enrolled in the Red Cross babysitting class yet. I let it ring.

"Pick up the phone, Danielle!"

It's Mrs. Raskin. I haven't seen her since Adrian pried my cell phone out of her hands in the ER. She gets right to the point. She's pretty sure the Dankers don't want me at the funeral.

Oh. Okay. 'Bye.

Dad comes downstairs. He's put on a suit and tie, which is not what he wears to work. He asks if that was Mom on the phone. I tell him it was Mrs. Raskin un-inviting me to Humphrey's funeral.

"There aren't invitations to a funeral, Danielle," he says.

"She said the Dankers don't want me," I say.

"Don't want you?" He turns his head to the side a little.

"So—do I not go?"

"Let me call her back," he says. It takes us a few minutes to track down Mrs. Raskin's number—she's not in our family telephone book (since she's not exactly a friend of my parents) or on our emergency phone sheet (ditto). But she's listed in a neighborhood directory. And she doesn't answer when Dad calls.

"Hmm." He calls Mom's cell. It goes right to her voice mail, which means she's on the phone, or the phone is turned off. "Hmm." He's not sure what to do. And I definitely have no clue.

He fumbles around in the neighborhood directory. Looking over his shoulder, I see he's turned to the listing for the Crenshaws, the Dankers' next-door neighbors. He punches in the numbers and waits.

"June?" So Mrs. Crenshaw answered.

The conversation is brief.

"Hmm," Dad says after he hangs up. "June Crenshaw says they didn't exactly say they don't want you. But they did say something about—about how hard it would be to see you. She hemmed and hawed, so I really don't know what, if anything, is going on. June didn't feel that whatever they said warranted calling us. She says the Dankers are breakable—no, *brittle* is how she put it—and she wasn't sure they actually intended to exclude you."

This is way above my head. And the phone rings again.

"Hello?" Dad says. After a beat, he mouths to me, "Mrs. Raskin." He listens. Then he says, "June Crenshaw had a slightly different impression." More listening. "Uh-huh." Pause. "Well, thanks for your insights." Pause. "No, I really do appreciate it." Pause. "We'll make our decision." Pause. "Okay, then." Pause. "'Bye."

She was in the bathroom when Dad first called her, which is more information than we need. She says she heard that the Dankers said they would be more comfortable if I were not at the funeral. She is confident that what they meant was that I should not come.

Oh, how this lady loves to tell people what to do.

"Danielle, like I said, there are no invitations to a funeral," Dad says. "We can go and sit in the back of the church. There will be a crowd. They won't even see us."

But what if they do?

Dad talks about my feelings about losing Humphrey. I suffered a loss, too. I am entitled to take part in our community's good-bye to Humphrey—more so than most of the people who will be there. The Dankers don't have to see me. And if they do see me, they will know that I'm there to honor Humphrey and they will understand. At least we hope they will.

I decide not to go to the funeral.

"It's your decision, Danielle. Make sure you're comfortable

with it." This is a total Dad-ism, like quality time. He's big on the decision-making process. Mom would just tell me what I should do.

But I'm sure. And Dad is not going to the funeral if I'm not going. In fact, he says, now that he thinks about it, he wonders if it wouldn't be better (*if it wouldn't be better*—another Dad-ism) for all of the Snyders to stay away from the funeral. Dad tries Mom's phone again, and Adrian's. It's one forty-five, and they're not answering. I send them texts: *Dankers don't want me at funeral, so Dad and I aren't going. Maybe you shouldn't either.*

Neither of us has eaten lunch, so I make tuna salad sandwiches.

"June Crenshaw also said that the Dankers were upset because someone put a football at that roadside memorial," Dad says. "A 'painful and thoughtless reminder,' June said. Look, it's an emotional day anyway. Maybe that put them over the top. So I hope you don't take to heart the fact that in their fragile state they've done something hurtful to you."

I cannot even swallow.

Ninety minutes later, Mom and Adrian walk in. They both saw my text, but it was too late. They were already in the church, and getting up to leave would have appeared strange.

"You could have come," Mom says. "It was a mob scene. And anyway, Danielle, you had a right to be there. You did nothing wrong. You should have been there."

"Understandably, Danielle was conflicted," Dad says. "And

we don't really know what the Dankers are thinking about Danielle's—role. You don't want to cause more pain. . . ."

"These people are in so much pain already, I don't think they could even feel more," Mom says.

"Jeez, guys," Adrian says. "Way to shore up Danny."

"I mean," Mom says, "of course they're mourning Humphrey. *And* they've got Clarice's health issues. Seeing Danielle, not seeing Danielle—I just don't think it's on their radar screen."

Adrian says he has to get going. I follow him outside.

"Do you want to hear about it?" he asks.

"Yes."

"It was seriously intense," he says. "I've never been to a funeral for a person who wasn't old. They use this tiny coffin."

The pastor spoke about God's mysterious plan. Someone read that poem about how, when a person is gone, they're not really gone, they're in the air, the mountains, the rivers, blah, blah, blah. Someone read a story that they said Humphrey loved.

"What story?" I ask.

"You know. The one that everyone reads to little kids. It doesn't make a lot of sense, when you break it down. *Goodnight Moon*."

" 'Goodnight noises everywhere,' " I quote. "I love that book."

"Marissa was there," Adrian says. "She said to say hello."

"Oh."

"It's more like she sent regards. It wasn't really a setting where people were just saying 'hey.'"

"No, I know," I say. "So she sent regards."

"Did you ever get back to her after she texted the other day?" Adrian asks.

I shake my head. "We're not—close. Anymore. If we ever were."

"Huh," Adrian says. "I always thought she was okay."

"A ringing endorsement," I say.

"No, I mean better than okay. She's kind of traditional, but not—Paleolithic. I liked that she usually brought a different point of view to the table."

"Yes, she did," I say. "Marissa does have her points of view. Which I haven't heard in seven months, and I'm okay with that." Adrian looks at me like he doesn't quite catch my drift, which he doesn't. How could he? I would never tell him what Marissa said about him and his bad attitude.

"Well," he finally says. "The last time I saw the two of you together was Rock Star Weirdness Day last winter. There were some, shall I say, twisted points of view on display from both of you on that occasion."

"I can't believe you're saying that."

"It was video game insanity," Adrian says. "It happens. Did you ever make it right with her?"

"Did she ever make it right with me?" I counter.

He looks at me again with that not-quite-getting-it squint.

"Am I missing something?" he asks.

"You're supposed to be on my side!" I cry.

"There's no side here," Adrian says. "Marissa said hello to you, through me, your trusted envoy. Maybe she doesn't know how to approach you right now. You just went through a really intense thing. Some people will reach out to you—"

"Yeah, newspaper reporters and the police are my bestest friends."

"—and some will hold back. Come on, Danny, you know that even in normal circumstances, you're not exactly the most approachable person."

"Not approachable?" Surely he's talking about someone else. "I'm totally approachable. Except when I am temporarily deranged by a stupid video game, which will never happen again, because you're all grown up and moved away."

"Hey, it's part of your charm," Adrian says. "It's who you are: a self-reliant person. It can be a little—daunting."

The whole time we're talking, we're standing next to his car. Suddenly I have to sit down. I sink into the grassy strip next to the curb.

"I'm always on your side, Danny," Adrian says.

I love that book *Goodnight Moon*. But Humphrey didn't love it. Maybe he listened to it before I knew him, but he never let me read it to him.

"That's from when I was a baby," he would say. "Let's read a more important book. A more interesting book."

"I put a football at that stupid memorial on Quarry Road," I tell Adrian. "I put it there because Humphrey loved to play catch with me, and that has a lot more to do with him than stupid stuffed animals and action figures. And now the Dankers think some insensitive moron put a football there as some kind of sick joke."

"A sick joke because . . ."

"Because, you know, he was running after a football when, you know."

Right. Of course he sees the problem. "It wasn't insensitive, Danny," Adrian says. "It has a meaning, a totally cool meaning, that the Dankers just don't get. That's not your fault."

"I guess I could have thought about how they would see it."

Adrian places his hands out, wide, palms up. The universal who-knows gesture.

"Don't they know the kid loved to throw a football?" he asks. "I mean, Mr. Danker must have played football with his own son."

I think for a moment. "No," I say, "and no."

Adrian shakes his head. "Parents," he says. "They are clueless."

14

Compass Points

I have another visit from the police. Not the same guy-'n'-girl team as the night of the accident, though. I mean, it's a man and a woman, but they're different people. They don't wear uniforms.

"We know you've already been interviewed by our colleagues, Danielle," the woman begins, "but we need you to tell us again what happened that evening."

"We were walking home from the park," I begin. "We were walking on the side of Quarry Road."

"Were you walking along the eastbound lane or the westbound lane?" she asks.

It's only the first question, and I'm stumped. When they see my confusion, they try again:

"Were you on the north side of Quarry or the south side?" the man asks.

Isn't that helpful. I know the points of a compass—but I don't think about north, south, east, or west when I'm going somewhere. I was on Quarry Road, heading home.

"She doesn't drive yet, detectives," offers Dad by way of an excuse as I sit there mutely. Mom and Dad are in the living room with us.

I have an idea: "I was on the same side of Quarry Road as the playground."

"Okay. You were on the north side of Quarry Road," the woman says. "Which puts you along the westbound lane. You were walking east along the westbound lane."

If they say so. I would say I was walking *up* Quarry Road, because there's a hill that you have to go up when you walk home from the park. When I walk from home to the park, or farther on toward the street that then takes you either to the mall or to the highway, I would say I'm walking *down* Quarry Road.

But I'll go with walking east along the westbound lane.

"To clarify, when you say you were walking on the side of the road, you mean on the shoulder?" the man asks.

Um—I look at my parents. They don't give me any clues.

"Well, I was on the side there," I offer, "where you're supposed to walk. To the left of the yellow line. Is that technically the shoulder?"

"No driver's education yet," Mom notes.

This is what you learn in driver's ed? The official parts of a road?

"Okay. And then what happened?" the man prompts.

"I dropped the ball and Humphrey ran after it into the street."

They pause. Appropriately, I think. It's like it's out of respect for Humphrey.

"When you say you dropped the ball," the woman says after our moment, "how did that happen? It slipped out of your fingers?"

I don't want to cast blame on a dead five-year-old, but they are making me.

"Humphrey tried to tackle me and the ball popped out," I explain.

"And then."

"And then the ball bounced into the street. You know how a football doesn't bounce neatly or predictably—it goes all over the place. That's what it did. It hit a couple of cars."

"So Humphrey ran into the street," the woman continues. "Did you run after him?"

Is this a trick question? I know better than to run into traffic. I'm alive.

I say: "No."

"Now, Humphrey ended up in the eastbound lane of Quarry Road. You say you were walking along the side of the westbound lane," the man says.

This eastbound and westbound thing again. It makes my brain hurt. Concentrate, Danielle. He ended up across the street.

In the lane with cars headed *up* Quarry. Which meant he first crossed the lane with cars headed *down* Quarry. Okay, we're on the same page. I wait for the question.

Which apparently they asked while I was mapping things out in my head.

"I'm sorry. What was the question?"

"Did you see any vehicle hit Humphrey as he was crossing the westbound lane?"

"No, I didn't."

I didn't see any vehicle hit Humphrey in any lane. Somehow, I was there, I was an eyewitness, and missed the whole thing.

"So you saw Humphrey cross the westbound lane and make it to the eastbound lane," the man says. "Did you see a vehicle hit him there?"

I shake my head. "I'm sorry. It was all a blur."

"Do you remember seeing a blue minivan on the scene after the accident, when emergency and rescue personnel were there?" This is the woman.

"Yes. I saw it. It was near Humphrey, at the head of the line of cars backed up to go up"—I want to be helpful—"to go *eastward* on Quarry Road."

"Had you noticed that car before?" she asks.

I shake my head again. "I'm sorry."

"You didn't see that car as it drove *up*"—the man detective trying to be helpful—"Quarry Road. Didn't see whether it was driving fast or slow, carefully or not carefully."

"No. I'm sorry." I pause, trying to remember anything. "I think I saw the football hitting a couple of cars. I noticed a white car, and a pickup. They were on the other side of the street—so driving, uh, driving east, in the eastbound lane. You know, it was still rush hour, and that's where most of the cars are in rush hour, I guess—heading east, toward Montgomery Heights. By then, Humphrey had run after the ball."

I try to re-create the awful scene.

"On our side of the street—in the westbound lane—I don't remember many cars. You know, because Quarry Road isn't so crowded going in that direction that time of day. And I remember some kind of silver car coming down the—um, westbound lane, but I don't remember the ball hitting it or anything."

I don't remember a thud or a thump or anything to indicate that Humphrey had been hit. I don't remember anything until the screech of brakes. Just—silence. Like a break in the sound spectrum.

"The silver car was where?"

"Coming toward us, on our side of the street. Driving in the westbound lane."

"Not in the same lane as the blue minivan."

"No."

"The silver car wasn't speeding away after possibly hitting Humphrey."

"No."

"Anything else about the silver car, or the white one, or the pickup?" the woman asks.

I push my brain to retrieve a memory. It lets me down.

"Can't the police tell how Humphrey was hit?" I ask. "By looking at his, you know, his body?"

"Forensic evidence is very helpful," the man says. "But so is eyewitness evidence."

Okay. But if we're going to be using words like "forensic," then, if this were a *Law & Order* rerun, wouldn't the cops be matching up the deceased's injuries to a particular type of car bumper or hood or something? Wouldn't they be taking paint samples and examining skid marks? Wouldn't the detectives be exchanging significant looks when I said something significant? These detectives haven't exchanged any looks, but it is possible that I haven't said anything significant.

They shift gears.

"What color was the pickup?" the woman asks.

"It was . . . I don't know," I say, surprised at myself.

Isn't that weird? You'd think color would be the first thing I would remember. It is what I remember about the white car, and the silver one. But all I can retrieve is: pickup truck. No color. Or some color. Just not white.

"Getting back to the blue minivan," the man says, "at what point in the chain of events did you first notice it?"

"When I was sitting in the road with Humphrey after he was hit."

"Really think hard, Danielle," the man presses. "We're trying to determine if the blue minivan was speeding or driving recklessly."

I shake my head for the millionth time. I only saw it stopped, afterward.

"What does the driver of the blue minivan say?" I ask.

"That he was driving normally—even slower than normal, because of the traffic—and never saw Humphrey coming," says the man.

"Did someone else see the accident?" I ask.

"We're not sure," the woman says. "There have been some reports from other drivers, but often people think they saw things that they really didn't in these situations."

There are more questions. Finally they're done. They leave me their cards in case I remember anything.

When the detectives are gone, Mom tells me I did as well as I could have. She means to be supportive. But when it mattered, out there walking east along the westbound lane of Quarry Road, clearly I did not do as well as I could have. As well as I should have.

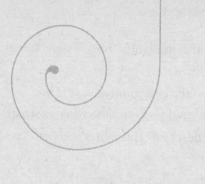

15

VRAIMENT, VRAIMENT

"Comment ça va?"

Camp is over, Becca's back, and we're at the bakery we like because it feels French and is not a chain.

"Really," Becca says. "Tell me how you're doing."

I take a sip of my café au lait. "I'm doing."

"Danielle, I'm sorry I couldn't be here for you."

"You were at camp."

"True, but now that I think about it, I could have gotten permission to come home for a day. That's what I should have done."

"You texted every day. That's being here for me. And you called after the funeral."

She did, that night, after Adrian went home. I've removed

those quotation marks I put around our "friendship." Becca's been a loyal friend.

"Texting, calling—they're not really being there. But you are *très gentille* for not being mad at me." She bites into her *pain au chocolat*. "Oh my God. This is to die for."

Her face freezes.

"I didn't mean to say that," she whispers.

I have to laugh.

"Becca, you can use the word 'die' in my presence."

"What I meant," Becca says, "was that camp food is definitely nothing like this."

"No," I say. "I seem to remember that."

"Bug juice," she says.

That would be watered-down fruit punch.

"Turds."

Translated: hamburgers. I know, disgusting, but true. Very hard hamburgers.

"Sticks and stones."

That's easy: fish sticks and overbaked macaroni.

"But really, Danielle, I can't imagine how you must have felt. And still feel."

There is too much to say. I feel like my head will crack open if I start talking about it. Which is an awful and stupid thing to say, given what happened, and it obviously would be worse to say out loud. So it's fortunate that I've temporarily lost the ability to speak.

"I want to know," Becca says. "That is, I want to know if you want to tell me."

I regain control of my voice. "I don't want to talk—I mean, about it. I'd love to hear about your summer. Being a CIT, being away for the entire eight weeks. Will you go back as a counselor?"

Becca peers at me. "Danielle, really? That's what you want to talk about? *Vraiment*?"

I assure her that it is. *Vraiment, vraiment.*

She rolls her eyes slightly.

"It was great," she says. "Really great. I had the youngest girls, the seven-year-olds. The counselors I was assigned to were really nice, and didn't just give me the grunt work."

"What would be the grunt work?" I ask.

"You know, if a kid needs bathroom help. Or like serving food."

"Okay."

"I was also assigned to arts and crafts—I told you that, right?—which was my first choice. Which I loved. So—clay, and beads, and collage, and leather work. Fun, *n'est-ce pas*?"

"Yeah. It's fun," I agree. "Did you have those beads you iron so they melt together into pretty little doodads?"

Becca nodded. "The girls love that! Which is funny, because they all have the bead kits at home, so they ended up doing the same thing at camp arts and crafts that they could do at home. I kept trying to push leather working—you know, because it's more camp-ish—and they were totally not interested. They just kept wanting to do beads. Making useless little trinkets—*les bibelots*! I think one girl made twenty-five of them."

Somehow I've become transfixed. I know I'm supposed to laugh or nod or somehow react to the girl who made twenty-five useless little *bibelots*, but all I can think of is Humphrey. He knew about the bead kits, and he wanted one.

"Danielle. Did I say something?"

I shake my head, which feels like it weighs about a hundred pounds.

"See, I knew I shouldn't be talking about this. We should be talking about *you*."

I shake my head again. "It's not your fault. I asked about the beads—"

But I can't go on. Suddenly, I am conscious of the fact that words that begin with *b* are particularly prone to leading a person to tears. Seriously. Maybe because what you do with your mouth to say *b* is so close to what you do with your mouth when you burst out blubbering. I am not just trying to change the subject, to get away from thinking about Humphrey. In fact, I can't help but think of Humphrey, because I am sure he would have enjoyed experimenting with *b* words to test out my theory.

"These macaroons," I say, "really are to die for."

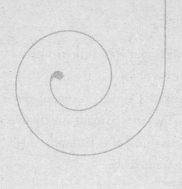

16

BAD, BAD BALL

I was on my knees next to Humphrey, in the field, in the park. This was a post-dinner, pre-dark outing, Saturday night, two days after Opposite Day.

"Okay. You want to sort of—tee it up. Tee it up here in your hand. Then launch it away from you."

"I can do it," Humphrey said. "I know I can."

I walked about ten paces away. "Launch me that spiral!"

It rolled out of his hand, dribbled on the ground. He pounced on it, readied it in his hand, attempted launch, and it rolled again. And again, five more times.

"Look, forget about teeing it up. Forget about launch," I said. "Let's see what you do when you just throw the football any old way."

It didn't go any old place. At all.

"I know you can teach me, Danielle," Humphrey said sweetly.

I wasn't so sure. Still, he was a good sport and I wanted to encourage his good attitude. "One way I can teach you to throw is to throw to you, Humphrey," I said. "That way, you get practice catching—"

"Oh, I can already catch."

"—and you get to watch how I throw." I told Humphrey to catch the ball, then run it to me. "As if you're running the ball down the field and I'm the goalpost."

I threw spiral after spiral. I threw as softly as I could, but he couldn't hang on to a single catch. He stood there waiting for the ball, or, if the throw wasn't right on target, he moved to get into its path—and then, basically, he tried to clap it. That's what it looked like to me, like Humphrey had been told to clap the ball. I studied him more closely. Maybe it wasn't so much that he was trying to clap the ball, as he was trying to grab hold of it with a pair of tongs, or tweezers.

"I almost caught that one!" Humphrey said.

No, he didn't.

It wasn't that hard to catch a well-thrown football.

"Humphrey, you're clapping at the ball," I said.

"No, I'm not," he said.

"You're slapping at it. You're slapping it away."

"No, I'm not."

I had taken a couple of juice boxes from the Dankers' refrigerator, and now he took them out of my backpack.

"Why do you want to slap that poor ball, Humphrey?" I said. "What did that poor, funny-looking ball do to you that makes you want to slap it?"

There went those gears clicking away in his head. In my three weeks with Humphrey, I had found I could best make a point by being funny and by playing with words.

"I'm slapping the ball because it's been bad. Very, very bad." Click, click. "It runs away from me when it's supposed to hold my hand. And it hangs on to me like a baby when it's supposed to run and get its exercise."

"What shall we do about these problems," I said, "other than slapping the ball?"

"I don't know," Humphrey said. "I think I'm just going to have to keep slapping, slapping, slapping."

"Ouch," I said. "Poor, poor, pitiful ball."

"Poor, poor, pitiful, poopy, poopified, putrid ball!"

"Wow. *Putrid.* That's not your everyday *p* word."

We drained our juice boxes. "Back to this football," I said. "I have an idea that might help you catch it. You know how you said the ball is running away from you when it's supposed to hold your hand?"

He nodded.

"Think of the ball as a baby. I mean, a little baby-baby. It doesn't know it's supposed to hold your hand. So when I throw it to you, you have to cradle it in your arms to catch it. You have to cradle it like it's a baby. Like this." I tossed the ball up and caught it in a cradling way.

"Like a baby," Humphrey said.

"Rock-a-bye baby," I sang out.

"In the treetop," Humphrey responded, also singing.

"In your arms, the football cradle," I said. He started to run out for a pass, but I stopped him. "Just toss it up, right here." He tossed it maybe five inches into the air. "A little higher," I said. He followed my instructions.

"Toss and cradle. Toss and cradle. That's good," I said. After a while, I took the ball and tossed it to him from just a couple of feet away. Then I moved a few more feet away.

"You slapped it," I said when the ball escaped Humphrey's arms.

"Because it's bad," he said.

"I don't think so," I called out in a singsongy voice. "Cradle that baby."

He did. I tossed it to him from six feet away, ten feet, fifteen feet. He cradled the baby and ran it back.

"Good. Great! Now go long!" I said, at the same time thinking, *Listen to me with the football lingo.*

He didn't know what "go long" meant.

"Go long—it means 'run far'! Then stop and look back for the throw."

Far, in Humphrey's case, meant running maybe twenty-five feet away. He turned, expectantly. I launched a sweet, gentle spiral his way. "Cradle it!" I yelled.

"Yes!" he rejoiced. He ran the football back. "Again!"

He didn't catch it every time. But he caught it enough of the time.

"I'm a football catcher!" he said.

The sun had disappeared behind the trees that rimmed the park. Time to head home.

He didn't want to go. "I still have to learn how to throw a spiral," he said.

"You do, and you will," I said. "Just not tonight. You don't want to be here in the park when it's dark, do you?"

"I like the dark," Humphrey said.

"I like it, too. But we need to start walking home. Look— you can already see stars."

I knew that the low-hanging white discs in the darkening sky were Venus and Saturn, although I didn't know which was which.

"Which one came out first?" Humphrey asked.

"I don't know."

"*Did* one come out first?"

"Well—yeah."

"How come I can never see the first star?" he asked. "When- ever I look, there's always more than one."

"I guess you'd have to pay really close attention," I said. "You'd have to just sit down and say, 'Okay, I'm not going to do anything but look up at the sky and wait for the first star to come out.'"

"Let's do that next time," Humphrey said.

"Okay, but—it's probably about as exciting as watching paint dry," I said. "If you catch my drift."

"I catch your drift," Humphrey said. He skipped a little to catch up with me on the path leading out of the park. "And now I can catch your football, too."

17

INCOMPETENT

Not to let me come to the funeral. Or not to want me there, since, as Mom and Dad said, there are no invitations to a funeral. They must really hate me.

They have a right to. They have a right to hate me. And they have a right to find me despicable. And to think I'm incompetent. That's not a strong enough word. Careless. Mindless. They're also not strong enough. There may not be a strong enough word to describe my failure. Because, honestly, how hard is it to keep a little boy from running into the street?

He was <u>not</u> an out-of-control kid. He was perfectly easy to control. Unless you were an incompetent, careless, mindless, <u>horrendous</u> babysitter.

After two sessions of sitting around looking at each other, one hundred minutes of me looking at her looking at me, for which my parents paid I don't know how much—my therapist, Dr. Gilbert, had an idea.

"Are you a writer, Danielle?" she asked.

"Not especially," I answered, truthfully.

"Hmm. But are you comfortable writing?"

"I don't mind writing."

"Do you think you might be more comfortable writing your feelings than saying them out loud, for starters?"

"You mean, sitting here and writing?"

"That's not exactly what I have in mind, although that's a possibility. What I meant was writing your feelings down at home, and then reading aloud what you wrote when you come to see me."

"So you mean, doing homework?"

"I guess it is like homework. But I wouldn't want you to feel burdened by it."

"But what if I did feel burdened by it?" I asked.

"I'm open to alternatives. Or we could continue to sit here as we've done for two sessions. Sometimes sitting in companionable silence can be very helpful, but I'm not sure that's what's happening here."

I didn't have a better idea. And she was right, it wasn't

companionable silence. It was just silence. Almost total silence on my part, punctuated by her occasional questions and conversation starters. I wasn't trying to be difficult. I just found the concept of sitting there and talking to this middle-aged lady who doesn't know me difficult.

Now, having just recited my first therapeutic work of literature, I'm looking at her again.

"Do you really think the Dankers hate you, Danielle?" Dr. Gilbert asks.

I sigh. "I wrote it," I say.

"No, you wrote that 'they must' hate you. And that they have a right to."

"I don't know," I say. "I don't know what they think about me. Maybe they don't think about me at all. Why should I even presume to think that they have any thoughts about me? How self-centered am I? 'Oh, poor me, the Dankers hate me.'"

Dr. Gilbert allows herself a small smile. "I wouldn't take it quite where you did, but, yes, maybe they aren't thinking about you. So if you think that may be the case, I suppose you could call yourself even more names and berate yourself for being self-centered. Or you could let yourself off *this* hook, at least—you could let go of the feeling that they hate you."

"Mr. Danker always hated me," I say.

Dr. Gilbert raises an eyebrow.

"He always made me feel stupid and clumsy and in the way."

"Did Mrs. Danker?"

"No."

"Did Humphrey?"

I shake my head.

"Maybe that was just Mr. Danker's problem," Dr. Gilbert says.

"His problem?"

"Maybe he's not great at interacting with a teenage girl."

"Or a five-year-old boy," I say.

"I don't know about that," Dr. Gilbert says. "Did you not like his interactions with Humphrey?"

I think back. There wasn't much to judge. My job was mostly to be at the Danker house when the Dankers weren't there. As for Mr. Danker and Humphrey—I never could figure that out.

"Sometimes it looked kind of—*off*, I guess, to me," I say. "Hot and cold. One day I'd think Mr. Danker was terrible at being Humphrey's father. Another day I'd think he was good at it."

Dr. Gilberts nods encouragingly.

"But what do I know," I say. "I was just the babysitter."

18

GOOD COOKIES

Back in the spring, Mrs. Danker had purchased tickets to a children's concert, intending to take Humphrey in the summer.

"It's the National Symphony," she explained to me the day before the event. "They have these wonderful programs, where they choose pieces that appeal to children, and they talk about the instruments and narrate the music. I've been looking forward to taking Humphrey to his first one."

But she couldn't reschedule her treatment. And Mr. Danker could not get away from work.

"So . . . unless you can't stand classical music . . ."

"I'd love to go," I said.

So there I was with Humphrey on the subway, on our way downtown.

"Why is it called the Candy Center?" Humphrey asked. "Do they have candy at the concerts?"

"The *Kennedy* Center," I said. "Not the Candy Center. The Kennedy Center for the Performing Arts."

"But they still might have candy," Humphrey said.

"You never know."

It was a long walk from the subway station to the Kennedy Center, but the weather was nice and we practically skipped along.

"Maybe we'll see Daddy," Humphrey said. "Since we're in Washington, D.C., and his office is in Washington, D.C. He said he was going to court today. Maybe we'll see him walking to court."

"You never know," I repeated. "But I doubt it. I don't think there are too many law offices in this part of the city."

"How about courts?"

I didn't know where the courthouses were.

"Well, then, you never know," Humphrey echoed.

We climbed the hill leading to the Kennedy Center's grand entrance.

"Lookit!" Humphrey threw his head way back to look up, up, up at the colorful flags lining the high walls.

We were in the Hall of States, I told him after consulting an informational placard.

"These are the flags of all fifty states," I said, "plus the five U.S. territories and Washington, D.C."

"These are really giant flags," he said.

"They are."

"I know our state's flag," Humphrey said. "I'm going to find it. Don't tell me if you see it first."

I didn't see it first. Humphrey pointed it out.

Our necks hurt after a while.

"I can't look up anymore," Humphrey said.

"Let's go to the Concert Hall," I proposed.

We found our seats.

"What are the five U.S. territories?" he asked.

I had wondered when he would come back around to this.

"I was afraid you would ask," I said. "I don't think I know them all."

"I bet you do. You know a lot."

"Puerto Rico is one."

"Okay. What's two?"

"Guam."

"G-wam?"

"Yes. Guam."

"Okay. Next?"

"American Samoa."

"I love Samoas," Humphrey said.

"Those are some good cookies, aren't they?" I said.

"Yup."

I didn't know the two remaining U.S. territories.

"Think, Danielle! Think hard!" Humphrey said.

"I don't know them, Humphrey. It's not that I've forgotten

them. I could think and think and think and still not know what they are. They're just not in my brain."

"I bet they are," he said.

"I am not that smart," I said. "I'm not as smart as you think I am."

The concert was about to start.

"Alay?" Humphrey whispered.

"Alay? What's Alay?" I whispered back.

"Is that one of the U.S. territories?"

Alay. Al-ay. El-ay. L.A.

"L.A.? The city L.A. Los Angeles?" I asked.

He shrugged. Sheepish. He knew he wasn't quite getting something.

"Whenever Daddy has to go there, he and Mommy make it sound so far away. I thought it was called Alay. Maybe it's a territory. Now that I know there are such things as territories."

I squeezed his hand. "L.A. is a city in California, Humphrey. But good try."

The concert was magical. The theme was "Summer Splash," and all of the compositions had something to do with water. The songs were about water, and the musicians also showed how they could make their instruments sound like water dripping, flowing, and splashing. Humphrey was mesmerized.

"I loved that," he said as we walked back to the subway. "Didn't you love that, Danielle?"

"I really did," I said.

"I loved the one especially by the one—his name is like a hand—"

"Handel," I said. "Me, too. That was so beautiful."

"Have you?" Humphrey said. "Have you ever?"

I'd been focused on getting us on the train and on my own thoughts about the music.

"Have I ever what, Humphrey?"

"Written a song."

"No. Not yet."

"I don't think it's too hard," he said.

"I don't know, Humphrey. I think it would be hard."

"You just said you haven't written a song 'yet.' That means you're going to write a song someday."

I laughed. "Oh, is that what it means?"

We were quiet on the ride back to the suburbs.

"We forgot about candy," Humphrey said. We were off the train now, off the bus from the subway station that brought us to the intersection of Franklin and Quarry Road, and walking in the neighborhood toward the Dankers' house.

I gasped in mock horror. "Oh, no! No Kennedy Center candy!"

"No can-e-dy!" he said.

"Maybe next time," I said.

"Next time, maybe there will be a concert about—candy music."

"You never know," I said.

It was four fifteen. I was scheduled to stay until six o'clock.

"What do you think, Humphrey? An early dinner for you?"

"Yes, please."

"You wouldn't want chicken tenders, would you?"

He smiled his answer. "And I'll write a song while they're cooking."

"Okeydokey," I said.

The Dankers had an old upright piano in the family room off the kitchen. Maybe once or twice I had seen Humphrey sit down at it and tinkle the keys. I'd never heard Mr. or Mrs. Danker play.

He was hesitant at first, and I could barely hear the piano from the kitchen. He struck the keys a little louder—not banging them, but hitting the notes more solidly. It wasn't a song, but it wasn't unpleasant or harsh. Just the sounds of someone noodling around on a piano.

Clang!

Clang-clang! Clang-clang-clang-clang!

Now Humphrey was banging. Now it was unpleasant.

"Humphrey, buddy," I called from the kitchen. "What are you doing?"

Clang-clang-clang-clang!

"Hey, I think you might be hurting the piano." I was standing next to him now. "You shouldn't be doing that."

"I can't write a song!" Humphrey said.

He seemed so surprised that I had to catch myself not to laugh.

"Maybe not yet," I said. "It takes practice. No one can just sit down at the piano and write a song."

"Yes, someone can," Humphrey said. "My daddy can."

"What's going on, guys?"

Mrs. Danker entered the family room. She looked wrung out.

"I'm sorry," I said. "I didn't realize you were resting. I mean, I didn't even know you were here."

"That's okay," she said. "I wasn't really sleeping. Humphrey, you sound like you're angry at that piano."

Humphrey just looked down at his hands. They were in his lap, no longer on the keys.

"Sorry."

The front door opened. Mr. Danker. He was earlier than I had expected. I heard him riffle through the mail on the table in the hall. I felt as though I was about to be caught red-handed. Doing what—not teaching Humphrey how to compose a symphony?

"Hello," he said. "Why are we all standing around the piano? Humphrey, are you giving a performance?"

"No," Humphrey said. "I can't write a song. Not even a tiny song. Here—this is all I can do."

Clang-clang-clang-clang. Clang-clang-clang. Clang-clang-clang-clang.

Inwardly, I cringed. *No, Humphrey. Don't get in trouble with your father.* Then I immediately felt embarrassed because I knew what I really meant was, *No, Humphrey. Don't get me in trouble with your father.*

Mrs. Danker excused herself and went back upstairs.

"Is that really all you can do?" Mr. Danker asked.

"Yes," Humphrey said.

"How about those songs we worked on?"

"They're *baby* songs," Humphrey said.

"Are they?" Mr. Danker said.

Humphrey nodded.

"You don't like taking baby steps," his father said.

Humphrey shook his head.

"But what did we say baby steps lead to?" Mr. Danker asked.

Humphrey sighed. "Big steps," he said.

"So, how about playing one of your songs?" Mr. Danker said.

"I wanted to write a song, not just play one," Humphrey said.

He was, I thought, coming dangerously close to whining—but not quite. Mostly, he just sounded so disappointed.

"I see," Mr. Danker said.

"Like you write songs," Humphrey said.

"Humphrey, I don't write songs," Mr. Danker said. "I just have fun on the piano. Sometimes I pick out a tune that I know, and then I improvise on it."

"What's 'improvise'?"

"It's making things up—making up notes and tunes that go with other music that someone else has already written," Mr. Danker said. "That's as close as I get to writing music."

"I want to improvise," Humphrey said.

"First, you have to take—"

"I know!" Humphrey interrupted. "Baby steps."

"Like your C-D-E song. The C-B-A song. After that you'll be playing the whole scale, and then the whole keyboard."

"And then the whole world!" Humphrey said. He seemed to be out of his funk. "And then the whole country!" He laughed and got up from the piano. "We saw the flags from the whole country today at the Kennedy Center," he said.

"Ah," Mr. Danker said, "the Hall of States."

"Plus the five territories," Humphrey said.

"Do tell," Mr. Danker said.

"Do you know what they are, Daddy?"

"As a matter of fact, yes, I do." Mr. Danker recited them: the Northern Mariana Islands, Guam, American Samoa, Puerto Rico, the U.S. Virgin Islands.

Humphrey looked at me. "There are the two you forgot!" he said.

"Forgot, or didn't know in the first place," I said.

"Sometimes I use tricks to remember things," Mr. Danker said. "I think of words or pictures in my head that remind me of the things I want to remember. Funny words or pictures work best."

"Can you teach me?" Humphrey asked.

Mr. Danker thought for a minute. "Try this," he said. "Aunt Mary Ann chewing gum and eating cookies on her porch in Virginia."

"My *real* aunt Mary Ann?" Humphrey squealed. "Chewing gum and eating cookies at the same time?"

"That's the idea," Mr. Danker said.

"But Aunt Mary Ann doesn't live in Virginia," Humphrey said. "Does she? I thought she lived in New York."

"But if you pretend she lives in a house with a porch in Virginia, it will help you remember the five territories," Mr. Danker said.

"How will Aunt Mary Ann eating—I mean, *chewing* gum and . . . eating cookies on her porch in . . . Virginia help me remember?" Humphrey asked, giggling.

"*Mary Ann* is for the Northern Mariana Islands. *Gum* is for Guam. *Cookies* is for—"

"I already know it!" Humphrey exclaimed. "Samoa Girl Scout cookies!"

"Try not to interrupt," Mr. Danker said, but not sternly. I could tell he was pleased that Humphrey got the concept.

"Sorry," Humphrey said. "I love those cookies. So does Danielle."

"As do I," Mr. Danker said. "Those are good cookies."

I had never heard him so—friendly. *He must have won a case today*, I thought.

"*Cookies* is for American Samoa," Mr. Danker continued. "*Porch* is for Puerto Rico. *Virginia* is for the U.S. Virgin Islands. So that's the trick. You remember a funny sentence that has clues to what you want to remember."

Humphrey thought this was the greatest thing. "Aunt Mary Ann chewing gum and eating cookies on her porch in Virginia," he repeated slowly. "Um . . ." He closed his eyes to think better. "Aunt Mary Ann . . ." He opened his eyes. "The only one I remember is Guam."

"That's all right," Mr. Danker said. "They are not easy names to remember. And now you know a memory trick. Next time we'll try it to remember something less complicated." He lifted his head a little higher and sniffed. "Is something burning?"

"Oh, no, the chicken tenders!" I cried.

They weren't ruined. But they were very well done.

"I like them this way," Humphrey said, his jaw working away at the leathery nuggets. Mr. Danker had gone to change his clothes and check on Mrs. Danker. I was to leave after Humphrey had his dinner.

"That's nice of you to say," I said.

"I like Daddy this way, too," Humphrey said. "Isn't he so, so, so smart?"

"*Yeah*," I said with enthusiasm. Smart and unpredictable.

"*Yes*," Humphrey said, correcting me.

"Of course—we say 'yes,'" I said.

"When we remember," Humphrey added.

We both burst out laughing.

"Northern Mariana Islands, Guam, American Samoa, Puerto Rico, U.S. Virgin Islands," I said. "I'll never forget them again."

"You're smart, too," Humphrey said.

"Not so, so, so smart?" I teased.

He considered this.

"Not yet," he said.

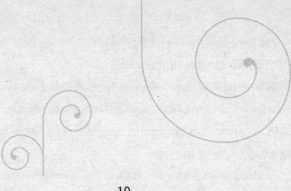

19

Doing Lunch

School is weird. School is also a relief, because at least I know what I'm supposed to be doing with my days.

The bus is weird: the first day back, the Tuesday after Labor Day, I feel like people are avoiding me—not that I've ever been a people magnet, but what I mean is, now I feel like there's a bubble around me and people are afraid to pop it. Some of the kids give me sympathy looks, some give me what's-wrong-with-her looks, some act like I'm not here, some seem to want to keep their distance because of an ick factor that now attaches to me.

Here are a few whispered tidbits:

"I mean—she chased him in the street."

"No. She threw the ball and he ran after it."

"I wouldn't take a stupid babysitting class. But it's not like you need a class to know not to do *that*."

"Killer essay for her college apps."

"That's a terrible thing to say."

Homeroom is more of a relief: Becca and I are in the same homeroom, since we both have *S* last names. We hug.

A guy from the newspaper staff distracts Becca by throwing a ball of paper her way.

"Let's do lunch together tomorrow," she says to me. "Today I have a newspaper thing."

I nod, and she turns to the newspaper guy.

We do meet up for lunch the next day. Our school is right in the middle of a busy suburban shopping area, and once you're a sophomore you're allowed to walk off-campus for lunch. We head for the less popular of the two coffee places, which isn't too crowded. It's not our French place, but it'll do.

"So," Becca says once we've got our food, "we're sophomores."

"Oh, yes, pinch me," I say.

We talk about school. We don't have a single class together this semester. Becca's newspaper duties take up not only a big chunk of her after-school time, but also a class period. She's already loving it. Newspaper people came back early to get organized.

"It was us and the football players rattling around here last week," she says. "So you can expect a lot of football stories in our first issue on Friday."

"I'll be sure to read every word," I say.

"I know you're a huge fan."

"Actually," I say, but then stop.

"Actually?"

I shake my head. Actually nothing.

"How're things?" Becca asks. "And by things, I mean—your state of mind."

"It's there, and it's in a state," I say. "You'll be happy to know I have broken my vow of silence with Dr. Gilbert."

"*C'est merveilleux!*"

"Yes. It's *merveilleux*. I'm officially in therapy. Now I'm a walking, talking modern cliché."

"I would concentrate on the 'walking, talking' part," Becca says. "You have to talk about all this, Danielle. If you won't talk to me"—she makes a disappointed pouty face—"for sure you should be talking to a therapist."

The lunch hour—the lunch forty-three minutes, to be exact—is almost over, and we start walking back.

"I know you're not ready," Becca says. "But when you're ready to talk, I'm here. I want to help if I can."

"I know, Becca. I appreciate it. I really do."

"I have an idea," Becca says after a few minutes.

"Of course you do."

"Really," she says. "Maybe this will be easier for you. Maybe you'll consider talking to me for the paper. It could be an amazing article."

"An *article*?"

"A human interest article," Becca says. "About how an experience like this affects a person. How it's changed you."

"Why would this be easier for me?" I ask.

"I'm just thinking it would be you getting outside of your head to look at what happened. You'd be talking to me as a reporter, not just a friend. Like you talk to the therapist as a professional, not just as a friendly adult. Maybe it helps to have that distance. You'd be stepping outside of yourself to think about it, to let other kids know what you've learned."

"Obviously I've learned nothing. Remember the article about the Red Cross babysitting course?" I say.

"No, no, that's not what I'm talking about at all. I mean what you've learned in a deeper way. You know, kids our age don't think about death. You must be so far beyond that now."

"Becca, I don't think so. . . ."

We're walking side by side, and she squeezes my shoulders. "It wouldn't be about the neighborhood conflict, or the immigration thing. Just you sharing your personal insights."

"There's an immigration thing?" I ask. "There's a neighborhood conflict?"

Becca stops to look at me. She seems about to say one thing; then I see her shift gears. Oh, how Humphrey taught me to read the little wheels grinding away inside people's heads.

"It's probably not a huge deal," she says. "I get all kinds of so-called inside scoop because I'm such a news junkie. I'm sure half of what I hear isn't true."

"Tell me the half that you think is true," I say. We're walking again.

"Just that some of your neighbors want to use the accident

as a reason to make changes along Quarry Road, and others say changes would ruin the neighborhood."

"And the immigration thing?"

"That the people in the van that—that hit Humphrey were illegal aliens. Or rather, undocumented immigrants. And that brings up a bunch of other issues, at least for some people."

So the accident has become an issue, or a bunch of issues, and I've missed them. Including something that some people say will ruin the neighborhood.

"I had no idea," I say.

"Like I said, probably *normal* people have no idea," Becca says. "But—speaking of 'walking, talking'—I'm a walking, talking blog. The neighborhood thing hasn't gotten any publicity yet, but it will. And the immigration thing—it'll probably come up at the county council, or even the state assembly."

"Why would that happen?" I ask. "What does the state assembly care about an accident in puny Franklin Grove?"

"Because," Becca says, "lots of other places have these laws against undocumented aliens who get in trouble for other reasons. For reasons other than being here illegally, I mean, like getting a traffic ticket. Like, if you're an undocumented immigrant and you get a speeding ticket, instead of just getting a ticket, you also end up getting reported to immigration authorities, and they could kick you out of the country. So now some people want a law like that here, too. They think that's a good way to fight illegal immigration. And whenever an undocumented immigrant is involved in a traffic accident, people always get up in arms and say things like, 'See, if it weren't for illegal aliens, that kid wouldn't have died.'"

I wince; I can't help it.

"Sorry," Becca says. "I talk too much."

I don't say anything to that.

"My point was supposed to be that my article wouldn't be about all that. Like I said, it would be about sharing your insights from going through something so profound. Very personal and deep. I think kids would really relate. I think it could help kids when they have tough stuff to deal with."

We're back at school.

"I'll don't know, Becca," I say. "Sharing my insights—not really my thing."

"It might be good for you," she says.

It might be good for you, I think, but don't say. Bare my soul for a newspaper article? Talk to Becca as a newspaper reporter, with some kind of "distance" that's supposed to make it easier? Easier for who? Whom?

I'm thinking I might need to put those quotation marks around our "friendship" again.

20

ANOTHER BRILLIANT CONVERSATION

Before Becca proposed that I become her ticket to a
Pulitzer Prize, or whatever prize it is that they give out
to fifteen-year-old journalists for writing a profound,
insightful article about my, um, profound insights—before
proposing that really appealing idea, she said it was good
for me to be talking about "all this."

I wonder if she meant something in particular by "all
this." There's the "all this" that's about what happened
with Humphrey, and there's the "all this" about me in
general. Right now I'm having a hard time separating
the two.

Then there's the "all this" about Humphrey as a
person, a cool little person, not just a kid who was killed
in an accident. But I know for sure Becca wasn't saying

it would be good for me to talk about that category of "all this." No one is.

I was an unspeakably incompetent babysitter this summer. I became a babysitter this summer because I assumed I would be an incompetent CIT. I assumed I would be an incompetent CIT because I was an incompetent Bat Mitzvah girl, and that unforgettable incompetence has clung to me and made me an incompetent high school sophomore.

I know that having a fear of speaking in front of people is not so very abnormal. But fear of raising your hand in class? Fear of leading a group of seven-year-old campers in a rousing rendition of "Kumbaya"? <u>Perculiar</u>, is what Humphrey would say.

"Would Humphrey have said that?" Dr. Gilbert asks. "Would he have said you were peculiar?"

I can barely bring myself to look at her after reading all that.

"Actually," I say, "I have more to read."

I suppose that I am, in fact, a fairly peculiar person. Here are a couple of random oddities: When I was six years old, I loved my turquoise corduroy pants but was distressed by how easily they got wrinkled, so when I wore them I tried not to sit or squat or bend or do anything to make them rumpled. I tried to wear the corduroys when I knew I'd be doing a lot of standing.

Then when I was nine, I loved one particular pair of perfectly faded and softened jeans so much that I rationed them. I did not allow myself to wear them more than once a week, because I didn't want them to wear out from washing. By the time I was ten, they no longer fit, and they weren't close to being worn out, and I have never found another pair so perfect. All those days spent wearing jeans that were merely adequate, when I could have been wearing the perfect ones.

What any of these random things have to do with "all this," I have no idea. Why they come to mind when I'm thinking about Humphrey and the accident, I can't begin to imagine.

"Now I'm done reading," I say to Dr. Gilbert.

"Why don't you try to imagine why these things are coming to mind?" she asks.

"I just said: 'No idea.'"

"If Humphrey had said to you that he had a favorite pair of jeans that he only wore once a week because he didn't want to wear them out, but you knew that he would grow so fast that he'd outgrow them before they wore out, would you think he was strange? Or peculiar, to use your word?"

"No. I would think that he was cute."

"But looking back at yourself when you were younger, you label that same behavior as evidence of something wrong with you. So Humphrey gets to be cute, but you have to be peculiar. Why don't see yourself as cute, too?"

Need I point out to her that being a string bean of a nine-year-old girl and being cute are mutually exclusive? Need I say that if there's one more heartbreaking thing I'd rather not imagine, it's Humphrey saving a pair of jeans to wear in a future he didn't get to have?

I don't have to; our time is up.

Later that afternoon, after I've stopped at home to drop off my stuff, I walk to the park. I have an overpowering urge to visit the Bumble-Boos in the land of Thrumble-Boo.

"Hey, Bumble-Boos," I say to the sad-looking faded little creatures on springs. "I come in peace." I bet no one has ridden them since Humphrey.

I'm too big to sit on the Bumble-Boos, so I plop down on the roundabout, our spaceship. In the trees over by the picnic table area, some crows are loudly arguing. I can hear the cars on Quarry Road, the evil eastward-bound rush-hour-traffic-carrying lane of Quarry Road.

When I think about the accident, it's like watching a movie with the sound turned off. Actually, that's not quite it. It's like watching a movie with the sound turned off and with one of those white noise machines turned on, so my ears are filled with *whoosh-whoosh-whoosh*. I can't hear the sounds of the street or of Humphrey saying anything. Did he cry out? *Whoosh-whoosh-whoosh*.

"Hey, there."

I jump a little; I didn't hear anyone approaching.

It's the same boy from last month, when I stopped here the Monday after the accident.

"Hi," I say.

"So—you're here again," he says.

The start of another brilliant conversation.

"The start of another brilliant conversation," he says.

Did he just say that?

"How're you doing?" he says.

"A-okay," I say. "And you?"

"Good, good. Just out for, you know, another day at the park."

Awkward. But not awful.

He's holding a football.

"Where are your friends?" I ask.

"They're not coming. I'm just out for, well—"

"I know, another day at the park," I say. "But you're carrying a football. Football isn't a solitary sport. Did they stand you up?"

"No. I'm just—carrying a football. I guess it's my security blanket."

"Huh," I say.

"Not that I'm feeling insecure," he adds.

139

"I'm sure you're not," I say, laughing a little.

"Want to throw it around?"

I wouldn't have thought so, but I do. It feels good to run around, to pass, to catch. We don't talk, other than the occasional "Nice." We back up from each other as we continue throwing, until we're far enough away so that we're launching bombs. Then he starts running from Point A to Point B so my passes have to follow him, and I do the same when it's my turn to receive. I do like a good game of catch.

My arm gives out before his. We move over to the picnic tables and perch on top of one of them.

"You're good!" he says.

I wait for the inevitable ". . . for a girl," but it doesn't come.

"Thanks," I say. "I guess I like to throw things."

He laughs at that. "What, other than a football?"

"Oh—I don't know. Darts. Baseballs."

"Rocks?"

"Could be," I say.

"Hmm. Interesting."

"Oh, sure," I say. "Utterly fascinating."

"I'm Justin Folgar," the boy says. "If we're going to be throwing things at each other, we should introduce ourselves."

"I'm Danielle Snyder."

He makes a face that I can't interpret.

"What?" I ask.

"What what?"

"Is there something about my name that made you make a face?"

"I have to confess, I already knew your name," Justin says.

"Did I mention it last time . . . ?"

"No. I just—you know, kids know your name. Now. Because of what happened."

"It wasn't supposed to be in the newspaper," I say. "My name."

"I didn't read it in the paper," Justin says. "Just—people talk."

"We're not even in the same school!" I say.

"Yeah, no," he says. "Anyway, hi, Danielle."

"Why *are* you here?" I ask. "You don't even live around here."

"That again?" he says. "You're still going to raise a geographical objection to my use of this park?"

This makes me laugh.

"But really, why are you here?" I say.

He tosses the ball to me, sideways, since we're sitting next to each other.

"I'm here to throw things at you," he says.

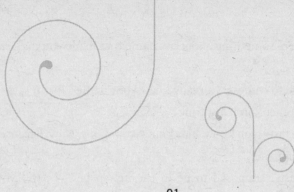

21

BOING-BOING

We had a playdate with another little boy who lived in a house with, reportedly, a huge basement playroom.

"I don't know him and he doesn't like me," Humphrey sulked when Mrs. Danker told him about the playdate.

"If you don't know him, how can he not like you?" Mrs. Danker said.

"To know you is to love you, buddy," I added.

He liked the sound of that. *To know you is to love you. To know you is to love you.* It made a very good chant. Mrs. Danker gave Humphrey a kiss and left for her treatment while he was still chanting.

"But what does it mean?" Humphrey asked after a while.

"It means you're so wonderful that a person who gets to know you will definitely like you. They can't help it!" I said.

"To know you is to love *you*," he said.

"Aw, shucks," I said. "Back at you."

Mrs. Danker had set up this date with little Christopher Battle. Christopher had a real nanny, a live-in, Darcy, from Scotland.

"Shall we go to the playroom, then?" Darcy said after answering the door. "Christopher has all sorts of things going on down there."

She spoke with a lovely lilt, and a little bit of a slur to her *s* sounds: "all *sh*orts of things going on down there."

Christopher did have all sorts of things going on in the playroom. He had what had to be every action figure he owned—and it looked like there were at least forty of them—arrayed in two lines, facing each other.

"Come on, I've got us set up for battle," Christopher said. "Look, you can be these guys." He pointed to one of the action figure armies laid out on the floor. "*Aargh*!" he growled, Iron Man in hand.

"*Aargh*," Humphrey said. He picked up the Flash.

"*Gaah*!" Christopher moaned, now holding G.I. Joe in his other hand. "Come on!"

Humphrey took up a Prince of Persia figure, and looked at Christopher expectantly.

"Don't you know how to do this?" Christopher said. "Come on, bring it on!"

Humphrey didn't seem to get what "bringing it on" entailed.

"Look, Humphrey," Darcy said. She danced the Green

Lantern around on the carpeted floor. Christopher danced his G.I. Joe energetically in front of Darcy's Green Lantern, and then had Iron Man pounce.

"Gotcha!" Christopher cried out.

Humphrey took an action figure in each hand and moved them about in a weak imitation of Darcy and Christopher.

"He—his parents don't buy action figures," I said quietly to Darcy.

"Oh—you mean—do you think they'd mind?" Darcy asked.

"No, no, it's fine. Just—as you see, he doesn't have a clue."

Darcy waved her hand, as if to sweep away doubts. "He's a boy, right? He'll get it. Christopher will turn him into a ninja or a special-ops guy or whatever soon enough."

Christopher was remarkably patient for a little kid, I thought. "No, look, like *this*," he corrected Humphrey, repeatedly, but not impatiently, adjusting the action figure in Humphrey's little paw. "Then go like *that*," he said, twisting and turning the figures in patterns that made total sense to him and, apparently, his nanny.

"Okay," Humphrey kept saying.

After a while, both boys lost interest. Christopher became engaged in a cartoon playing on the big-screen television. Humphrey wandered to an alcove at one end of the playroom, where an elaborate dollhouse was set up on a dining-room-size table. The interior was filled with finely detailed furniture and fixtures and accessories, from carved beds to wing chairs to desks to toilets to a tiny teakettle.

"Awesome!" Humphrey breathed out.

"Yeah, it's Emma's," Darcy said. "Christopher's big sister."

"Can I play with it?"

"Um—" Darcy looked back at Christopher, in front of the television. "Don't you want to—" She looked at me. I shrugged. "Okay, I guess," Darcy said. "Very carefully."

"Oh, I'll be extremely, extremely very careful," Humphrey said.

Humphrey explored every inch of the dollhouse.

"It almost gives me tears," he said quietly.

Darcy looked at me for translation.

"It's fabulous," I explained.

"Are there any—dolls?" Humphrey asked.

Darcy hesitated before answering. "Up in Emma's room. I don't think we should get them."

"That's okay," Humphrey said. "Maybe . . ." He hurried over to the action figures. "Maybe this guy." He picked one up. "And this one."

"What'cha doing, Humphrey?" Christopher asked.

"Taking these to the house."

"To the *doll*house?"

Humphrey nodded.

"Action figures don't go with the dollhouse," Christopher said. "They're action figures, not dolls."

"They're kind of like dolls," Humphrey said.

"No, they're not!"

"They're little pretend people," Humphrey said. "Like dolls."

145

"You know, guys, maybe we should have some outside time," I said. Darcy agreed. We went out the playroom door.

"Scrimmage!" Christopher yelled, grabbing a football off the grass.

"Does Humphrey have any interest in sports?" Darcy asked me quietly.

"He likes football," I said. "Hey, Humphrey, go long and I'll pass to you." There was a second football on the ground and I launched a spiral across the lawn. He missed the catch, but then retrieved the ball and ran it back to me.

"Again," he said.

"Go!" I said, and he went.

He caught that pass, and a few more after that. Christopher was impressed with my throwing ability, and asked for some passes, too.

After a few minutes of passing, Christopher and Darcy convinced me and Humphrey to play a game.

"Two-on-two," Christopher said. "Me and—" He pointed at me.

We dragged lawn chairs to the opposite ends of the yard to serve as goalposts and formed up on a line of scrimmage.

"Two-hand touch," Darcy said. She and Christopher explained the rules to Humphrey.

A coin toss gave Darcy and Humphrey the ball first. Her first pass to him—incomplete. Her second—way beyond his reach. Her third—Humphrey completed a reception. *A miracle*, I thought.

"Run, Humphrey, run!" Darcy called. He ran toward the lawn chair, Christopher right on his heels. Christopher reached both hands out to touch him; Humphrey dodged the touch by twisting his body away. As a result, Humphrey stumbled. He recovered his balance and didn't fall, but the ball popped out of his hands. He didn't run after it.

"Fumble!" Christopher screamed happily. The ball ricocheted a few times—*BOING* this way, *BOING* that way—and Christopher followed it and grabbed it. Holding the ball tight against his side, he ran toward the lawn chair at the other end of the yard. Humphrey just stood and watched him. "Touchdown!" Christopher yelled.

"I thought—I thought you start over if you drop the ball," Humphrey said. "I thought you hike the ball again."

"That's if it's an incomplete," Christopher said. "But not if you drop it after you've caught it. Then it's a fumble, and anyone can get it. Like I did."

"When the ball is dropped, no matter who drops it, you don't even stop to think about it, Humphrey," I said. "Fumble! You just pounce on that ball."

"Fumble and pounce," Humphrey repeated. "Fumble and pounce."

"You got it," I said.

It took a few more plays, but Humphrey figured out the difference between an incomplete pass and a fumble. And on the last play of the game, a pass by me to Christopher, Christopher ran only a few steps before losing the ball.

"Fumble!" Humphrey immediately cried, following the *BOING-BOING*-ing ball until he could pick it up. He ran all the way for a touchdown. "Touchdown!" It was his only one, but it was sweet.

On the way home, I asked, "Was that fun?"

Humphrey shrugged. "Sort of."

"Christopher's a nice boy," I said.

"Yeah," Humphrey said. "But if we go there again, maybe it should be when his sister is there."

"That dollhouse, huh, Humphrey?"

He nodded. "If I had it, I would play with it all the time."

"Maybe your mom and dad will get you one for your birthday," I said.

"I think they'll think it's for girls," Humphrey said. "Like that bead project set." Humphrey and I had seen it at the mall when we shopped for Mrs. Danker's birthday present. "Dad said no when I asked for it last Christmas."

"Maybe he didn't want you playing with tiny beads," I said. "Maybe he thought you were too young back then. Really little kids sometimes put things in their mouths that don't belong there."

"I would never put the beads in my mouth," Humphrey scoffed.

We walked for a few more minutes in friendly silence.

"At least I learned about fumble and pounce," Humphrey said.

Funny, I thought. *At least*. "At least you did."

"Fumble and pounce. They sound like names of cats to me," Humphrey said. "When I get my kittens, I'm going to name them Fumble and Pounce."

"I love that!" I said. "You're getting kittens?"

"One day," Humphrey said. "The only problem is, my daddy's allergic."

"Bummer."

"But sometimes allergies go away," Humphrey said.

"I hope that happens with your dad," I said.

"Also," Humphrey said, "Mommy says there are shots. Daddy could get shots and then he wouldn't be allergic and we could get our kittens."

"Well—then maybe that's what will happen," I said. I had my doubts.

"I hope the allergies just go away," Humphrey said. "I wouldn't want him to have to get shots."

"Very thoughtful of you, Humphrey."

"Yes," he said sweetly, "I know."

22

In Light Of

Franklin Grove
Community Hall Meeting
IMPROVING SAFETY ON QUARRY ROAD
7 p.m., Thursday, September 17
Franklin Grove Community Hall Main Meeting Room

In light of the tragedy this past summer, many Franklin Grove residents have raised safety concerns about Quarry Road. At this community hall meeting, residents will present their concerns. The Franklin Grove Board has also engaged the services of an engineering consulting firm, which will present preliminary findings of its study of the Quarry Road corridor.

If you would like to speak at the community hall meeting, please contact the Franklin Grove Board office.

The telephone rings; against my better judgment, I answer it.

"Danielle, you saw the flyer for the community hall meeting?" Doris Raskin asks.

No "How are you?" No "How is school?" She just launches right in.

I tell her I did, that it showed up in our mailbox yesterday.

"I'd like to urge you to speak," she says.

"Oh, I don't think so, Mrs. Raskin," I say.

"I think the Franklin Grove Board—and all of us in the neighborhood—would benefit from hearing from you," she continues.

She's not saying what needs to be done—sure she's not—since we need to hear from the engineering consultants, respect the character of the neighborhood, encourage diversity of opinion, blah, blah, blah—but she's thinking sidewalks, streetlights, and a crosswalk with a blinking light.

"Would you like me to call the office to tell them that you'll be speaking?" she says.

"No, thank you, Mrs. Raskin," I say.

"You'll call them yourself?"

I hesitate. She jumps in.

"Danielle, you're a young woman now. Not a child. And

I think you can understand that you owe it to your neighborhood to speak up. Everyone wants to make sure something like this never happens again."

"I've talked to the police, Mrs. Raskin. Twice."

"Oh, my dear, this is not about the police. This is not about assigning blame to you. I would hate for you to think that anyone in the neighborhood is looking to blame you."

Oh, that's a relief.

"We are concerned about the absence of certain safety features along Quarry Road," Mrs. Raskin says, "and about making improvements that will benefit us all."

She says the Dankers are interested in the issue of safety on Quarry Road. They lost their son and they want to make sure no one else ever has to suffer such a loss.

"Don't you think you owe it to the Dankers, Danielle?"

"I don't think they really want to hear from me," I say.

"Given Tom Danker's status in the legal community, you might think about how best to make clear that what happened is a result of the woeful condition of our street, and not of your . . . caregiving."

Whoa, there. Whoa. First: *Woeful*? And second: Is she saying that Mr. Danker, lawyer extraordinaire, might *sue* me? She just said that no one was looking to blame me.

She's still talking.

". . . and I think that after all Clarice Danker risked for her boy, it would be a blessing if some good could come of his death," Mrs. Raskin says. "You would be doing a mitzvah."

Mrs. Raskin isn't even Jewish. She should leave the concept of mitzvah alone. This is not some good-deed mitzvah project for Sunday school. Plus, I have no idea what she's talking about: Mrs. Danker risked something for Humphrey? But I'm not going to ask Mrs. Raskin to explain. I just want to get off the phone.

"I'll think about it, Mrs. Raskin," I say.

"And you'll let me know?" she says. "You'll get back to me before next Thursday?"

"Yes. I'll get back to you."

Okay, so I'm crossing my fingers when I tell her that.

"What's the point of a community hall meeting about something that's already been investigated? It's not like the Franklin Grove Board can *do* anything about anything."

Adrian just gives me a look. He came for dinner, our parents have gone to the living room to watch *Jeopardy!*, and now he and I are cleaning up.

"You know I'm right, Adrian," I say. "All they have any power over is trash pickup."

"Don't forget snow removal," Adrian says.

Right. I wouldn't want to forget the single plow in their vast empire. "So a bunch of neighbors want to put sidewalks and streetlights and whatever on Quarry Road—as if that has anything to do with anything. As if a sidewalk would have kept Humphrey from running into the street."

"Then maybe you should tell them that," Adrian says. "Maybe you need to give them a reality check."

"But, Adrian—it's the Franklin frigging Grove Board! What a waste of breath!"

"They'll end up passing a resolution calling for these so-called improvements. They'll send the resolution on to the county council," Adrian says. "That's what they do. So, yeah, the Franklin Grove Board can't directly build anything, but they can make a formal request. And then the county council will debate the issue. And the council will want to do something, because people always want to do something when bad things happen. So you're saying you're saving your breath for the county council?"

"I can't believe you're on Doris Raskin's side."

"You and your sides! I'm not on Doris Raskin's side," he says. "I'm on your side. But the point is, you do have a side, Danny. And I don't want you and your side to just fade away."

The thing is, I'm not sure. What do I know, really? I feel like I barely know what happened. To talk about it in front of a bunch of people feels impossibly hard.

"You know I hate to talk in front of people," I say.

"I know, Danny," Adrian says. "Sometimes, though, you do what you hate. If there's a good enough reason, you just suck it up and do it."

"You have no idea how impossible that feels for me," I say. "It's not like, 'Oh, I hate this.' It's not like I can just suck it up. I totally can't do it. I will implode. Or explode."

Adrian nods sympathetically. "I know it feels like that."

He can't know, really. He can't know because he hasn't felt it.

"What if I break down and cry in front of everyone? Get hysterical. Lose control."

"I don't think that would happen," Adrian says, "although if it did, it wouldn't be the end of the world."

I stare at him.

"Okay, maybe it would be the end of *your* world, losing it in front of a community hall meeting," he says. "But if that's what's stopping you, then the thing to do is to let go and bawl and get hysterical beforehand. Like—right now. Go ahead. It's okay."

I shake my head. "I can't let go. It would be totally, completely overwhelming."

Adrian finishes washing out the pot he's been working on. "Danny," he says, "you are about the least overwhelming person I know."

I feel a sting, like I've been insulted.

After Humphrey's funeral, Adrian said I was "daunting." I remind him of this.

"I don't think a person can be both daunting and underwhelming," I say.

"It's all part of the intriguing, endearing puzzle that is Danielle Snyder," he says.

Before he leaves, Adrian pokes his head in my room, where I'm reading my history homework.

"How's the head shrinking going?" he asks.

"It's going," I say.

"How did I know you would say that?"

"That's me," I say. "Utterly predictable."

Adrian gives me a little bit of a cross-eyed look, signaling *Come on.*

"Okay," I say. "The thing about it is, it's utterly unpredictable."

"Interesting," Adrian says. "Meaning?"

"Meaning I think I'm going to talk about one thing, and I end up talking about something else."

"That makes sense."

"It's more than that, really," I continue. "It's more like I'm in therapy to deal with how I feel about the accident, but all kinds of other things from my life come up. I don't know whether I'm just avoiding talking about the accident, or . . . what."

"Well—everything's connected," Adrian says. "You know. The head bone's connected to the neck bone, et cetera."

"Yeah," I say. "I guess that's part of it." I hesitate, then tell him how I ended up talking to Dr. Gilbert about things that make me feel like I've been a weirdo since birth, like the obsession with my perfect corduroys and jeans.

"Pretty tame, as obsessions go," Adrian says.

"Compared to what?"

"Pulling out eyebrows. Repeated hand washing. Tame compared to the typical manifestations of obsessive behavior evident in certain high school students."

He did manage to take AP psychology during his junior year.

"But the pants obsession—is that not weird?" I press.

"If you got a group of friends involved," he said, "you could call it a sisterhood and write a blockbuster book and movie."

Adrian can always make me laugh.

"Look, Danny," he says, turning serious. "About not wanting to talk at that community meeting that's coming up, if you're saying you're too raw, I get it."

I am. I am too raw.

"Just—don't put yourself outside what happened. It happened to you, in your life. Don't let everyone else shape what it means."

I shrug. It's the best I can do.

23

THE TREES

I never get back to Mrs. Raskin, and—thank you, God—she doesn't call me again. September 17 rolls around. My parents have an event to attend for Mom's job—she teaches writing and rhetoric at the community college—so they're not going to the Franklin Grove meeting.

"I can skip this thing at the college," Mom said this morning. "It's just a reception for a visiting scholar. Dad and I would be happy to go with you to the meeting."

"I don't know if *I'm* going to the meeting," I said.

"But if you do, we'd like to be there with you, Danny," Mom said.

"We want to support you," Dad said.

"*A,* I don't think I'm going," I said. "And *B,* if I do end up going, I won't be doing anything that requires support. Really."

It's six fifteen. I'm still weighing whether or not to go when my phone rings. I look at the display; no, not the dreaded Mrs. Raskin. Becca.

"I'm an idiot," she says.

"Hello to you, too," I say.

"Let me say that again in case you didn't hear me: *Quelle idiote je suis!*"

I laugh. "No, I heard you."

We haven't talked too much since the second day of school last week when she surprised me with her article idea. We've checked in with each other on how classes are going, and that's about it. Nothing significant, and nothing about putting my life story in the school newspaper.

"I don't know what I was thinking," she says. "I mean, I know what I was thinking. I can't deny that. I was going to present you and your experience to the world. Or, to the world of Western High School. But really, sometimes I need a muzzle."

"A muzzle so you don't say what you're thinking?" I say.

"Yes. An internal censor. Just, shut up, Becca. Keep it to yourself."

"But—why would you be thinking about writing an article about me in the first place? I mean, okay, a muzzle. A censor. But you'd still be looking at me and thinking what a good headline I'd make?"

The phone is quiet.

"Becca."

Still quiet.

"Hello, hello," I say, "can you hear me, Joe?" This is our private signal, borrowed from Dr. Seuss. *One Fish Two Fish Red Fish Blue Fish*.

"I'm beyond being an idiot," she says finally. "A *très grande imbécile*."

"Well, you don't have to call yourself names," I say.

"I think I do," Becca says.

"Usually, I feel like you push me to do things because you think they'd be good for me," I say. "But this felt different. This felt like you cared more about your story than me."

"That's terrible," Becca says. "And I'm sorry. I don't want you to think that. Please forget I ever did that. Please?"

"Okay," I say. "Apology accepted."

I tell her about tonight's Franklin Grove meeting. Becca doesn't live in Franklin Grove, but in one of the neighborhoods next to ours, so her house didn't get the notice of the meeting.

"I would have gone with you if I'd known," she says.

"It's starting in five minutes. So I think I've made my decision to stay away," I say.

"Maybe—" Becca begins, then stops.

I wait, but she doesn't say any more.

"Becca, *maybe* what? Just because I don't want you to see a headline every time you look at me doesn't mean I don't want your opinion. What did you start to say?"

"Honestly, nothing," she says. "So, are we good?"

"We're good."

"You're not just saying that?"

I promise her we're good and we say good-bye.

Maybe—I'll just walk over to the community hall, which is less than ten minutes from my house. It's a quaint old building that houses a couple of meeting rooms, a couple of offices, a tiny post office, a rec room with an old Ping-Pong table that is very close to my heart, and, of all things, an indoor basketball court. It might seem a strange combination—*you want stamps with that free throw?*—but it's part of what makes Franklin Grove Franklin Grove.

The meeting has begun and I can ease unnoticed into a chair in the back row. The five people who make up the Franklin Grove Board are sitting, facing the audience, behind a couple of long tables that have been pushed together. Two men are seated at a long table facing the board members, backs to the audience. One of them is speaking into a microphone, and he has one of those voices that alternates between really loud and really soft, so certain words come booming at us—"LUMENS" and "CIRCUITS" and "SCOTOPIC" and "PHOTOPIC"—while others are lost. He finishes up. Then the other guy at the table talks, reading, as far as I can tell, from a study of the traffic on Quarry Road. Peak hour trips. Directional split. Pedestrian facilities.

Next up are some of the neighbors. Mrs. Raskin is first. I slouch way down in my seat so she doesn't see me. She says some nice things about the lumens guy and the traffic guy. But what the Franklin Grove Board mustn't forget, she says, is the need for a sidewalk study. She's not an expert, she says in a voice that suggests she actually thinks she is, but sidewalks along Quarry Road are absolutely necessary to make Franklin Grove safe for our children and families.

Other neighbors say other things about the benefits of street-lights, crossing signals, and sidewalks. Then old Mrs. Joseph, who lives on Quarry Road, and who probably has been there since the beginning of time, has her say. In her quavery voice, she talks about the character of the Franklin Grove neighbor-hood and the rustic feeling of its streets. We may be a suburb of Washington, D.C., but we've managed to hold on to a small-town atmosphere and we should be vigilant about maintaining that atmosphere. More artificial light, Mrs. Joseph says, will take away from Franklin Grove's simple charm. More artificial light means we won't be able to see the stars. A sidewalk will mean taking down trees and clearing out the brush alongside Quarry Road, and all that means less wildlife.

Some people are shaking their heads at Mrs. Joseph's com-ments. I imagine some are rolling their eyes, although I don't really know, since I only see the backs of people's heads. I won-der if anyone agrees with her.

Well, yes, others do agree with her. Another neighbor, a younger man, goes to the microphone and says basically the same things that Mrs. Joseph did, only shorter. A woman speaks, and says that not everyone knows this, but the first Littleleaf Linden trees on Quarry Road were planted in 1938 on the twentieth anniversary of the end of World War I in honor of Franklin Grove's veterans of that war. Over the years, more of the trees were planted to recognize the neighborhood's World War II and Vietnam War veterans.

"If you go to the archives," this woman says, "you will see that every tree has a name. A name of a person. Even if you don't agree that the trees deserve our consideration, think about the people behind the trees. I strongly urge the board not to destroy these living monuments."

Wouldn't Humphrey have thought it was cool that the trees had names? I almost want to say something to this tree lady. But I don't. I just slip home before anyone notices that I'm there.

24

INFAMOUS

My understanding is that the family, the
Guzmans, are from Colombia, and they've
been here nine years. I don't know if
they've been illegal the whole time. He
works in a medical lab. I think she works
in elder care. Two kids, both elementary
school age. —Doris Raskin

They live east of Franklin Grove, I
believe in Montgomery Heights. That's where
you find most of them. —Sonny Green

Sonny, what do you mean by "them"?
Undocumented aliens? Foreign-born people?

Working-class people trying for their shot
at the American dream? —Dotty Engleman

The logic of what you're saying, Dotty,
defending the right of illegals to have
their shot at the "American dream," eludes
me. By definition, the American dream
belongs to Americans. Come to this country
legally, become a citizen, and then you can
chase the American dream. —Sonny Green

Legal immigrants, not just citizens, also
have the right to work toward this so-
called American dream, don't you think?
Once we say, okay, you may live here, then
why would we draw a distinction between
their rights and ours? —Eric Templeton

How about minor details such as voting?
Are you saying we should open up the right
to vote to immigrants who aren't citizens,
who haven't pledged their allegiance to
this country? —Nan Kimmel

I was referring to economic rights, Nan.
Of course you have to be a citizen to
vote. I was saying we don't want to put

economic barriers in front of the
immigrant population. We want them to
integrate into the economy, contribute
to it, and not end up needing public
assistance and other costly social services. —Eric Templeton

The plain fact is that they are, overall,
a drain on our resources. This is the
logical outcome of the clash of cultures
that our nation is becoming. Don't learn
English, and you can't get a decent job.
Don't adopt American culture, including
basic things like maintaining your
property so it doesn't drag down the
neighborhood, and you will remain
outsiders, clueless as to how things work
in this country. —Sonny Green

Hey, Sonny—who "maintains" your property?
Seems to me it's the same brown-skinned
men who cut my lawn. They seem to know
what they're doing. —Tim Watkins

Hey, Tim—take a drive through beautiful
eastern Montgomery Heights. Messy

vegetable patches in front of the houses
instead of front lawns. Tacky ceramic
statuettes. If you like that kind of
"maintenance," I think I counted eight For
Sale signs when I was last there. I'm sure
they'd welcome you. —Sonny Green

Sonny, haven't you seen the articles
recently about the stupidity of front
lawns? They waste precious water, they
spread chemicals, and otherwise are a
complete waste. Maybe those people in
Montgomery Heights have the right idea
with their front yard gardens. —Jennifer
Hernandez

Maybe lawns aren't a *complete* waste,
Jennifer—they allow people like Sonny to
display their shameless hypocrisy. Yes,
Tim, that is Manuel's truck you see
outside Sonny's house every week. . . .
—Michael Hunter

Neighbors, just a friendly reminder from
your Franklin Grove Listserv administrator
that we keep things civil and respectful

here. Thank you all for your cooperation.
—Moira McGillicudy, Listserv administrator

I don't usually lurk on the Franklin Grove e-mail list. But this whole illegal immigration thing has become kind of a hot topic in our neighborhood, and I can't help but want to know what all the heat is about. An article in the *Observer* said that someone brought it up at the community meeting after I left, but the Franklin Grove Board chairman said the subject wasn't on the agenda, and shut down any discussion. By the way, don't you just love it when people (like Sonny Green) use the word "logical" to describe their arguments, as if calling them "logical" settles everything? And how 'bout that sarcasm (Sonny Green, Michael Hunter)? I've never been averse to a good sarcastic jab. But some of this stuff I'm reading seems more mean than anything else.

Actually, the argument is reaching way beyond our neighborhood. The *Washington Post* had an article about it—that is, how the accident is triggering debates in Meigs County and even in the state assembly over undocumented immigrants.

There's a video, too. Not of the accident itself. Jeez, thank the Lord. And not of me sitting in the street, either. The video is of Mr. Stashower, when he was yelling at the kids who gathered on the side of the road to gawk at the disaster. "Stay there!" he yells in the video. He's looking right at the camera. "You kids stay there!" Funny thing is, there are no kids visible in the video at all. You do hear someone off-camera muttering, "Chill. No one's going anywhere." And if you listen really carefully, you can hear—at least, I think I can hear—someone saying "Oh my God. Oh my God," over and over again. That would be Mrs. Stashower.

"Hey, Danny."

Adrian's come by for dinner again. He looks over my shoulder. "Ah, the infamous Franklin Grove e-mail list."

"It's infamous?" I say.

"It should be," he says. "This is a perfect example of why adults should be barred from any communications technology more advanced than the touch-tone phone."

I smile, although I don't exactly know what a touch-tone phone is.

"Want to cook with me?" Adrian asks.

"Uh . . ." I'm fairly incompetent in the kitchen.

"I amend my invitation. Want to watch me cook?"

Sure. Adrian isn't just here to eat dinner; he's here to make dinner, which is great. Mom won't be home for another hour. Dad, who almost always gets home from work before Mom, is most often the cook now that Adrian's moved out. He makes edible meals, my father does, but Adrian is the true chef in our family. Tonight's menu includes his famous (to me) Moroccan chicken, couscous, honey-glazed carrots, and a green salad. Dad's in the basement, exercising.

As he browns the chicken in a big pot, Adrian tells me about a restaurant-bar type of place that some guys he knows want to open. I haven't heard him sound so excited since Guitar Hero first came out.

"It's in the boonies," he says, "near where I live. There's no decent place around there where people can get good food and listen to live music. So we thought—actually, really, *they* thought, I'm definitely the junior guy on the project—why not open a place that *we'd* want to hang out in? Not a rowdy bar scene. Not a dump, but also not fancy. And definitely not another chain restaurant."

"Would you—cook?" I ask, watching him chop an onion and a green pepper "And what's that spice you put in this chicken that makes it taste the way it does?"

"Cumin," he says. "It goes in when I put the pot on simmer. And—would I cook? I'm not really qualified to do anything in the kitchen other than be a helper, but I'd do that. I'd wait tables. And—here's the amazing part—I'd play music." He adds the onion and green pepper to the pot and stirs them to the bottom.

I give out a whoop. "Really!"

"Yup. Since I took my drum set out to my place over the summer, I've been playing with a group of guys. Some of them are also part of the group that wants to open the restaurant. We wouldn't be the only act to play there, but we'd play there some of the time." Now Adrian is draining and rinsing a can of chickpeas in the sink.

"Bluegrass?" It's Adrian's favorite. Not exactly what he got to play in high school band class.

"Bluegrass." He adds the chickpeas, along with crushed

tomatoes and seasonings, to the browned chicken. Once they boil up, he turns the heat down under the pot and covers it.

"Wow," I say. "It sounds great."

"I'm really excited about it," he says.

"What about plumbing?" I ask him.

"Less excited about that," he says. "It's earned me some money. I don't mind it. But it's not what I want to do with my life. For now, I'll keep doing it. Once the restaurant opens, I'll try to do both. We'll see."

When Adrian told our parents he was apprenticing to a plumber, you would have thought from the looks on their faces that he was joining al-Qaeda. Afterward, when he vented to me, I said, "Adrian, what reaction were you expecting? I mean, we know them by now."

"Look, if they hadn't shut me down with their inane questions—*Do you intend to make plumbing your life's work? Do you not have higher dreams than this?*—we might have had a reasonable discussion," he said.

And the thing was, he wanted to have that reasonable discussion.

"Maybe Mom's work is the fulfillment of her highest dream," Adrian said. "I mean, it definitely fits her personality. Lecturing. Telling people what the rules are."

Oh, yes.

"But Dad—you can't tell me that he, or anyone, ever dreamed of looking at people's feet day after day." Dad is a foot doctor. "Does being a foot doctor really ring his chimes?"

"It might," I said. "It's Dad, Adrian. His chimes are easily rung."

I didn't mean anything mean by it. Just, Dad's easy. It doesn't take much to satisfy him.

"Point taken," Adrian said. "And actually, Dad's a good example here. He doesn't love feet. He's not fulfilled by feet. He likes being his own boss, and being good at something."

"Even if it's feet," I said.

"Exactly. Feet, toilets, whatever. So, to answer the question you were tactful enough not to ask me, no, snaking drains isn't the fulfillment of my highest dream. I don't know that it will be my life's work. The point is, I feel the need to stake out on my own. So I learn a trade, I make money, I support myself, and *that* makes me happy. Because I can't live under this roof."

"Why?" I couldn't stop myself from asking, even though I knew I was practically whining. "Why can't you live under this roof? I like you under this roof."

He moved over to me then and hugged me.

"I can't *take* from them anymore," he said.

"Is that different from I can't take *them* anymore?" I asked.

"It's close, but different," he said. "I can't take their money or food or a room in this house. Because then I have to take all that comes with it. Especially all that disapproval I see in their faces."

I wanted to disagree. But he was right. Sure, they were right that Adrian had higher dreams than being a plumber, but it's just too bad that they couldn't lay off enough to let him work his way toward those dreams while living under the same roof as the rest of us. Down the hall from me, where he belonged.

The front door opens and closes.

"It smells wonderful in this house!" Mom says. "I detect the presence of Adrian Snyder!"

"Hi, Mom," Adrian calls out.

"How great to come home to my talented son cooking," Mom says as she walks into the kitchen. "Danielle, are you taking notes?"

"Copiously," I respond.

Mom goes to change. Dad pokes his head in the kitchen and makes appreciative noises on the way from his basement workout to a quick change of his own. Ten minutes later, we all sit down at the kitchen table to eat. Adrian serves; when he cooks, the food even looks attractive.

And, of course, it's totally delicious. As always.

We talk about the buzz on the neighborhood e-mail list a little bit. Mom and Dad aren't exactly in total agreement with each other on immigration issues. Mom has become more negative about undocumented immigrants ever since a day labor center opened up near the mall. As for Dad, he likes to remind us that we're only two generations away from being immigrants ourselves; both his and Mom's grandparents came from Europe in the 1930s.

After some aimless back-and-forth on all this, Adrian says, "I have exciting news."

This is not the smartest strategy for him. With an introduction like that, you know my mother is thinking that he's announcing his decision to go back to school. I can already see a smile beginning to form around her eyes.

Instead, he tells Mom and Dad about the restaurant thing.

Dad repeats something Adrian says: "Seven people are starting this restaurant?"

This is a Dad-ism. He repeats a piece of information, and cocks his head as if he doesn't get something. But, Adrian and I both know, he almost always does get it. This is his way of expressing his doubts about whether something is a good idea.

"Yeah," Adrian says. "There are seven guys in total, including me. Five of us have been playing music together."

Pause. Their carefully arranged faces give my parents away. Dad, especially, is trying to keep his face expressionless, but he's so not good at it. Mom exercises less self-control, and I see her attempt to maintain neutrality break apart, one eyebrow at a time. I know she will go in for the kill. *Resist*, I message her telepathically.

She doesn't get the message.

"Does anyone in this group of seven have experience in the restaurant business?" she asks.

"Yeah," Adrian says. "Two of the guys have managed places. Applebee's, I think."

"Where's the money coming from? Creating a business isn't

cheap. There's rent, probably renovation, equipment, supplies, labor costs—"

"We're all putting in some money. And we're getting investors. We might also get a bank loan."

"You're putting in some of your own money?" Mom's voice rises to a higher register on this question.

"Some," Adrian says. "I've saved. But it's not like I'm putting up an equal share of the money. We're forming a kind of partnership, but with different levels of participation. So I risk less of my own money than some of the other guys. Which also means I'll make less when we start earning money."

"Adrian, did you know that the majority of new businesses fail within a year?" Mom says. "And the percentage is significantly higher for non-chain restaurants? The likelihood that this place will earn money is—not great."

Adrian briefly closes his eyes. He doesn't answer.

"Son—the place will serve liquor?" Dad asks.

"Yes," Adrian says. "It will. That's how most restaurants make money."

"And it's not a problem getting a liquor license for you, one of the owners, to be under the legal drinking age?" Dad asks.

"No," Adrian says. "We checked. You can own a restaurant that sells liquor if you're nineteen. You can bartend if you're nineteen in Meigs County. You just can't drink."

"Who are your outside investors?" Mom asks.

I see Adrian's jaw tighten. "So far, only one's for sure. My bass player friend's parents."

"Uh-huh," Mom says.

"Don't worry," Adrian says. "I'm not asking you to invest in this."

I see the gears clicking in Mom's brain, and here's what they signal: Adrian is doing something unwise. She disapproves. She will not support this. He tells her it's happening anyway. He tells her he doesn't need her support—her money, in this case.

Wait for it. If he doesn't want her to invest, then, of course, she'll go in the opposite direction.

"Why *aren't* you asking us to invest?" Mom says.

Bingo. She can't help herself.

Adrian just shakes his head. It's almost unnoticeable, but I notice. Other than that, he doesn't react. And Mom doesn't press for an answer. So there isn't a big unpleasant scene, but the rest of the meal isn't exactly a barrel of laughs.

After dinner, Adrian doesn't stick around. Before he leaves, though, there's another debate between him and Mom about, of all things, leftovers. She wants him to take them. He cooked, after all. He pushes back: He was happy to cook. She: There's enough for one, not three. He: Plenty of food at his place. She: Don't be stubborn. He: Now he's stubborn because he's not taking food out of her house.

Mom gives up, says good night, and goes upstairs.

"Adrian," I say as he shrugs on his jacket to leave. "Take the poor Moroccan chicken. Otherwise Mom will deport it."

He doesn't laugh, but he does smile. A little. And he takes the chicken.

25

JUST SAYING

After Adrian leaves, I see that I missed a call on my cell: Marissa.

I haven't heard from her since she texted after the accident. Wait, that's not quite true. I got a Rosh Hashanah card from her—yes, even though she's not Jewish. Marissa is big on everyone's "heritage," as she puts it. My "heritage," according to Marissa, is being Jewish. Hers is being Mexican American, at least on one side of the family. Her great-grandparents—her father's grandparents—came from Mexico way back in the day.

Anyway, Marissa usually knows the dates each year for the High Holy Days—Rosh Hashanah and Yom Kippur—before I do. Do you call someone when she sends you a Rosh Hashanah card? I did not.

I consider not calling her back now, too. But there's her Rosh Hashanah card, this call, and the message Adrian relayed from her the day of Humphrey's funeral—I can't not call Marissa back. Unless I want to close the book on five years of flamenco-playing afternoons. I dial the phone.

"How are you?" she asks.

"You know," I say. "Fine. Not fine. It depends."

She murmurs sympathetically.

"Thanks for the card," I say.

"You're welcome."

"And—thanks for calling today."

"I should have called earlier," she says. "I guess—I don't know. We've grown apart. I wish we hadn't. I don't want to. But I felt like it would be strange for me to rush in as if—as if you needed me."

"You texted me," I say. "Thanks for that, too." I pause. "I'm also sorry we've grown apart."

We push through an *I-feel-bad-no-I-feel-bad* exchange, in which I cannot, cannot bring myself to mention, much less apologize for, last winter's video game idiocy. She, of course, doesn't apologize for the things she said about Adrian. Why would she? She has no idea that they bothered me. So we talk as if there was nothing in particular, no precipitating event that pushed us apart.

No particular precipitating push. Are you listening, Humphrey?

But soon we're on the other side of all that, and talking about ordinary stuff. My school, her school. Movies. Music. She does ask about Adrian. I hesitate, then tell her about the jobs he's been working and the restaurant, although I don't fill

her in on my parents' reaction. She's already heard from someone else that he moved out of our house.

"Wow. He's busy," she says.

"He really is."

"How are he and your parents getting along?"

"Oh," I say. "Pretty well. When he comes over, he cooks
dinner, and it's—nice."

"He cooks dinner?" Marissa asks. "Has he become a good
cook?"

"The best," I say.

"That's great."

"Except that I miss having him around," I say. "You know,
you have brothers—they're fun to have in the house."

"Some of the time." She laughs. Then, more seriously: "Most
of the time. But at least you don't have to be the peacekeeper
between Adrian and your mother anymore. There's a job at
least as tough as being a plumber."

Is that what she thought she saw me doing when she sat at
our dinner table or joined us for post–hockey game pizza
outings—peacekeeping?

"I don't know," I say. "I don't know about being a peacekeeper."

"Okay, but *something*. Some kind of go-between." When I
don't say anything in response, Marissa adds, lightly, putting
on a fake accent, "And zat is zee doctor's p-sychological analy-
sis of zee Snyder family dynamic." She laughs. "Because I'm
such an expert on family dynamics."

I laugh, too, relieved, somehow, that she backed off from telling me what role I play in my family. We move on to talk about her own brothers.

"Martin got his license last spring," she says. "Which means Matt has to share the car he thought was his God-given birth-right. You know how some families have 'chore wheels' up on the refrigerator, so everyone knows whose turn it is to take out the garbage? So, we have a 'car wheel,' to settle their arguments over whose turn it is to take the car. And a 'gas wheel' so they know whose turn it is to put gas in."

I think about this. "What if it's Matt's 'car wheel' turn but Martin's 'gas wheel' turn?" I ask.

"A gold star for you, Danielle! That is exactly the problem with this system," Marissa says.

"I suppose then Martin could just give Matt money for gas," I say.

"A reasonable person would suppose that." Marissa laughs. "And yet, oddly, that is not how M&M interpret it."

I have always liked hearing about her family. As you may have noticed, everyone's name begins with *M*. With *M-a-*, to be exact. From youngest to oldest, Marco, Marissa and Martin— who are twins—Matt, Manny, and Malcolm. It matches their last name, too: Martinez. Yes, Marissa's twin brother lives with the name Martin Martinez.

"I got my license over the summer," she says, "and any day now they're going to make new wheels for the refrigerator and put me on them."

"You use their car?"

"It's not really 'their' car. It's the car that our parents don't use. So it's just as much mine."

"Uh-huh."

"Okay, yes, I use *their* car."

In this way, we circle around to the accident. Not the accident itself, but the fallout. Marissa is especially bothered by the illegal immigration issue, and not in the way you might think. She embraces the "Mexican" part of her Mexican American heritage—food, music, history, art. She's a fanatic about the paintings of Frida Kahlo. But she's also always been very clear about the "American" part, too. She's proud of the fact that her great-grandfather, the one who came here from Mexico, fought in the U.S. Army in World War II and even got some kind of medal. His son, Marissa's grandfather, joined the U.S. Army, too, and was in the Vietnam War. I can't say that we've ever had a full-fledged conversation about immigration issues before, but today she wants to talk about it.

"Remember last year, when that gardener guy was arrested after he tied up some of his customers—all old people, living by themselves—and then stole things from their houses?" she asks.

"Vaguely, I guess," I say.

"It turned out he was here illegally," she says. "Mexican, I'm very sorry to say. He shouldn't have been here, and he shouldn't have had the chance to hurt those people."

It's hard to argue with that.

"And remember that accident, which was all over the news

last year, where that drunk driver crossed into the wrong lane on the highway and crashed into a car being driven by a middle school teacher? And another teacher was the passenger?"

I do remember that. The teachers both died.

"That was awful," I say.

"One of them used to teach at my school," Marissa says.

"Oh my gosh," I say. "Did you know him?"

"*Her*," Marissa says. "No, she left before I started there. But Malcolm had her. Anyway, that driver was also here illegally. So, think about it. If he hadn't snuck into the country—two times, the papers said—those two teachers would be alive."

It's hard to argue with this, too, but I feel like there's some sort of disconnect about what Marissa is saying. The drunk driver wasn't drunk and driving *because* he was here illegally, was he? If the guy were a legal U.S. citizen, it would be kind of like arguing that the teachers would be alive if the guy hadn't ever been born. Which is technically true. But then what, would you say people who are going to grow up and become drunk drivers shouldn't be born?

I am not sure that my arguments make any sense, either, so I just say, "It's awful."

"It is," she agrees. "I don't want to sound intolerant, but I'm starting to really kind of resent these people."

"Resent?" I say. "Why would you resent them?"

"Because . . . my family followed the rules when they immigrated here. Everyone should have to."

"I wouldn't have guessed you'd be on the anti-immigrant side," I say.

"Danielle, I'm *pro*-immigrant!" Marissa says. "How could I be anti-immigrant, with a name like *Martinez*? But the people who are here illegally hurt the legal immigrants. They make people think that all immigrants are bad news, because, honestly, who takes the time to figure these things out? All foreigners just end up with a bad name. All Hispanics, anyway."

"I—I don't think people think all Hispanics are bad news," I say.

I hear Marissa exhale through the phone. "I shouldn't get on a soapbox about it," she says. "And you're right: not *all* people think that. But I still don't like knowing that thanks to undocumented immigrants, people with my family's background are looked down on, even just by *some* people."

"I understand," I say.

"You probably would feel the same way," Marissa says.

"I don't know," I say. Lightly. "Maybe. I mean, I understand how you feel, but I'm not sure how I would feel. Or how I do feel. I haven't really been focused on the immigration status of the people in the car that . . . hit Humphrey."

"No, of course not," she says. "You've had so much to deal with. I'm just saying. It's an issue you've ended up in the middle of because, as everyone now knows, those people are undocumented immigrants. I thought you might be thinking about it."

"Marissa," I say, "it's great—I guess—that you've become an anti–illegal immigration activist. And—"

"I'm not an activist. I'm reading and thinking about things."

"Well, okay," I say, and add testily, "think away."

Marissa does not like sarcasm. "I'm in favor of legal immigration," she says. "Like how my family came here; probably yours, too. It's not fair to turn it into something negative. Something *anti*. I'm not *anti*. I'm pro–legal immigration. I'm pro-immigrant."

"That's fine," I say. "But I don't have to become pro or anti anything just because the people who were unlucky enough to have hit Humphrey are here illegally."

The air between us hums for a few seconds.

"I could send you links to a few very interesting websites," Marissa says.

"That's okay," I say, meaning *please don't.*

"This didn't just happen to Humphrey. Or to you. It happened to the community," she says.

Wow. That almost sounds like some kind of political campaign slogan.

We say good-bye quietly ("I have to go"; "Me, too").

Marissa says she isn't anti. She's pro.

Well, I'm both.

Here's what I'm anti: random deadly accidents.

Here's what I'm pro: do-overs.

Send me the website for that.

26

Journalism II

AFTER ACCIDENT, LOCAL SPOTLIGHT ON NATIONAL DEBATE

by Caroline Touey

Washington Post staff writer

A fatal accident in the Franklin Grove neighborhood of Meigs County is causing repercussions well beyond initial concerns about pedestrian safety on a busy thoroughfare, catapulting the quiet, stately bedroom community just outside the nation's capital into the national debate on illegal immigration.

The driver of the vehicle that struck and killed five-year-old Humphrey T. Danker has been living in the country illegally for many years, according to officials close to the accident investigation. Eugene Folgar Guzman, 43, of Calvert Hills, is believed to have entered the United States on a student visa some years ago to pursue graduate studies in bioengineering. Whether he obtained his graduate degree while legally on his student visa is not clear, but sources involved in the investigation say that the visa expired at least a decade ago.

Guzman is a native of Colombia, as is his wife. They have two young daughters, both of whom were born in the United States. Mrs. Guzman and the two daughters were in the automobile when Mr. Guzman struck Humphrey Danker.

Guzman was driving on an expired driver's license obtained when he was a graduate student.

"Mr. Guzman apparently did not seek to renew his license when it expired, presumably because he thought such an action would have exposed his by-then illegal status to authorities," said a person with knowledge of the investigation who spoke on condition of anonymity because he is not authorized to speak about the case.

According to Cynthia Hardisty of the Meigs County Police Department, Guzman has no record of traffic violations or other legal infractions in the state.

Anti–illegal immigration activists are disturbed

by the fact that an undocumented alien driving without a valid license killed young Humphrey Danker.

"If it were not for this illegal immigrant, a child
who is now dead would be alive," said Geoffrey
Merryman, executive director of the Federation for
Lawful Immigration, which advocates for tougher
immigration law enforcement. "He was driving without
a license. And we don't even know everything about
this Mr. Guzman yet. He studied bioengineering—
then what? He's from one of the more violent countries
in South America, a center of drug trafficking. What
has he been doing all these years?"

Susan Lester, spokeswoman for Americans for
Secure Borders, said, "Look, let's assume that this
driver has not been up to anything nefarious. I'm
happy to give him the benefit of the doubt. But that's
not the point. The point is, he's here illegally, and he
has been for many years. How has he been able to
work and live here illegally for so long? Because of
indefensible loopholes in our legal system."

Under existing law, Meigs County police do not
take action when they suspect or determine that an
individual who is cited for a misdemeanor traffic
violation may be an undocumented alien. In several
adjacent jurisdictions, county and city police follow
a policy of determining the immigration status of

individuals who are stopped for traffic violations. Those police departments then share information about undocumented aliens with federal authorities for possible prosecution and deportation.

"Our community so far has resisted the temptation to blame all its problems on immigrants," said Simon Lytell, director of the Immigration Rights Center. "Obviously, law offenders are held to account here. Federal immigration policy is a federal matter. Our concern is that efforts to get local police involved in immigration enforcement not only divert scarce community resources to problems that are the responsibility of the federal government, but also can be used as a screen for intolerance and bigotry, pure and simple. That's not what our county is about."

Last year, an undocumented immigrant with a criminal record that included a drunk driving conviction killed two middle school teachers when the car he was driving crossed the median on Interstate 595 and crashed into their car. The immigrant, Hassan Mansour, had a blood alcohol concentration of .15 percent, nearly twice the legal limit. That incident spurred debate throughout the region about the role of undocumented immigrants in deadly accidents.

Earlier this year, Delegate William Foster (5th District) introduced legislation in the Meigs County Council that would authorize, and in some cases require, county police to inquire into the immigration status of any person stopped for a traffic offense and to report any apparent violations to federal immigration authorities. Hearings have not been held on the proposal, and prior to the Franklin Grove accident, it did not attract significant attention. Nor has it been considered likely to pass, as a solid majority of the council members are considered friendly to the county's immigrant population, which generally opposes the idea. The Humphrey Danker accident may change this calculus.

"We will be going to the council on this," said Merryman, of the Federation for Lawful Immigration. "And if they are afraid of offending the immigrants in this community, we'll take it to the state assembly. Enough is enough. Let's act before another innocent child is killed."

The parents of the child killed in the Franklin Grove accident, Thomas R. and Clarice Danker, declined to comment. Thomas R. Danker is a prominent Washington, D.C., attorney known for his advocacy before the U.S. Supreme Court. In the past, he has been counsel of record in at least two cases in which he represented the Immigration Rights Center.

27

ANOTHER SATURDAY NIGHT

"Another Saturday Night." The song, from one of Mom and Dad's Jimmy Buffett records, played in my head as I walked to the Dankers' house for another weekend out with a five-year-old.

Another Saturday night, and I ain't got nobody.

Which reminded me of the funny tune that Adrian sometimes played, "Poor Poor Pitiful Me." He liked the cover recorded by the country singer Terri Clark. Mom and Dad have the Linda Ronstadt version on an old LP, and it's one of Mom's favorites. The differences between the two have been a source of heated debate between Adrian and Mom. Naturally.

"Dan-ielle-y!" Humphrey sang out when he opened the door.

"Hum-phrey-y!" I said.

They'd been playing dominoes, Humphrey and his parents; their game was spread out on the kitchen table.

"I already ate my dinner!" Humphrey said. "So we can play, play, play all night!"

"Sounds great!" I said.

"And we can go to the park if we want, right, Mommy?" Humphrey said.

"That's the beauty of summer," Mrs. Danker said. "It stays light late out there."

Mr. Danker came downstairs. A get-together at some friends' house, Mrs. Danker said. They would not be home late.

"So—what shall we do first?" I asked Humphrey after his parents left.

"Want to play dominoes?" Humphrey asked.

We played a few hands, and then Humphrey blew out a long sigh.

"What's wrong, buddy?" I asked. "If you don't like this, we don't have to play."

"I do like it, and I don't like it," Humphrey said. "I like the way they feel. But playing is a little boring."

"If you want to go to the park, now's a good time for that," I said. "If we head out now, we'll have a nice long time before it gets dark."

As we made the turn onto Quarry Road, Humphrey said, "Let's talk about something. Something interesting."

"Okay," I said. "First we have to think of something interesting."

"Something highly interesting," Humphrey said.

Of course the son of a brilliant lawyer would have high standards for making conversation.

"What would you like to talk about that's highly interesting?" I asked.

"No—*you* talk about something highly interesting."

Oh, yes, I thought, *I'll just delve deep into the treasure trove of sparkling ideas that have made me such a dazzling conversationalist.*

"Hmm," I said.

We walked.

"Danielle!" Humphrey said.

"I don't have anything," I said. "Sorry. I'm coming up empty. I have nothing highly interesting to say. I have nothing even a little bit interesting to say."

"Of course you do!" he squealed. He thought I was joking; I could tell from his squeal, which was part laugh. He thought this was some kind of game: me withholding highly interesting conversation. It became his mission to find the key to my highly interesting thoughts.

"What do you think about . . . dominoes?" he asked.

"I think . . . they should be called domi-*yeses*," I said.

"Yes!" he said. "And what do you think about . . . that tree?"

"I think . . . I'm glad we didn't invite it over for dinner, because we'd have to wait so long for it to wash its hands before eating," I said. "If you catch my—"

"I do! I catch your drift! Ha!" Humphrey said. He craned

his neck way back to look at the branches and leaves, which caused him to swerve a little. I caught his hand. "How many leaves, I mean, *hands*, do you think that tree has?" he asked.

"I don't know," I said. "Eight hundred and eighty-eight?"

"Nine thousand and ninety-nine," Humphrey said. "That's what I think."

I could see he was turning something over in his mind.

"Trees don't eat with their hands," he announced. "They eat with their feet. So the tree wouldn't have to wash its hands before dinner."

"They eat with their feet? You're right! Now I'm even more glad we didn't invite the tree for dinner!"

We were at the entrance to the park.

"See how interesting you are?" Humphrey said.

"See how interesting *you* are!" I said.

"We should be on TV," Humphrey said.

It's Saturday night and I ain't *ain't got nobody*, I thought.

As Humphrey and I walked up the path into the park, we realized that we'd forgotten the football.

"Aargh!" Humphrey groaned. "I wanted to play catch."

"Me, too," I said. "Next time."

"I guess we'll just have to visit the Bumble-Boos."

We took our imaginary journey to Thrumble-Boo. We swung on the beat-up swings, with their beat-up black rubber planks for seats. We climbed the little jungle gym, pretending it was Mount Olympus of Thrumble-Boo.

"You know what else I want to do?" Humphrey said.

"See the first star," I said. "I didn't forget." I'd checked online for the exact time when the first star—Venus—would be visible that night. We had half an hour until it was scheduled to appear.

"Let's play hide-and-seek while we're waiting!" Humphrey said.

I didn't think hide-and-seek could be much fun with two people in an open field with no hiding places. So we made up our own game, a land-based version of the swimming pool game of Marco Polo. In our game, both people had to close their eyes. The person who was "it" called out "Thrumble!" The other person had to respond, "Bumble!" No one could take more than twenty steps per turn.

"This is the best game!" Humphrey said after we played a few rounds. "Now let's look for Venus."

But clouds had rolled in.

"It looks like rain, Humphrey," I said. "I don't think we're going to see that first star tonight."

"Hmm," Humphrey said. "I know what. Let's do a don't-rain dance."

If there is one thing I am not, it is a dancer. There just never seems to be a right place to put my long legs and arms. Plus— could you be more on display than when you're dancing?

"I don't really dance, Humphrey," I said.

"Everyone dances," Humphrey said. "Just do what I do."

What Humphrey did was to gyrate wildly, twisting his little body, shaking his butt, punching his arms in the air, kicking his feet.

"Rain, rain, go away, come again another day," he sang. "Rain, rain, go away, come again another day." He kept repeating the line, changing the style and tune each time. "Come on, Danielle, you can do it!"

"I really don't dance, Humpty."

"You *have* to dance! I need a dance partner!"

I had to laugh at him. He hadn't stopped twisting and turning. "You *need* a dance partner?"

"Yes, I do. Be my partner, Danielle. You can do it!"

I did it.

"Rain! Rain! Go away! Come again! Another day! How's that, Humpty?"

"Go, Danielle! Go, Danielle!" Humphrey cheered.

I rapped, I crooned. I rocked out. Somehow dancing outdoors felt easier than in a school gym or hotel party room. Plenty of space for my arms and legs. I let myself lose control, and danced like crazy on the planet of Thrumble-Boo.

"You look like a beautiful daddy longlegs!" Humphrey said.

"I'll take that as a compliment, Humphrey!"

"You're a good dancer! Not as good as me, but as good as anyone else!"

Then the skies opened up, and we hurried home.

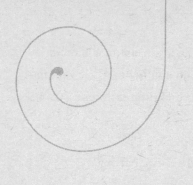

28

NEED TO KNOW

I can't ignore the ringing telephone on the wall, because I'm sitting right here in the kitchen next to it. I missed a call on my cell phone from Adrian when I was in the bathroom; when I called him back, he didn't answer. So I'm thinking this is him and pick it up without looking at the display to see who's calling.

"Danielle?"

One day I will answer the telephone and it won't be Doris Raskin. But today is not that day.

"I'm calling to urge you, to strongly urge you, to go before the county council next month when they take up the question of Quarry Road improvements."

And how are you, Mrs. Raskin?

She goes on (and on and on). She understands I may still have been feeling too "traumatized" to speak at the community hall meeting last month. Fortunately, as a result of that meeting, the Franklin Grove Board passed a recommendation in favor of the safety improvements that are needed to prevent another tragedy. But the board doesn't have the power of the purse, and action by the county council is required to make things happen, and the county council has many other priorities, but we must make this a top priority for them, and the way to do that is with a strong showing, blah, blah, blah, blah.

And I am a key figure in the accident. And I have experienced firsthand the tragic consequences of etc., etc. And I can surely make a compelling statement about blah, blah, blah, blah.

"I'll think about it, Mrs. Raskin," I say when she takes a breath.

By which I mean no.

"I hope you will, Danielle. You're a young person. But I know you're mature enough to understand the obligation you have to the community and especially to Clarice and Tom Danker to try to make something good come out of this tragedy. I'm sure your parents would agree with me."

Could she lay it on any heavier?

"After what the Dankers have gone through," she adds. So yes, she could lay it on heavier. "What Clarice risked . . ."

My cell buzzes itself awake on the kitchen table. A quick glance tells me it's Adrian.

"Mrs. Raskin, I'm sorry, I have another call," I say.

"I urge you to think—"

"I will," I say, and hang up.

"Hi, Adrian," I say.

"How's it going?" he asks.

"Tip-top-terrific," I say.

Don't even ask who introduced that line into our family vocabulary.

"So glad about that," he says.

"How are you? I miss you." He hasn't been around much lately.

"Miss you, too, Danny-boy. I'll come by this weekend, I promise."

"Is something going on, or is this a purely social call?"

"Both," he says. "What's going on is that we've almost reached the level of funding we need to make the restaurant thing happen."

"Wow," I say. "That's great!"

He tells me about who the new investors are, and about plans for how the place will look and what kind of food it will have, and how other local businesses in the neighborhood are supportive and helpful, happy to have a decent place open in a desert of fast-food chains. He sounds so excited.

"And I'm taking cooking classes at night," he says.

"*You* could teach people how to cook," I say.

"Restaurant-quality cooking classes," he says. "Like—how to be a chef. Not how to make dinner at home."

And, yes, he's still plumber-ing during the day.

I am wondering about whether the cooking school he's in cares that he didn't finish high school. I mean, I know he's brilliant, and he's no less brilliant for dropping out four months before graduation, but I wonder what the world out there thinks about it. I hate to ask. It's a Mom-ish thing to press him about. But—I do.

"Danny, I got my diploma. And I don't mean a GED. I was so far ahead in my credits. Mr. Farley"—that would be Adrian's guidance counselor, and a huge fan of Adrian's—"helped me work it out. I even took my APs."

"Get *out!*"

He laughs.

"So—it only *looked* like you dropped out when you moved out of the house," I say, slightly incredulous.

"Yup. It only looked like it."

Should I even ask— "Do Mom and Dad know?"

"No," Adrian says. "They're on a need-to-know basis with me. I decided they didn't need to know."

"Jeez, Adrian." I can't help it. "Why would you not tell them something that they'll think is a good thing?"

He doesn't answer immediately. I hope he's not mad at me for asking.

"Not really sure," he says. "And of course, you're sworn to secrecy."

"As if you have to tell me that," I say.

"It's like—if I tell them I actually did graduate," Adrian says, "*and* with an above-4.0 average, they'll say, 'So, why aren't you applying to Yale?'"

"Maybe," I say.

"And if they know I'm in cooking school, they'll say, 'Why don't you apply to Le Cordon Bleu in Paris? Or the Culinary Institute in New York?'"

I actually can't imagine Dad saying that. But Mom—sure. And she'd come to the conversation prepared with websites and brochures. And Adrian knows that Dad, her loyal soldier, would back her up.

We talk a little bit more. Adrian doesn't really ask about me, which is fine. I just love hearing him so energized.

After we hang up, I hear the mail drop through the slot.

Is Doris Raskin clairvoyant? There's a formal letter addressed to me from the chairman of the Meigs County Council requesting my "testimony" at a council hearing in November regarding improvements on Quarry Road. The letter gives me the date, time, place, directions—and, oh look, someone to call with any questions. I don't have any questions. But I call anyway. I want to make sure I'm not going to be arrested when I don't show up.

The phone number belongs to an aide to the council chairman.

"It's nothing to worry about," she says lightly. She explains that the council just wants to understand what problems with the street might have led to the tragedy. They already have all the information gathered at the Franklin Grove community meeting. And, of course, the police report.

Of course, the police report. This chills me. I am in a police report.

"It won't be a grilling," the aide, who is nice and whose name is Jen, says. "No one thinks you're at fault."

Unless you count Humphrey's parents, Mrs. Joseph, Mrs. Raskin, everyone at school, and, I would guess, undocumented immigrants everywhere.

I think about that hint Mrs. Raskin dropped last month— the vague possibility that Mr. Danker might use his powerful lawyering skills to sue me for what happened. I haven't mentioned this to my parents. I think Dad would freak and Mom would . . . Mom would froth. I wonder if Jen might know something about this. For half a second I think of asking. Then I drop the idea.

I gather from what Jen tells me that the council can't make me testify—or maybe she's saying they can but they won't.

"But, Danielle, you should. Really."

"I just don't think I have anything"—I pause to gather my thoughts—"anything *useful* to say. So much of it was a blur, like I told the police."

"That's okay. You can tell the council that."

"What's the point, then?"

"Sometimes," Jen says, "when you tell your story again, little details come back to you."

"I don't think that's going to happen."

"You'll feel better. . . ."

How in the world does this Jen know how I'm feeling when I don't even know how I'm feeling?

"I'm sorry," I say. "I can't."

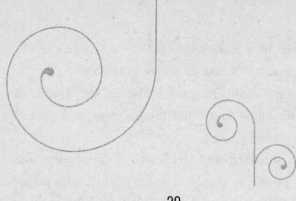

29

THERE ARE WORSE THINGS

The next day. Do I answer the kitchen telephone, or have I learned my lesson?

I look at the display; I don't know the number. That's good news, since by now I'm able to recognize Doris Raskin's number. This is not her. I answer.

It's Justin, from the park.

"How's it going?" he says.

"It's going," I respond. Then, because I'm a little put off to find him on the line: "You're calling my house." No, not the start of another brilliant conversation! "To state the obvious."

"Yes, I am. I didn't have your cell number. But you did tell me your name. It wasn't hard to figure out which Snyders in the phone directory were your family—I just looked for the address closest to Quarry Road Park."

He engaged in *sleuthing* to call me?

"So," he says, "I heard you might be speaking at the Meigs County Council hearing next month."

Okay. What is he, some kind of stalker?

He apparently reads my mind. "I'm not a stalker," he says. "I talked to one of the assistants there."

That's not stalking? "Why would you be talking to people at the county council?" I ask.

"Doesn't everybody keep in touch with their elected representatives?" he asks.

I have no response to that.

"Joking," he says, and then tells me he has to do a report for his government class. The Franklin Grove safety debate is government in action, so he thought he would use it for his assignment.

"If you're going to ask to interview me, given my last experience being interviewed, I think I'll be keeping my mouth shut until the hearing," I say.

He's not asking to interview me. And actually, he's not doing his report on the Franklin Grove thing after all. He doesn't think the county council will make any decisions in time for his report.

"So I'm doing my report on something that already happened—a law in Congress," Justin says.

"Then you're not calling to talk about me testifying at the county council."

I must sound—relieved, confused, *something*, because he

laughs. "Yeah, no, the pressure's off. I was just calling to say hi. And to say it was fun throwing the football around with you. But it's supposed to rain for the rest of the week and into the weekend, so I'm wondering if you'd like to get together for coffee or something."

Huh. Is Justin-from-the-park asking me out?

"Okay," I say. "I'll meet you for coffee or something. What's the 'or something' option?"

"Uh—"

Now I've confused him.

"Coffee would be nice," I say.

"Great."

I ask what the weather forecast has to do with getting together for coffee.

"I figure you won't be at the park if it's raining," he says. "So we can't meet up there."

We settle on a place, a coffee shop neither of us has been to before. We agree to meet there; it's on bus routes for both of us.

"See you Saturday," Justin says. "Three o'clock."

I don't think it's a disaster. The place is in one of these new fake-downtown areas that are getting built all over the suburbs. We're both perfectly on time. We both like our coffees pretty simple. We both like to eat something when drinking coffee.

He tells me about his paper for government class. It's about laws passed by Congress that concern toxic substances making their way into drinking water and food. This subject clearly gets his engine going.

"It's a huge problem," Justin says. "And we're so far behind on solving it, even though there have been laws around for decades. The thing is, people—all kinds of people, from folks in their homes to big companies—have been pouring poisons down drains and in sewers forever. Eventually they can contaminate drinking water sources. And then another problem is how everyone wants their fruits and vegetables all pretty, and farmers want to have big crops, so we use pesticides. But you can end up with a plateful of pretty food that has some pretty bad stuff in it."

"Mm-hmm," I say.

"I get a little carried away," he says. "Sorry—end of speech."

"No, it's fine," I say. "Feel free to speechify."

He takes a bite of his apple muffin. I take a sip of my café au lait. Our eyes meet while our mouths are full and we almost burst out laughing. We're having the same unserious thought about all that "pretty bad stuff" Justin was just speechifying about.

"Uh-oh," he says with his mouth still slightly full.

"Ruh-roh," I say around my half-swallowed sip.

"Is it on apples that are cooked in muffins?" he says.

"Is it in coffee?" I say.

We recover without spitting out our mouthfuls. Now we do burst out laughing.

"I'm sorry," I say. "I know it's a terrible problem. Nothing to laugh at."

"I'm laughing, too," Justin says. "What else can we do?"

What else, he adds, getting serious again, is we can have strong laws. But what he's even more interested in, he says, is figuring out new ways to fix the problems with scientific solutions.

"Like bioremediation," he says.

I have no idea what that means.

"Speaking of the food chain," he says as he gets up from his chair, "I'm still hungry. Do you want something else?"

I decline.

When he gets back, Justin mentions that he has a hockey game tomorrow morning. "Does your brother play anymore?" he asks.

I forgot that I'd mentioned Adrian's hockey playing when we talked in the park.

"Well, you know, he's not in high school. . . ."

"Yeah, but he can keep playing," Justin says. "There are all kinds of leagues."

I don't actually know whether Adrian is playing hockey. I suppose it could be one of those things that he's picked up again but decided not to mention at home because then Mom would want to know if he's going out for the NHL.

"I'll ask him," I say.

"So he's working at this new restaurant?" Justin asks. I mentioned it earlier.

No. I explain that while the restaurant is a work in progress, Adrian's still doing plumbing. "If he plumbs like he does everything else," I conclude, "then he's probably a great plumber.

A plumber of prowess. Proficiently practicing the profession of plumbing."

I could bite off my tongue. I'm doing *p* words in front of Justin?

"I like it!" he says. "Wacky and wondrous wordplay."

You must be kidding me.

He looks embarrassed. That makes two of us.

"So, are you—are you going to Western's homecoming?" he asks.

A sputtering laugh bursts out of my mouth before I can stop it. At least I wasn't trying to swallow coffee. This boy has a lot to learn about me.

"Is that a funny question?" he asks.

"No. Sorry," I say. "It is a perfectly reasonable question. No, I am not going to homecoming."

"You like football," he points out.

"I like throwing a football," I correct him. "Two different things."

"I can see that," he says.

"And I don't—I mean I really, *really* don't—dance," I say.

"Huh," he says.

This leads him to talk about his sister, who's older, and who *does* dance. She's at a performing arts conservatory, where her major is dance.

"I've been to a lot of ballet recitals," he says, half laughing. "I can tell you what an arabesque is. And a pas de deux. And a chassé. I could go on."

"Impressive," I say. "Do you speak French?"

"Nope," Justin says. "Just random ballet terms."

We talk about what it's like to have brilliant older siblings. It's fine, we agree. Better than fine. He seems to idolize his sister as much as I idolize Adrian.

And so we chit and we chat, meandering around our lives. Before I know it, two hours have passed.

"I should get home," I say, although I don't have any particular reason to get home.

"Yeah," he says. "Me, too."

When we reach my bus stop on the corner right outside the coffee shop, he says, "Want to walk a little? You can pick up the bus down at Greenway Road and Maplewood Avenue."

There's not too much talking as we walk. To be honest, I'm kind of talked out. But it doesn't feel too awkward to be walking in the light drizzle without saying much. Not too terribly awkward, anyway. A little. A little perculiar. I smile.

"What?" Justin asks.

"What what?"

"You just laughed a little."

"Oh—nothing. Just—nothing."

"It must feel good to walk around and feel like laughing for no reason," he says.

Do I detect hurt in his voice?

Oh, all right.

"Sometimes I remember something about Humphrey— something funny or cute. And it makes me smile."

Justin nods.

"It makes me feel like crying, actually," I say, "but that would be embarrassing, wouldn't it? Walking around and suddenly bursting into tears? I mean, this happens multiple times a day."

The next bus stop is in sight.

"I don't know," Justin says. "There are worse things, I think. Not worse than what happened to Humphrey and you. I mean, worse than crying. Sometimes a person needs to cry."

What does he know about it? Maybe there aren't worse things, for me. Maybe if there are worse things, I don't want to go there.

This is starting to remind me of being in a therapy session. And that is not where I want to be, so:

"Since we were talking about homecoming," I say, "here's something more embarrassing than me bursting into tears in the middle of the sidewalk. That would be me dancing."

We walk for a bit, while he either ponders or ignores that comment.

"I saw you dancing in the park," he says finally. "With Humphrey. Didn't look bad to me."

He saw me dancing? It had to be the rain dance. To be precise, the do-not-rain dance. Our crazy, out-of-control do-not-rain dance. Mortifying.

"You were there that day?" I ask. I didn't see him. And I thought he'd only seen me and Humphrey throwing the football—the wrong kind of football, as he informed me that first time we met.

"I was over on the basketball court. I was supposed to meet my friends, but they bailed on me. I thought about coming over, but I figured—"

"You figured you'd better stay away from the peculiar girl doing a bizarre do-not-rain dance with a five-year-old," I say, "in case peculiarity is something you can catch."

"Catch, as in a football?" he says.

"As in a disease."

My bus is here.

"You just had this look on your face, like you're thinking I was spying on you," Justin says. "Which I was not. I just like that crummy little park. In fact, I was going to that park before I ever saw you there."

"Okay," I say. "You win. It's *your* park."

The bus doors are open.

"Well—thanks," I say, and step up.

"And I thought about coming over that day, but didn't want to break up your fun," Justin calls after me. "The kid was looking at you like he thought you were a rock star. You looked like you were having a great time. I didn't think you were perculiar at all."

The bus doors close.

Did I just hear that?

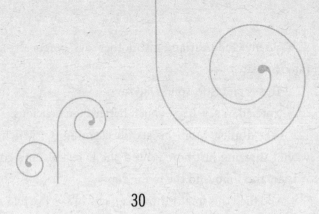

30

DEFINE "ANGEL"

When I get home, Mom and Dad are both there. Since I never
go out on—this isn't the right word for what this was, but I don't
have another one—*dates*, I can tell they're kind of curious about
how it went. Mom especially, surprise, surprise.

But their attention is diverted away from me by an actual,
and better, surprise: Adrian shows up. He's here to cook dinner; we'll be his guinea pigs for dishes he's learned from—as I
know and our parents do not—his cooking class. Pan-roasted
halibut with chopped-up salsa-like stuff on top. Sautéed broccolini with garlic. Mashed potatoes. I hang around him as he
cooks, and learn the difference between pan roasting and sau-
téing; broccolini, broccoli, and broccoli rabe; and the important question of when to cook fish with its skin on and with its
skin removed.

"Oh my God, Adrian," my mother says, practically melting into her plate.

"This is fantastic, son," Dad says.

"Not bad," I say. It's so much better than delicious.

After dinner, Mom insists on cleaning up, which is her way of showing just how wowed she is by Adrian's cooking. Adrian and I move to the living room.

"And then this freaky thing happens," I say. I've told Adrian who Justin is, and about meeting him for coffee. "Actually, it happens twice. We're talking, and he says these things—just a couple of words, but I'm telling you, it's strange—that were Humphrey words. Things Humphrey and I used to say."

Adrian raises his eyebrows. "And those words were?"

"He says 'yeah, no'—wait, this was when we were on the phone," I say.

Adrian cocks his head to one side. "Okay, Danny, I hate to tell you. That's not exactly a unique expression."

"I know, I know," I say. "It doesn't sound like anything. *Yeah, no.* But there's a certain way to say it, a certain time when you say it—that was Humphrey's and mine."

"What's the other thing?" Adrian asks.

"Just as I was getting on the bus, he was saying that he didn't think something was peculiar—"

"Wait. That he *didn't* think something was peculiar?"

"Yeah. It sounds like a weird conversation, but it made sense. In context. Anyway, so he's saying the word 'peculiar,' only instead he says 'perculiar,' with an *r* stuck in the middle."

"Which was something you and Humphrey used to say?"

"Well, which Humphrey used to say. He had a whole string of *p* words in his vocabulary—don't ask—and they were mostly these hard, high-level words, which a five-year-old wouldn't normally know. And he always got them right, all except the word 'peculiar.' He said 'percular,' every time, and he insisted that this was the right way to say it. Insisted, even, that Mr. Danker told him so."

"That's really pretty cute," Adrian says.

Yeah. It really was.

"So." My voice is a little shaky. Hold on. Take a deep breath. "So, I know it's just a coincidence that Justin, who, also coincidentally, hangs out at the same park that I did with Humphrey, happened to speak in Humphrey-speak. I know. But it also felt like, I don't know, Humphrey was there. Like some kind of Humphrey-angel was there."

I can't believe I just said that. It's ridiculous, and I don't believe in angels. I don't even know what it means to say that you do or do not believe in angels.

"So." There it goes again, all shaky. Breathe. "It's just weird. And a little creepy. And I feel sort of mad at this guy for making me think Humphrey's around."

Adrian is quiet.

"But, Danielle," my mother says. She's standing in the doorway. "What's wrong with thinking Humphrey is around?"

I didn't know she was there. Obviously. By now, Dad's in the room, too, but he's quiet, like Adrian.

What's wrong with thinking Humphrey is around? Isn't this obvious, too? Talk about peculiar. Perculiar. Whatever. Do I really want to be seeing the angel—or ghost—of a five-year-old boy hanging around the only high school boy who's ever paid any attention to me, ever, ever?

"I really don't think I need an angel in my life," I say quietly. "At this particular time."

"Define 'angel,'" Mom says.

Perfect. My mother thinks it will be helpful to analyze my vocabulary of the supernatural. Of the spiritual. Or whatever.

Mom sits down in the chair across from the sofa, where I'm sitting. I don't offer her a definition.

"Okay, then, I will," she says. "Or at least I'll try to tell you something about—about angels."

Mom and angels. This is unusual.

"My father died a long time ago," Mom says. "As you know. Adrian was less than a year old. You, Danny, weren't born yet."

Yes. I know.

"We were sitting in the kitchen of my parents' house—where Grammy stayed on to live until she died. Grandpa had died that morning. It was late afternoon, and he had already been taken to the funeral home. We were waiting for the rabbi to come talk to us.

"You know how Grammy's house had that big window in the kitchen looking out to their little backyard? As we're sitting there, a big, beautiful red cardinal flew into the dogwood tree. He sat there on the tree branch for the longest time."

"I remember this, kids," Dad says.

"The next day, we have the funeral. It was a pretty day. Afterward, we go back to Grammy's house, where we're going to sit shiva. Grammy and I and Uncle Harold are there, sitting in the living room in those special shiva chairs—the ones that are so low to the ground. Because we're only a few inches off the floor in those chairs, our point of view is a little different than usual. We're looking up, if you can picture it. So I'm looking up and out the bay window in the living room, to the front yard. And there's that cardinal again, this time in the cherry tree."

"You know it's the same one?" Adrian asks.

"I have no doubt," Mom says.

Adrian and I share a look. Of course she has no doubt. She's Mom.

"Every day of shiva, during daylight hours, I see the cardinal," Mom continues. "He's always on a branch or windowsill as close to the house as he can be. 'Mom,' I said to Grammy, 'if we open the door, I think that cardinal will fly right in.' 'What are you waiting for?' Grammy said."

Mom smiles. I can hear Grammy saying that.

"Grammy had never seen a cardinal around the house before," Mom says. "Chickadees. Blue jays. Finches. Sparrows. But not cardinals. They just weren't seen much around that neighborhood."

"But Grandpa dies and suddenly a cardinal appears," Adrian says.

"Yes," Mom says. "And doesn't just appear; he makes his presence known. He preens. He doesn't flit around like the other birds. Every other bird flies away when we approach the window. He stays put and acts like he's perfectly at home."

"So you're saying this cardinal was an angel?" I say. "It was Grandpa?"

Mom sighs. "To this day, when I'm stressed—but also when I'm very happy, or just feeling emotional in some way—I find that I'm likely to see a cardinal. Do I think it's Grandpa in the form of an angel? I don't know. That's why I said 'define angel.' When Grammy and I were sitting shiva, I just might have said that, yes, the cardinal that suddenly showed up and acted like he owned the joint, he was Grandpa, coming back to make sure we were all right. My father was a good-looking man, and meticulous about his appearance and dress. And he liked a little dash of flash. Special cuff links, a good tie, a silk hanky in his jacket pocket—something. If he were to come back as a bird, it would be as a cardinal, a bird so bright you can't miss it, and with that dashing crest on its head."

Adrian is looking at Mom with his mouth half-open. I think he can't believe what he's hearing. I saw it in his face when Mom said she sees cardinals when she's feeling emotional.

"But do I really and truly think the cardinals I see today are all Grandpa? Heck, I know they're not the same bird we saw all those years ago during shiva. I guess they're not really Grandpa. I guess they're not truly angels, if an angel is defined as some kind of ethereal being." Mom has been looking at her hands, and at Dad, mostly, while she's been talking. Now she looks at me. "But when I see a cardinal, I feel like the universe is communicating to me. Not that my father is physically present, or even present in spirit, but definitely that his life force, his impression on the universe, is very much present. Present and available to me."

We all just sit there for a few minutes. Mom gives me a cockeyed little smile. Adrian looks blown away. Here is what I gather he's thinking from the gears I see grinding away through his transparent skull: *She feels! She thinks about the universe communicating! She talks about life force!*

"Thanks, Mom," I say.

We sit quietly for a few more minutes.

"There's dessert," Adrian says. "Warm apple crisp, anybody?"

He brings it into the living room.

"Speaking of angels in heaven," Mom says after she takes a bite. It is, like the rest of Adrian's dinner, so, so, so good.

"In other news of the day," Adrian says after he finishes his dessert, "I'm a high school graduate. I just wanted you guys to know."

He explains. I know this already, of course. But I won't let on. This is Adrian's offering to Mom. His acknowledgment that she is, after all—human. That she isn't just cold-blooded, driven, and prestige chasing.

Wait for it.

"Now you can apply to colleges!" Mom exclaims.

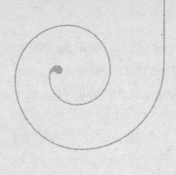

31

A MISHMASH

I never considered that I was a peacekeeper or any other
kind of go-between in our family between Adrian and
Mom. In the last conversation that I had with Marissa,
though, she said I was. I was less than thrilled to hear
more of her opinions, of which I think she has too many,
about our so-called family dynamics, so I was happy when
the conversation moved on. Although I wasn't happy with
where the conversation went, about illegal immigration,
but that's a whole different subject.

If I was a peacekeeper between Adrian and Mom, is
that a bad thing? I love Adrian and I love Mom, and I just
wanted them to love each other more. To <u>like</u> each other
more, is what I mean, because I'm sure the love is there.

But Marissa made me start thinking that my

go-between-ness was something more than just trying to get Adrian and Mom to like each other. I don't know what, exactly. Something.

When I think about how I have reacted to Marissa's comments about my family, I wonder about myself as a friend. Friends should be able to tell each other things honestly. I know Marissa wasn't trying to put me or my family down. I don't like that she seemed to be saying that her family is superior—but maybe she didn't mean to say that. Maybe she was just trying to be a helpful friend.

And speaking of being a friend, how strange is it that I, a high school sophomore, should have felt so close to Humphrey, who never even made it to kindergarten? I almost feel like he was my best friend. How can I feel like this about a kid who isn't my age and doesn't know enough to have conversations about things like family dynamics and immigration?

I should say who <u>wasn't</u> my age and <u>didn't</u> know enough.

"This was a total mishmash," I say.

"Mishmashes can be helpful," Dr. Gilbert says. "Sometimes the most important thing isn't to say something in a neat and logical way, but just to say it, period. In any way it comes out."

"But I don't even really know what I'm saying."

"Do you think there's some truth to what your friend was saying about the role you play vis-à-vis Adrian and your mother?"

My "friend," or my "former friend." But that's not the issue here, so I concentrate on Dr. Gilbert's question.

"I'm not sure, but I guess I must think there's some truth there because she said this two weeks ago and I'm still thinking about it," I say.

"Let's not put a label on the role—like 'peacekeeper' or 'go-between,'" Dr. Gilbert says. "Let's just try to think about the function itself. What is it you would do, or still do, with respect to Adrian and your mom?"

"I try to get them to like each other."

"By doing what?"

I can't think of anything specific. "I guess if I can't come up with examples, I'm not really doing much of anything," I say.

"Not necessarily," Dr. Gilbert says. "Do you carry messages from one to the other?"

"Like—do I tell Adrian what Mom thinks and tell Mom what Adrian thinks?"

She nods. I think.

"No, not really," I say. "That's not it."

"Do you try to change the subject when everyone's together if you see things are going in a hairy direction?"

"I've done that," I say. "Not a lot, but sometimes."

"Do you translate for them?"

I laugh a little, because I'm thinking of Becca and me and our French.

"Not literally," I say.

"No, of course not literally."

"But, yes, I've been known to take what Adrian is saying and put it in terms that won't offend Mom so much. And to rephrase something Mom says so that Adrian won't just hear *nag-nag-nag-nag-nag*."

"Do you try to protect them from each other?" Dr. Gilbert asks.

Do I try to protect them from each other? "I don't know what you mean," I say.

"I don't have anything in particular in mind," Dr. Gilbert says. "The question is whether that question resonates with you—whether, even if you can't yet say how or what, you think there might be an element of you protecting them from each other in how you relate to them or behave or things you say."

"I guess there might be an . . . element like that," I say.

"And, on the flip side, do you ever protect yourself from them?"

"No," I say. "That doesn't sound true at all. They don't bother me enough for me to need to protect myself from them. They really don't bother me at all."

"And how about this: Do you ever protect them from you?"

I'm about to say no, but I stop.

"Like how?" I ask.

"You tell me," Dr. Gilbert says.

I want to say no. But there is something there. Maybe not *protection*, exactly. But I'm having the same uneasy, unsure feeling I felt when thinking about what Marissa said about my being a go-between.

"I don't protect my mother from me," I say. "But I also don't want to give her any trouble, because I know how much Adrian's stuff bothers her."

"Adrian's stuff being . . ."

"Taking the opposite position to whatever position she takes. Not letting things she says slide. Not living up to her and Dad's expectations in school and all."

"So you don't protect your mother from you," Dr. Gilbert says. "But you do protect her from potentially being disappointed by you."

"I guess I try," I say. "I'm not saying I'm any good at it."

"And how about protecting Adrian from you?"

It pains me, this question, almost as much as hearing Marissa bad-mouth him last winter.

"Again, I wouldn't say I protect Adrian from me," I say. "But maybe I don't want him ever to feel like Mom and Dad are happier with me than with him. I don't want to do things that make him look bad."

"That make him look bad by comparison, you mean?" Dr. Gilbert says.

"Yeah."

"You don't want to upstage him," Dr. Gilbert says. "If you're an accomplished student who makes her parents proud at school and in the community, then how will he feel?"

It sounds messed up to hear her say it.

"Kind of," I say. "I mean, obviously I'm not out to be a total screw-up. I do well in school. I don't get in trouble."

"But are you living up to your full potential, or are you living small out of deference to Adrian?"

"Adrian isn't living small. He's working jobs, playing music he loves, starting a new—"

"*I* don't think he's living small," Dr. Gilbert says. "But are you living small and taking as few chances as possible out of some notion of loyalty that has you not wanting to outshine your brother?"

"I *couldn't* outshine him," I say. "He's a great guy."

"Then you have no reason to limit yourself at all. Any accomplishments you might have, any passions you might develop—they'd only be about your own growth and achievement. They wouldn't reflect poorly on him."

I don't understand how we ended up here.

"I thought I'm supposed to be dealing with my feelings about the accident," I say. "I shouldn't have dragged Adrian into this. Or even Marissa."

"But if they're on your mind, then that's what you should be dealing with," Dr. Gilbert says.

"They don't have anything to do with the accident, or my feelings about the accident," I say. "I just wasted a session."

Now here is something I haven't seen before: a look of exasperation on Dr. Gilbert's face.

"What?" I say. "Are you even allowed to be mad at me?"

She laughs. "I'm not mad, Danielle. I'm just thinking, Really, this was a wasted session? You expressed some important insights."

"I can't think of one."

"I'll refresh your memory," Dr. Gilbert says. "In earlier sessions, you talked about feeling incompetent, especially after the accident. Today, when you talked about not wanting to outshine your brother, I couldn't help but think about whether this meant that you get in your own way of rising above those feelings of incompetence."

"Isn't this kind of off track?" I say.

"In earlier sessions," Dr. Gilbert continues, "you talked about feeling, to use your word, 'peculiar.' Today you asked whether it's strange—which, I'm sure you'll agree, is a synonym for 'peculiar'—for you to feel so close to a five-year-old. Exactly the same track."

"Okay, I'm on track," I say, "but am I strange?"

She rolls her eyes—who knew that therapists did that to their patients?—and laughs. "You are not strange," she says. "You're interesting."

"Oh, yes," I say, "highly."

She laughs again and gives me a sort of questioning look. "Until next time, then," she says, "keep on thinking your highly interesting thoughts."

32

EARNESTNESS

Me, Becca, a Ping-Pong table. Defeating the guys. I am in my childhood heaven.

Okay, defeating the guy, singular. Not guys, plural. Defeating Justin, to be exact. It is very satisfying. And unlike twelve-year-old boys, Justin doesn't tell us that we won only because of my freakish height or because of Becca's tricky serve or because he wasn't really trying.

"You two are good!" he says, at twenty-one to nineteen. This is the second game he's lost to that score.

He doesn't mention that maybe we won because we were playing two against one. I point this out.

"Right! Let's not forget that," Justin says, laughing.

"Oh, I think we could put some other guy across the table with you and still beat both your pants off," Becca crows.

There's no other guy around to draft into this challenge. We're the only ones in the rec room of the Franklin Grove Community Hall.

"Another time," Justin says.

I introduced Becca and Justin this afternoon for the first time. They like each other, I think. Sometimes he seems a little surprised by—let's see, what shall I call it?—her assertiveness. Not bothered by it, not at all. Just mildly surprised, and maybe amused, too. I understand. Becca's earnestness can be kind of funny. For sure, it helps keep her assertiveness from having sharp elbows.

Justin is earnest in his own way, too, which I'm finding kind of funny also, and also kind of—appealing. Before we came to the community hall this afternoon to bat around the Ping-Pong ball, we met up at my house. Justin walked in with a small grocery sack.

"I come bearing gifts," he said.

"I like him already," Becca said.

"Gifts of food," Justin added.

"Oh," Becca said.

He set the bag on the kitchen table. "Five kiwis, three mangoes, and a pineapple." He unpacked them, one piece at a time.

"Fruit! I'm very touched. Thank you," I said.

"Not just any fruit," he said. "These are among the top low-pesticide fruits out there. In light of our conversation last week at the coffee shop, I thought I'd, um, I thought you'd like—"

He was distracted because Becca was holding up a kiwi and a mango like she'd never seen them before.

"Pay no attention to me," she said. "I'm just looking to see if maybe you're hiding chocolates inside of them."

"Pay no attention to *her*," I said. "Thank you for the pesticide-free fruit."

"*Low*-pesticide fruit," Justin said. "I don't know if a pesticide-free fruit exists in our grocery stores."

We peeled three kiwis and two mangoes, and halved the pineapple.

"Good," Becca said, popping a pineapple chunk. "I'm sorry I made fun of your fruit, Justin."

"That's okay. I have a thick skin," he said. And pointedly looked at the peelings in the sink, waiting.

Becca and I groaned.

"That may be the only pun I think of all year," Justin said.

Taking a break from our serious table tennis competition, Becca and I rally the ball back and forth. Justin stands at the side of the table and tosses us new balls when we hit out of bounds.

"So I hesitate to ask this, Justin, but . . . ," Becca says.

"As if you ever hesitate to ask anything." I laugh.

"This passion for pesticide-free fruit that you two share—"

"I don't think it's fair to say Danielle shares it," Justin says. "I think she's just been polite."

"Excuse me, I can speak for myself," I say.

"Okay, speak," Becca says.

"Yeah, no, I'm not passionate about fruit," I say. "I like fruit, though." I silently mouth to Justin, "*Sorry.*"

"I'm not holding it against you," he says.

"*So*, then," Becca says, "Justin, *your* passion for pesticide-free fruit . . ."

"Jeez, that makes it sound pretty, um, peculiar," he says. "It's really more an interest in . . ."

And he gives a little speech on toxins in our food and water supply. Becca's interested, especially when Justin mentions some journalists who apparently are famous for their writings on environmental issues like these.

"So you don't just have a thing about fruit," Becca says.

He laughs. "No, I also have a thing about water."

By now, Becca and I have stopped hitting the ball back and forth, and we're sprawled on the shabby chairs in the lounge. I think the community hall gets its furniture from neighbors who donate stuff they don't want anymore.

"Did you see the movie *Erin Brockovich*?" Justin asks us.

Becca turns to me and bugs her eyes out.

"Did I see it?" I say. "You mean, did I memorize it. I've seen it twelve times."

"At least," Becca chimes in.

"Really?" Justin says. "Why?"

"I thought it was so cool, what she did," I said. "Figuring out what made all those people in that town in California sick. . . ."

"Toxic substances in their drinking water," Justin said. "That was my point."

Yes. I hadn't made the connection between his government paper and my hero-worship of Erin Brockovich.

"Danielle's going to go to law school to become Erin Brockovich's boss," Becca says.

Justin smiles, but looks puzzled.

"Becca's got it all planned out," I say. "She's going to be a big-time investigative journalist. And I'm going to be a big-time lawyer battling the forces of evil. According to Becca."

"But 'Erin Brockovich's boss'?" he asks.

"Because she was a law clerk, not an actual lawyer," Becca explains. "And wouldn't you rather be the lawyer making the decisions—telling the law clerk what to do—"

"Because I'm so talented at telling people what to do," I interrupt her.

"—cross-examining witnesses in court, making arguments before a jury?"

"Now, those are really my strengths, aren't they," I say.

Justin is still looking puzzled. He doesn't know about my illustrious history of public speaking. It hasn't come up.

"They *could* be your strengths," Becca says. "I know you have it in you."

"Well, Erin Brockovich was definitely as important, or more important, than any lawyer in that case," Justin says. "She was the one who led the investigation and figured out it was hexavalent chromium in the groundwater that caused cancer in all those people. And that it was the power company leaking the chromium into the ground."

Even Becca can't argue with that.

"But, I mean, if you want to be a lawyer," Justin says to me, "you should go for it. I can see it. I can see you making closing arguments."

"It's all settled, then," Becca says. "How about you, Justin? An environmental lawyer?"

"I'm more interested in the science side," he says. "Like bio-engineering. Or chemical engineering. There's this thing called bioremediation, where you use bacteria to clean up poisons in water and in the earth."

This is what Justin mentioned that day we had coffee.

"There are bacteria that will basically eat toxic substances," he continues. "Even hexavalent chromium, the stuff in *Erin Brockovich*. They eat the poisons, digest them, and what's left is water plus a harmless gas."

"Magic," I say.

"Really complicated magic," he says. "Because it's not easy to figure out what bacteria will work. If you get it wrong, they eat the poisons, yeah, but then digest them into another type of poison."

"Black magic," I say.

"And even once you find the right bacteria," Justin says, "you've got to make sure conditions are right for them to stay alive. Without the right temperature, without the right amounts of oxygen and nutrients, they'll just die."

He gets so earnest and lit up when he talks about this. But

as soon as the words "they'll just die" are out of his mouth, he turns somber. He looks at me apologetically.

Ah, the problem of mentioning life and death in front of Danielle.

"Guys, it's okay," I say. "People are going to talk about living and dying. You don't have to worry about me falling apart just because someone says something about dying. Especially when the subject is bacteria."

They smile, a little.

"Just trying to be sensitive," Justin says.

"I know."

"It would be fine if you did fall apart," Becca says. "Especially around your friends. Around me, to be specific, who has known you a long time. No offense, Justin."

"None taken."

We sit there in silence for a few moments. I know that when Becca realizes I'm not taking this strand of our conversation any further, she'll move on.

And she does.

"So, Justin, how'd you get interested in all that?" Becca asks him. "In toxic whoevers and bio-whatevers."

Justin thinks for a moment. "I guess I'm just a nerdy science guy." He smiles, big.

Yes, his earnestness is definitely appealing. His smile is definitely not nerdy.

Becca gets up from her chair. "Feel like getting clobbered again?" she asks. "In Ping-Pong, I mean."

Justin picks up the paddles. He offers one to me and one to Becca, extending them handles-first.

"You think you can beat me again?" he says. "Get a grip." And waits.

We react in the only way you can to a bad pun, which is by groaning.

33

HUMPTY DUMPTY HAD A GREAT FALL

Here we are, on our fifth date. Well. It's our fifth if you count hanging out with Becca at the community hall. And it's a date if just coming to the park after school in the middle of the week qualifies as a date. I can say that it's our favorite park, which may make it more date-like. It's the "our favorite" part that tips the balance, at least a little bit. Rounding out the count are our initial coffee rendezvous, an afternoon at a chai place, and meeting at a bookstore to hear an author speak. Nothing at night, but must a date be at night?

I am overthinking this, I know.

We scramble to the top of the little climbing gym.

"Humphrey and I used to pretend this was a mountain," I say.

"Yeah?" Justin says. "I can see that. It would be a mountain to a little kid."

I remember that when Humphrey and I first climbed it, I was nervous. I didn't know how coordinated or strong a five-year-old was, and I had visions of him slipping through the bars and falling on his head. The drop to the ground couldn't be more than four feet, but still.

I soon learned that Humphrey was both coordinated and pretty sturdy. I also learned that if you spend enough time around a five-year-old, eventually you'll see him fall down on his head.

"That sounds right," Justin says when I tell him this. "If you stopped kids from doing everything that could possibly hurt them, they wouldn't ever get to do anything."

"I was so relieved that the one time Humphrey had a really bad accident while I was around, his parents were there, too, and it wasn't my fault," I say. "I mean—before *the* accident. My accident. Isn't that ironic? Or something?"

"Or something," Justin agrees. "Did it happen here at the park?"

"No," I say. "Nothing bad ever happened at the park."

"What happened?" Justin asked. "When Humphrey's parents were there, I mean. That accident."

I can tell him about *that* accident.

I had just arrived, and Humphrey and his mother were outside. Humphrey was riding his little bike. It was early evening—after kids' dinners, before parents went out, if they were going out. There were other kids riding bikes, too—on the sidewalks, into the streets. It was nice. There were no cars. Not because there were no cars on their street, just—no one was going anywhere in a car right then.

When he saw me, Humphrey stopped and got off his bike. He was on the sidewalk. Another boy wasn't paying attention and rode his bike right into Humphrey. Right into him, knocking Humphrey down. This boy was a little kid, too, and it was a little bicycle, but the impact would have hurt anyone.

Humphrey picked himself up. His face wore a shocked expression. Like—*ow!* But he squared his jaw and pulled back his shoulders. The other kid's father saw what happened and ran over. Mrs. Danker was soon there, too, hugging Humphrey.

"I'm all right," Humphrey said. "It's okay."

He had scrapes on his palms—those rough, corduroy type of scrapes that really sting. He had blood on his knees. He had a bump on his head.

After fussing over Humphrey for a while, the Dankers decided that an emergency room trip wasn't called for. Because he'd hit his head, though, they wanted to stay home—just in case. They canceled their plans to go out.

"You can go home, Danielle," Mrs. Danker said. "Of course, we'll still pay you for tonight."

I didn't care about getting paid.

"I'd be happy to stay," I said. "If you want, you and Mr. Danker could still have a 'date night' at home."

"Yes, let Danielle stay!" Humphrey said. "We'll pretend that you and Daddy are out, but you'll really be right here."

So that's what they did.

Later, I was helping Humphrey get ready for bed. When he took off his T-shirt, I saw the tire tread marks on his chest.

"Humpty!" I said.

He looked down and saw the marks.

"I really got run over!" he said. "Cool!" He went running downstairs. "Daddy," I heard him calling, "I really got run over and I have tire marks to prove it!"

He ran right into the wall. I didn't see it, because he was downstairs and on his way to the dining room, where the Dankers were eating Chinese food, and I was up in his room. He ran into the door frame, and cut a gash right in the middle of his forehead. The noise of the impact carried upstairs to me, followed by the scrape of chairs as his parents jumped up.

I jumped up, too, and ran downstairs.

There was Humphrey sitting on the floor looking a little surprised and a little amused. Even if, magically, the wound didn't hurt, anybody would have had a right to be hysterical just from the sight of all the blood. Humphrey didn't shed a tear. Not a single whimper.

"Ow," he said. But even that wasn't a whine.

How can there can be so much blood in a forehead, I wondered, but there it was, gushing all over. And the bleeding wasn't stopping. Clearly, Humphrey had to go to the ER.

Since he was shirtless, I ran upstairs to get a shirt—one with buttons, so it didn't have to go over his head. By the time I returned downstairs, Humphrey was already in the car with his parents. I peered in. Mr. Danker looked perturbed. Mrs. Danker looked tired. And Humphrey was crying, crying, crying. Mr. Danker started to pull away, but then he stopped and the windows came down on the passenger side of the car, front and back seats.

"See, Humphrey, she's right there," Mrs. Danker said.

Humphrey looked at me. I realized that I'd never seen him cry before. "It hurts, huh, buddy?" I said.

No. That wasn't it.

"I thought you left without saying good night." He was just this side of hiccups from crying so hard.

"I wouldn't do that," I said. While I had run upstairs for a shirt for him, someone had found his Baltimore Ravens jersey and put it on him. "Nice shirt, Humphrey," I added. I knew he liked it because it was purple, not because he cared one way or another about the Ravens.

"Laundry room," Mrs. Danker said.

"Good night, Humpty Dumpty," I said. I was whispering, as I didn't think Mr. Danker would appreciate the nickname.

"Good night," he whispered back. "Humpty Dumpty had a great fall." His eyes were all sparkly—not with tears anymore, though. He was perfectly pleased with his little joke.

"He did, didn't he," I said. "But *you* will be put back together again."

⸙

"He sounds like an awesome kid," Justin says.

"Yeah," I say. But I can't form another word. If I try to say anything else I will absolutely lose control. I need to keep my face a mask. Tight. Tight. Hold on.

But I can't hold on to my thoughts. And my thoughts go back to Humphrey's little chest with the bicycle tire tread marks on it. The black of rubber against his pale skin. The pink sandpaper of the scrapes. Tender, tender. Tender and trusting. His tender, trusting little chest.

The kid got run over by a bike, didn't cry, cracked his head open, didn't cry, but when he thought I'd left without a proper farewell, he cried as if—as if he'd gotten run over by a bike and cracked his head open.

Now that I think about it, I never saw him cry again.

I can't hold on. Finally. Finally, I cry.

I rush to climb down from the jungle gym, driven by a need to hide my face from Justin. And once I'm on the ground, I might as well run, right? Where to? Obviously, I have no plan; I blindly make for the picnic tables. No. For the field. No—home. So I head for Quarry Road.

Here's what I discover: it is very hard to run and cry at the same time. At least it's hard for me. I could stop running and cry. Or I could run to stop myself crying.

Or I could trip over a tree root. Which is what I do, falling on the ground just inside the entrance to the park.

"Hey," Justin whispers. "Hey." He's kneeling next to me. "It's okay."

"It's *not* okay," I choke out.

"It's not your fault," he says.

"It *is* my fault," I say. "Why did I think I should play football with him? Stupid, stupid football. I don't even like the game. I hate that game."

"For him—you did it for him," Justin says. "It made him happy. And then—sometimes terrible things happen, and there's nothing anybody can do."

"Why did I bring him to this stupid park?" I say. "I should have kept him right there on his own street, so he could . . . get run over by a stupid *bicycle*, get mowed down by a bicycle, and get up afterward and say 'Cool!' and—and—"

That tender little chest.

That trusting little brain, with those gears. Learning and remembering. Fumble and pounce.

"It's okay to cry," Justin whispers. "You just told me. Even Humphrey cried when he didn't get to say good-bye."

Okay or not okay, I am sobbing. Crouching there in the scrabbly grass, shielded from the street by the watchful Littleleaf Linden trees, I am grateful, at least, for the shadows that are settling over us as afternoon turns to night, the darkness not illuminated by the false glow of streetlights.

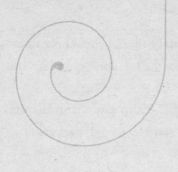

34

IT IS NOT BAD

I am not one of those eyes-only criers. What a gift that
would be. No, my eyes are the last to get in on the action.
My mouth wobbles and, basically, disintegrates. My face
becomes red and contorted. The only thing to do is to
hide it.

So, am I saying that <u>vanity</u> is what made me run
away from Justin when I cried in the park yesterday?

Dr. Gilbert looks at me expectantly. When I don't read any
more, she says, "No more?"

"That's everything I wrote down."

"And that's fine," she says.

"I do hate the way I look when I cry," I say. "So of course I wouldn't want this guy I'm kind of interested in to see me crying, when my face falls apart."

I sit for a few minutes without saying anything. She waits. Dr. Gilbert is a patient person.

"And maybe I didn't want to cry about Humphrey—about Humphrey in particular—in front of him. In front of anyone, really."

"Because you think it might seem strange that you felt so close to a five-year-old," Dr. Gilbert prompts, "who doesn't know enough to have conversations about family dynamics and immigration?"

Wow. I said that two weeks ago. "Do you memorize the things I say and write in here?"

"The memorable things, yes," she says, with a hint of a smile.

"Well," I say, "it felt okay for Justin to know how great I thought Humphrey was. How cute and smart."

I am aware that I am not saying whether I did or didn't want Justin to see how close I felt to Humphrey. I'm only saying that I was okay with Justin knowing how much I liked Humphrey. Two different things. And I know I'm the one who raised this issue with Dr. Gilbert in the first place, this matter of feeling too close to Humphrey—but I don't want to talk about that with her anymore. I'm not sorry I said it when I said it, but I'm not going back to it, either.

"So then why do you think you didn't want to cry in front of Justin about Humphrey?" she asks.

"It's a little confusing," I say. "Maybe I do feel some embarrassment about what—about what—"

This is hard to say. I'm stumbling.

Dr. Gilbert is sitting there, her usual patient self.

"Not embarrassed, exactly, but I am aware that it might seem, I'll say, *unusual*, what Humphrey and I—what we . . . had."

There, I said it. We *had* something. We weren't siblings. We weren't exactly friends. But we were something. I would say we were soul mates, but I don't want to say that out loud.

"What I'm trying to say is that what Humphrey and I had—maybe I feel something like embarrassment about it. But mostly, I want to protect it. I feel protective of its . . . perfection. I don't want to say and show everything out loud about it to people. Especially people who didn't even know him."

"Even Justin, a new friend whom you like and, presumably, trust."

"Is that bad?" I ask. "Does that mean I don't know how to be friends with someone my own age? I did share *some* with Justin. More than usual. A lot more. Just not everything."

"No, Danielle," Dr. Gilbert says. "It is not bad. We aren't in the territory of good and bad here."

No, we're not, are we. After all the times I've gone over the accident, I've got north, south, east, and west down pat. But I sure could use a compass to navigate whatever territory it is that I'm moving into—with Justin, but also, if it's not too strange to say this, with Humphrey. And with my ideas about what is and what is not too strange.

35

How a Hero Acts

"This could be awkward," I say to Justin.

We've just entered the nearly empty stands at the ice rink, and who do I see sitting there waiting for the game to start but Marissa.

"Awkward because . . . ?"

How much do I tell Justin? Do I describe the original rift, where Marissa was angry about my rude behavior and I was angry about her attitude toward Adrian, only she didn't know I was angry about her attitude toward Adrian? Or the phone call, with the strain over her strong feelings about illegal immigration and my strong feelings about her trying to guilt me into having strong feelings? This relationship—or whatever it is—with Justin is nice. I like him. He's taller than me. He doesn't seem to think I'm incompetent or boring or clueless about how you treat your friends. He doesn't need every sordid detail.

So I just tell him that Marissa and I were friends but have grown apart.

There are so few people in the stands at 7:15 on a Sunday morning that I would be making some kind of pointed statement if I sat apart from her and the clump of hockey player parents clustered around the center line. So we go over.

"Hi, Marissa," I say.

"Danielle!" She hugs me.

"It's good to see you," I say.

"Same here," she says. "It's been way too long."

Marissa is a hugger. But she also gives me an extra squeeze at the end of our hug, like a punctuation mark. If hugs could speak, hers would be saying "Starting now, let's not be mad," and that works for me.

"Marissa, this is Justin," I say. "Justin, this is Marissa."

"Do you have a brother or someone in this game, Justin?" Marissa asks. "Because I can't imagine why else anybody would be here at this ungodly hour."

We explain that we came for Justin's 7:45 a.m. game, but it's been pushed back an hour. Trouble with the Zamboni messed up the league schedule today, only Justin didn't know about it. So we're here early. The younger teams, who were supposed to play at 6:20 a.m.—welcome to youth hockey—will play their game first, whenever the ice is ready.

"Is Marco still playing?" I ask. Marco is thirteen.

"That's why I've been here since six o'clock," Marissa says.

"Ouch," Justin says.

"Do you play high school hockey, too?" Marissa asks Justin.

"No, just MHC," he says. "I go to MacArthur. We don't have a hockey team."

MHC is Meigs Hockey Club. And although my high school, Western, has a hockey team, not all the schools around here do.

"Too bad," Marissa says. "Neither does ours. But I love watching hockey." She looks at me. "We used to go to Adrian's games."

There's nothing meaningful in her look. Just—*Remember. That was fun.*

"And Malcolm's baseball games," I say. "And Manny's soccer matches."

"And Matt's triumph last year as quarterback," Marissa says.

"Wait a minute," Justin says. "How long is this list?"

We explain about Marissa's five brothers and how they all play different sports—hockey, soccer, football, baseball, lacrosse.

"Who's the lacrosse player?" Justin asks. "I follow the high school and college teams."

"That would be Martin," Marissa says. "My twin. Who also plays basketball in the winter. I should say, he plays when he feels like playing."

I look at her questioningly.

"Long story," she says.

"Your twin, for real?" Justin asks.

"For real."

"Do any of the older brothers play college sports?" Justin asks.

"Malcolm, who's the oldest, is a D.C. police officer," Marissa says. "He didn't go to a traditional four-year college, so he kind of gave up baseball."

"And he was awesome," I say.

"A policeman?" Justin says.

"Yes, he is," Marissa says proudly. She adds that Manny plays soccer at his college in Pennsylvania. Matt, who's a freshman at the community college—living at home, so he and Martin can torment each other over sharing the car—was a fine high school player but not athletic-scholarship material. He's playing club sports.

By now, the teams are on the ice warming up.

"How about you—do you do a sport?" Justin asks Marissa.

"Some tennis. I'm on my school's team this year."

I didn't know that. "Marissa, you must have gotten really good!" I say. "We played a few times. . . ."

"And you're thinking, how is she good enough to be on a high school team, playing a varsity sport," she says.

"No!" I object. But, yeah.

"I'm reading your mind, Danielle," Marissa says. "And you're right, and the answer is, when you go to a little private school, it's a lot easier to make the team. *Any* team."

"Oh, come on," I say. "You're being modest."

"I'm better than I was," she says, "but I don't think I could be on Western's team."

"It's great you're on the team," Justin says.

"Thanks," she says. "It's fun."

There's a face-off on the ice, and we watch the action.

"Marco is almost as tall as me now," I say. He was always kind of little.

"Of course, three inches of that comes from his skates," Marissa says.

"Even allowing for that," I say. "He's taller."

"Bantam level hockey is kind of freaky," Justin says. "I mean, look at the players—their sizes are all over the place. There are thirteen-year-olds who look like babies. Then there are fourteen-year-olds who are bigger than me."

It's true; there are guys out there who look like men, and guys who look like boys dressing up for Halloween in hockey uniforms. Marco is in between, but closer to the boy-boys than the man-boys.

Up and back they skate, chasing the puck. There are a few shot attempts, all failing. The first period ends with no score.

"Are your parents coming?" I ask Marissa. I like her mom and dad.

"They try to come to most games. But Manny has a match game up in Pennsylvania, and they left around the same time I did to come here, and it's still preseason here at the hockey rink, so . . ."

"Sounds like it's always game day at your house," Justin says.

"Pretty much," Marissa says. "Never a dull moment." She stands and says, "I could use coffee. Would you like some?"

"I don't think the snack bar's open yet," Justin says.

"There's the machine," Marissa says.

"Right."

Justin and I both pass on coffee.

"Are we coffee snobs?" he says after Marissa leaves the stands.

"Guilty as charged," I say.

"She seems nice," Justin says.

"She is nice," I say.

"No awkwardness that I noticed," he says.

"You're right," I say. "I'm glad."

Marissa returns with her steaming paper cup.

"Not terrible," she says, and carefully takes a few sips. "Where did you say you go to school, Justin?"

"MacArthur," he says.

"So how do you two know each other?" she asks.

"Well—" Justin begins.

"We met in the park," I say. "The Quarry Road park."

"Danielle can really toss a football," Justin says.

"*Aww*," Marissa says, "what a nice compliment." She smiles and looks at Justin more carefully. "You remind me of someone I know from school," she says. "He comes from South America. From Argentina."

"Well, I'm not from Argentina," Justin says. "And we don't have any relatives from Argentina. But maybe your guy from school is my doppelgänger."

"Your doppel-*what*?" Marissa laughs.

"My doppelgänger. My non-twin twin. The double that everyone in the world may or may not have."

"Great word," I say.

"Agreed," Marissa says.

Justin shrugs, like he's a little bit shy about showing off.

"So, but, Justin, is your family from here originally?"

I turn my head to look at Marissa more directly. This would strike me as a really strange question, except for Marissa's undying interest in everyone's heritage. So, instead, it strikes me as only a moderately strange question.

Justin pauses. "Originally . . . my family is from Colombia."

Now I turn to look at him head-on. "As in, the *country*?" I say. "The country of Colombia? Or, like, a city in South Carolina?"

"As in South America," he says.

"I didn't know that," I say.

"I don't know where your family is from," he says. "So we're even."

"My mother's family is from some region of Eastern Europe that took turns being Russia and Poland back when they lived there a hundred years ago," I say. "And my father's family is from Hungary originally. And we feel absolutely no connection to either of these places."

"I've told you, Danielle, you're really missing out," Marissa says. "Pierogi. Goulash. And let's not forget the polkas!"

"Yes, I would not want to forget the polkas," I say. "Because embedded in my DNA is a girl who just wants to bust out and dance the Polish polka." I turn to Justin. "Marissa is unusually fascinated by the cultures and heritage of everyone she meets."

"I am," Marissa says. "So . . . Colombia. Fantastic prehistoric cave art. Home of Gabriel García Márquez. Two separate things, of course; I'm not saying his home was in a cave."

Ha. Even I know who the famous writer is.

"Well, sort of the home of Gabriel García Márquez," Justin says. "Since he mostly lived elsewhere once he was an adult."

"Have you ever been there?" Marissa asks. "To Colombia?"

"Never traveled there," he says.

"*Hablas español*?" Marissa asks.

"Some," Justin says.

As we're talking, we're watching the ice. The second period has started. Justin hasn't asked Marissa about her own ethno-geo-anthro-cultural profile—because who but Marissa asks about these things—and I'm about to tell him about her Mexican great-grandparents as a way of explaining her questions, but we're all suddenly distracted by the game.

"Oh, look! Go, Marco!" Marissa calls out.

Marco just stole the puck from the other team, which is a good thing, since they're dangerously close to his own team's goal. He passes to a teammate, who heads toward the center line, but then the teammate stumbles and a player from the opposing team gets it. Marco is still back, a few feet in front of his own goalkeeper. The boy with the puck, who's one of the man-boys, turns and gets off a quick slap shot.

"Wide!" Justin says. The puck is airborne.

"Yes!" Marissa says.

"Breakaway!" yells a parent behind us as Marco recovers the ricocheting puck and makes for the other end of the rink.

"Go, Marco!" Marissa yells.

There aren't enough people here to say that the crowd roars at the goal that Marco scores, but there are cheers.

"Score!" Marissa cries. "Marco scored!"

"Great breakaway," Justin says.

"Way to go, Marco," I say.

On the ice, the players aren't lining up as usual for a face-off.

"Huh," Justin says.

I look where he's looking.

"That ref is down," Justin says.

"I think he might have caught the puck in the chest," says the same person behind us who first cheered Marco's breakaway. "The puck from the other team's missed slap shot."

"That can really sting," Justin says.

There's another referee in the game; he's standing over the man on the ice. One of the coaches has slid out on the ice and is bending over the downed referee.

The other referee skates over to the stands. "Is there a doctor here?"

No, there isn't.

"Should we call 911?" someone calls.

"Everything seems okay," the ref says. "Just want to be on the safe side."

But now the coach is waving the ref over, and the coach does not look like a man who thinks everything is okay.

"Call 911!" the coach yells.

I see, or sense, a dozen hands reaching into pockets and purses for cell phones. But what I feel is Justin clambering over my legs to get to the aisle. He jumps over benches to get down on the ice. I watch him run-slide over to the injured referee, and practically fall on the ice next to him. Justin elbows the coach aside and starts pushing down on the referee's chest. I may not know how to do CPR (thanks to the Red Cross baby-sitting class that I did not take), but I can definitely recognize it. I turn to Marissa to tell her, but now she's down on the rink, too; she slips at first, but then gets the hang of running on a sheet of ice and is soon by Justin's side. I remember—she knows CPR, too. She took a class in it.

I can't go over there. I can't go and kneel by another person who's been hit by a moving object. Besides, what good would I be?

In what seems like forever, but really isn't, a man and a woman who work at the rink—they're wearing matching bright blue jackets—rush onto the ice. The woman is carrying a small machine. She speaks briefly to Justin. The man takes over from Justin. The woman attaches the machine's pads to the ref's chest, the man stops the compressions, and then the woman presses something on the machine. I see the ref kind of twitch, and the man gets back to doing CPR on him. After a few more compressions, he stops.

The ref lifts his head. The people in the bright blue jackets speak with him; the woman squeezes his hand. He bends his knees as if he wants to sit up, but the woman says something to him and he relaxes his legs again. Soon a crew from the Meigs County Fire Department bounds onto the ice. A couple of police officers have arrived, too, but they seem to know that there's no need for them and they don't enter the rink.

Marissa comes over to where I'm standing, which is in the front row right next to the boards.

"I've never seen that happen," she says. "The ref was completely out—but Justin—"

Where is Justin?

"If he hadn't started CPR so quickly . . ." She doesn't finish her thought. "He reacted so quickly. Meanwhile, I sat here on the bench . . . ," she says. The EMTs are moving the ref onto a stretcher. "Where did Justin go?"

"I don't know," I say.

"He must be talking to someone about what went on," Marissa says.

But we don't see him on the ice or in the stands. We go to the waiting room to look for him, but he's not there, either. After a while, Marco and his team come out. The remainder of their game has been called off.

"My goal probably won't even count," Marco says glumly.

"Hi, Marco," I say.

"It was a beauty," Marissa says. "But don't you think we should just be praying for that poor referee who got hit?"

"Yeah," Marco says. "Sorry. He's a good referee. Everyone likes him."

"We're going to head out," Marissa says to me. "Tell Justin I think he's a hero."

"Who's Justin?" Marco asks.

"The guy who did CPR. He's Danielle's friend."

"Wow," Marco says. "Super-quick thinking."

"Make that a superhero," Marissa says to me. "Tell him."

The appearance of the Zamboni seems almost offensive after what's happened, but I guess the show must go on. Marco's game may have been called off, but there's a whole lineup of games waiting to be played today, including Justin's. It's funny how an event can totally leave a small group of people in shock—*please*, no pun intended—and yet be completely invisible and irrelevant to the rest of the world. The EMTs and the cops are gone. A small knot of parents from the game are still standing around, no doubt rehashing what we all just witnessed. But basically the rink is back to normal.

I go back to the rink looking for Justin. He's not there. Then out into the main waiting room again, where I sit among its rows of benches and lockers. There are more people here than when we first arrived, but still not many. The rink doesn't open for free skating for a few hours—I think not until 11:00 a.m. on Sunday. The parents have moved to the door of the main office. Now they're reliving the drama with the man and woman who took over from Justin.

"There have been a few cases where a puck, if it hits really hard just beneath the chest protectors, has basically caused cardiac arrest," the woman is saying.

"Is that what happened?" one of the parents says. "That's horrendous!"

"I can't say for sure," she says. "By the time Tim and I got there, that young man—"

"He plays in the rec league, but I don't know his name," the guy named Tim says. "And Cindy has seen him around, too, but doesn't really know him, either."

"Well, that young man had begun CPR," the woman, Cindy, continues. "Jerry had a faint pulse by the time we got there. Did he lose it after the puck hit him? Don't know. But the fact that the defibrillator, when I attached it, determined the need to administer a shock, that tells me he may very well have gone into cardiac arrest. Which would mean the CPR kept him from slipping away until we got there with the machine."

Maybe Justin needed to go to the bathroom to pull himself together after such an upsetting experience. Should I go into the men's room? Maybe he went home. But without telling me? Sure, if he's shaken up enough. I'm about to text him when he plops down next to me, dropping his hockey bag on the floor.

"You were a hero!" I say. "And then you disappeared. Are you all right?"

"I'm fine," he says. "I needed to get ready for my game."

The team changing rooms are down a corridor off this main area. But—the thing is, he didn't get ready for his game.

He's still dressed in his regular clothes, and his bag is still stuffed with his gear.

"But, Justin, you didn't change into your hockey gear," I say.

"No," he says. "I decided not to after all."

"Are you sure you're all right?"

"I'm fine," he says again.

Maybe he's feeling disoriented. I decide to take a different approach.

"You're amazing!" I say. "You may have saved that referee's life."

"I know CPR," he says.

"Knowing CPR and springing into action are two different things," I say. "And you sprang!"

"Like some sort of action figure, right?" he says.

He seems unusually tense, but how should a person feel after something like this?

"Do you know him?" I ask. "Does he referee at your games?"

He's not really listening. "Look, let's get out of here," Justin says.

"But your game?"

"I'm going to skip it," he says.

As we're walking out, Tim and Cindy see us. They hurry out of the office, both extending their hands as they approach.

"Great work, my man," Tim says, pumping Justin's hand.

"Really quick thinking," Cindy says, shaking Justin's other hand. "You may have saved a life here."

Justin hems and haws. But every modest denial on his part

stimulates a new recitation by Tim and Cindy of his wonderfulness. After a few rounds of this, he seems to figure out that if he just accepts their praise, this conversation will actually end. And it does.

"Marissa wants me to tell you that you're a superhero," I say once we're outside.

"Okay," he says. "Thanks."

"Like Superman," I say. "Complete with disappearing into a phone booth after the heroics."

"Thanks."

"Actually, she didn't say that. About the phone booth. That was me. Please ignore me."

We walk toward the bus stop without speaking.

"Look, I need to get home," Justin says. "Can we talk later? Or tomorrow or something?"

"Sure," I say, thinking that "or something" can have a wide variety of meanings, including "or never."

"Great."

His bus comes first. He drags his bag up the steps. He doesn't turn to wave or say good-bye.

I guess this is how a superhero acts in real life.

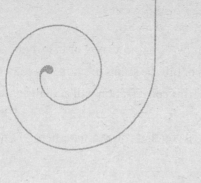

36

A Technical Truth

And that was the last time I saw Justin.

Is what I fully expect as the bus carries him away.

Fortunately, my expectations are not met.

I have just settled in the seat on my own bus when I feel the phone vibrating in my jacket pocket.

Sorry.

No apology needed.

I think there is. But thanks.

If anyone understands how spooked you must be, it's me.

There's more to it.

I'm listening.

Not really textable. If that's a word.

I'm listenable. If that's a word. In person.

We meet at the park. I get there first, and when I see Justin hobbling along with his big hockey bag strapped over his shoulders, my heart goes out to him as if he were a little boy. What a weight that is to carry around.

"So," he begins.

"So," I say.

"Your friend Marissa and her interest in where I'm from," he begins.

"You have to understand Marissa," I say. "I started telling you, she has this thing about everyone's 'culture' and 'heritage.' Including her own. You can expect to get a *Cinco de Mayo* card from her next year."

"That's Mexican, not Colombian."

"What?"

"*Cinco de Mayo* is Mexican, not Colombian."

"I know. Marissa is very into being Mexican American. Hence the *Cinco de Mayo* card. Actually, now that she thinks you're a superhero, who knows what she'll send you. A signed edition of a Gabriel García Márquez novel. The sky's the limit."

"Danielle, my point is that Marissa was on to something. My parents are from Colombia. It's not just the place where my long-ago ancestors came from."

"Okay. Your parents are from Colombia."

"And they're not here legally."

I have to admit, I did not see that coming.

His parents came here, Justin tells me, fifteen years ago as graduate students. They came on perfectly valid student visas. Then when they were no longer students, they started taking steps to get documents—green cards—to live here permanently and one day become citizens. They needed to find employers to sponsor them, and they did. But then they both switched jobs before the papers came through, and had to start over again with different companies.

To finalize the whole green-card thing, they needed to leave the country, go back to Colombia, and reenter the United States with their new documents. That's the way the rules said it had to be done, even though it sounds like a waste of a whole lot of airplane tickets. There was never a good time to do it. So they never did. Mr. Folgar's company decided to look the other way, even though they could have gotten in trouble for employing an undocumented immigrant.

"I'm sorry, Justin," I say.

I am. But I'm not getting why this would make him such a cranky superhero.

"And, see, about what happened today," he says. "About hiding when the EMTs and cops came."

When he says the word "hiding," his eyes turn into two dark platters of pain. Pain and shame. I don't like that he feels ashamed in front of me.

"My older sister and I, we were both actually born in Colombia. In Bogota," he continues. "So . . ."

I suppose I'm really dense, but I can't fill in the blanks at the end of that sentence. I'm not getting it.

"So that means we're both here illegally, too."

Okay. Really didn't see that coming.

"But—" I say, and stop for a moment. I'm reviewing the conversation from early this morning. "But you told Marissa you'd never lived in Colombia."

"No," he says. "I told her I'd never *traveled* to Colombia. Which is true."

True, in a hair-splitting sort of way.

"I don't like to lie. It is true that I have never been back to Colombia. They brought me here when I was a baby. I have no memory of anyplace but here."

I'm glad he doesn't like to lie, but I think sometimes you're lying even if you tell a technical truth.

I'm being too harsh. None of this is his fault, is it? And he has to protect his parents and sister, not just himself. Do they have an official Folgar Family Lie, a story that they all have rehearsed and consistently tell outsiders? I wonder how it feels to go through your life having to be always just a little bit dishonest.

"So—has something new happened?" I'm still not

understanding why Marissa's questions this morning have made him so upset.

Justin hesitates before answering. "It's not really about Marissa's questions. I'm explaining to you why I disappeared. Why I didn't want to be around when the rescue squad came— because they almost always come with police."

And he does not want to have any interaction with police. He does not even want to be a hero in the presence of police.

I feel like there's more he wants to say. Although the gear shifts of Justin's brain are not as transparently evident as the clickings and clackings of others, I'm feeling like there's more.

"I'm so sorry, Justin," I say. "If only—"

"If only my parents hadn't let this become such a mess," he says. "That's the only 'if only' that counts. Two adults with master's degrees who speak perfect English, and our life is a disaster waiting to happen."

He sounds so bitter. So not Justin.

"I hate feeling like I have to hide. I hate that I ran away— and that's after I did something *good*. I have to be invisible. Which is absurd, since the rest of them are so totally visible."

Okay, now I'm back to not getting it again. *The rest of them are so totally visible.* The rest of *who* are so totally visible?

"Danielle."

That's my name, don't wear it out.

"They were the ones in the blue minivan, Danielle."

In *my* blue minivan?

"They were in the car that hit Humphrey Danker."

They were on their way back from a dance recital. Justin's parents had left work early to see their two little girls up on stage. They had taken videos—of course—and were looking forward to sending the film to Justin's older sister, the conservatory dance student. They were just promising the girls that they would transfer the video to the computer as soon as they got home, even though they needed to rush to get to a neighbor's house for a dessert-and-coffee party. Justin would be staying home with his two sisters.

And then a little boy ran into their car.

"*You* were in the car?" I croak. I think back to that night. I saw the shadows of four people in the minivan, two adult-size shadows in the front seat, two little kid–size shadows in the backseat.

"No. Oh, God, no. I wasn't in the car. I was hanging out with my friends. I needed to be home by eight thirty to babysit my sisters."

I'm going over the time line of our so-called friendship in my mind.

"So when we first met in the park," I say, "you knew who I was . . . and what happened."

We'd joked about it, hadn't we? Like: ha-ha, you're stalking me, what a nutty idea.

"No. No. That was my park, too, you know. I'd seen you there with Humphrey, like I told you. But when you and I met there, I was just there—because. It's a place I like to hang out."

"But," I say, "you knew! You acted like you didn't know who I was, but you knew."

"I wasn't sure at first. I wasn't sure if the girl and boy I saw in the park were the girl and boy involved in the accident. I was afraid you were—but I couldn't be sure until you told me."

"Right—and I told you," I say. "But you said nothing to me!"

He looks away from me.

"And I don't get it," I say. "The articles I read said the family in the blue minivan had two daughters. Not two daughters *plus* an older son *plus* an older daughter."

"They were wrong," Justin says. "But it's not the sort of mistake that my parents were going to write a letter to the editor to complain about. My older sister and I aren't exactly standing up to be counted. We're trying to stay—invisible. That's what my parents want."

This still isn't adding up. The newspaper said the people in the blue minivan were named Guzman. And Justin's last name is Folgar. At least that's what he told me.

"Another thing they didn't get quite right," he says. "Another thing we saw no reason to correct. They did, at one point, say my father's name is Eugene Folgar Guzman, which is true. But then they only called him Mr. Guzman. He's not Mr. Guzman. We're not the Guzman family. Hispanic names don't work like that. He's Mr. Folgar Guzman, or—to make it easier—just Mr. Folgar."

"How could you say nothing to me!" I say. "We see each other, we talk, and you've got this huge secret!"

Now Justin turns to look me full in the eyes. And he looks so forlorn.

"I didn't want to ruin it," he says.

"Ruin it? Ruin what?"

"I didn't want to ruin us," he adds. "I know I was wrong."

Wrong? Not just wrong. Something deeper than wrong. Did he become my friend—excuse me, my "friend"—just to get the inside scoop on what I was telling the cops? To see if he could find out what the authorities knew—whether they knew about the existence of him and his older sister, the dancer?

"Wrong" doesn't begin to describe it.

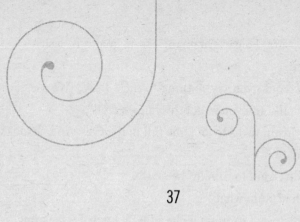

37

Us, Too

Later that week, I'm at the public bus stop near school when I see Becca walking toward me. The school day was done almost ninety minutes ago. Becca, I figure, is heading home from her newspapering work. Unlike me, she lives within walking distance of school. As for me, I wasn't staying after school; I had an appointment with my therapist, whose office is in a building on this street.

I didn't go in there with a piece of paper today. There's too much to write down. Too much confusion, too. I should at least have written a word cloud, with words like *betrayal, empathy, disbelief, understanding, suspicion, trust,* all in larger or smaller letters depending on their importance in my mind. Only I couldn't say which of those words is more important to me right now. And I didn't want to tell Dr. Gilbert about Justin and his family. I don't know if I wanted to protect myself from feeling naïve or to shield Justin from being found out. So we were back to sitting there and mostly just kind of looking at each other.

Now, seeing Becca approach, part of me wants to run and hide. She'll know something is bothering me. Dr. Gilbert knew, too, but she's not the type to grab hold and shake and poke and prod you until you spill the beans. I don't think therapists do that. Becca, though—that's her all over.

"What's wrong?" she says the minute she sees me.

"I'm just tired," I say.

She looks at me skeptically. "Are you coming from therapy?"

"Yeah, that'll wear a person out." Great, now I'm just making things up. "What are you working on for the paper?"

I succeed in diverting Becca from the question of my appointment. She tells me about the article she's working on, which—I guess I am not meant to get away from this—is about immigration issues.

"There's this new group. They're called 'US-2.'" She spells it out for me. "As in, the words 'us, too.' But also like the U.S., second edition, you know—US-2. Clever, *n'est-ce pas*?"

I saw the flyers announcing today's first meeting. "US, Too!" at the top of the sheet, "US-2" at the bottom.

"What are they doing?" I ask.

"So far, they're gathering information about the anti-illegal immigration proposals in the county council and the state legislature. I think they're going to have a rally. You know, about the accident stirring up debate about undocumented immigrants."

I nod. I don't tell her that by now I could write my own article about it all.

"So this is part of that. And for some of the kids, it touches really close to home."

"It does?"

"Some of the kids who came to the meeting are actually undocumented immigrants. You'd never know it—" She stops herself. "I don't mean anything by that. I don't mean there's a typical way an undocumented alien looks or anything. . . ."

"It's okay, Becca," I say. "I am not the Politically Correct Police."

"Anyway, two kids were brought here as babies by their parents. They're all undocumented, the whole family, but it's not as if these kids did anything wrong themselves. I mean, as far as they feel, they're Americans, you know?"

I nod again.

"Then three other kids were citizens themselves, because they were born here, but their parents are here illegally."

"So, but—"

"So the undocumented kids, now that they're teenagers, have issues. They can't get driver's licenses, because you need to show that you're in the country legally to get a license. And the legal kids, they're always worried that something is going to happen to their parents."

"What I don't get," I say, "is how the accident or all the racket about it in the papers and online affects these kids. I mean, I know it's hard for them, but it's no harder today than it was six months ago, right?" Unless those kids happen to be Justin and his sisters, but I keep that part to myself. "They couldn't get driver's licenses back then, either, could they?"

Becca thinks this over. She hadn't really considered that. "True. They couldn't get licenses. Or after-school jobs. I guess I have to make that clear in my article."

But what is harder, and what is different, she says, is the new attention on immigrants and the focus on uncovering whether foreigners are legal or not.

"So, let's see. Here's what could happen under some of the proposals," she says. "Say you're at a party with your friends and it gets rowdy," she says. "And the police are called. All the other kids get sent home. If there's been drinking, maybe some kids get citations. If you're undocumented, though, you get handed over to the immigration authorities. And next thing you know, you're deported back to a country that you don't know anything about, and that you've probably never even visited."

"There's got to be a more sympathetic scenario that the US-2 people can come up with than rowdy teenagers," I say.

"There is," Becca says. "In my notes somewhere."

"Like," I continue, "Adrian once got a ticket for jaywalking."

"Are you serious?" Becca asks.

"Yup. For crossing Wisconsin Avenue downtown in the middle of the street, not at the crosswalk."

"That's crazy!"

"Anyway, he wasn't arrested," I say. "But it was a ticket, like a parking ticket. Only unlike a parking ticket, you know, he was face-to-face with the policeman. Actually, policewoman. And so I suppose if he were here illegally—"

"If the policewoman thought he might not be a citizen," Becca says, "one of the proposed laws would have her ask for proof that he was actually legal. And if he wasn't, if he didn't have that, then—"

"He'd be turned over to the immigration police," I say.

"That's it," Becca says. "And that's just one example."

"But, Becca," I say.

"But, Danielle," she responds. An old pattern for us, from our middle school days.

"How is it that all this—all this *stuff* comes out of what happened to Humphrey? I mean, these kids you're talking about were going about their merry way, and now they're worried about being deported because of—" I won't blame Humphrey. "Because of *me*?"

"*C'est dommage*, I know." Becca sighs. "It's such a shame. But I'm not sure they were going about their merry way. Their problems just felt less—immediate, I guess. Now illegal immigration is this big cause célèbre around here."

We hear a bus approaching and look down the street to see if it's mine. It's not. Becca keeps her eyes looking away from me, and says, "I thought you might be at the US-2 meeting, actually. . . . But if you had therapy . . ."

When I don't say anything, Becca picks up where she left off. "Of course it's not your fault, but—remember that guy arrested last year for crashing his car into those teachers? He was here illegally. That's when it all kind of started. Now your accident has pushed it all to the surface again."

Ouch. *My accident.* Well, it is.

"The point is, it's not just what happened this summer that started it all," Becca says. "So don't take that on. But—maybe instead of staying on the sidelines, it might be really good if you got involved, don't you think?"

"Some of us aren't joiners," I say. "Have you ever known me to join things?"

"I know," Becca says. "I guess I think this isn't about being a joiner or not."

My bus rumbles down the street. I let it pass.

"What, then?" I press.

"What, then, is about taking the next step. Doing it for you; not for some group that's holding meetings. I mean, take camp. You *loved* camp, Danielle. Loved it, loved it, loved it."

Yes, I did.

"And I understand why you didn't take the next step and become a CIT," she says. "But what if you had tried? I'm not saying you could have just pushed yourself past your problem with putting yourself out there—with public speaking, or semi-public speaking, or being the center of attention. I know it's not that simple. But what if you had put yourself in that position as a CIT?"

I shudder. I mean, I physically, visibly shudder.

"I know how awful that sounds to you. But, believe me, you

would not have melted. You wouldn't have self-destructed. I know you have it in you."

Have it in me. That's what she says about my becoming a lawyer. But I wasn't shuddering at the thought of public speaking or semi-public speaking or my usual phobic worries. I was shuddering at the thought that I could have saved Humphrey by the simple act of going back to camp last summer. Yes, Becca, it *is* that simple.

"Look, forget it," Becca says. "Forget I said anything. I talk too much."

She's said this before. Not that it stops her.

"No, it's okay," I say. "It's just that, Becca, all this just feels like too much. All these issues stirred up by the accident—I know they're important, and they matter, but to me the accident is about Humphrey, not a bunch of issues."

"You can talk to me about that, Danielle," Becca says quietly.

Can I? I know she would listen. Would she get it? Maybe; she's a people person, and she's a kid person. But it's Humphrey. Can anybody really get Humphrey if they didn't know Humphrey?

Anyway, I'm not even sure I know what I mean when I say that the accident is about Humphrey. I don't know how that translates into words.

And now there's the whole Justin complication. I just told Becca that to me the accident is about Humphrey and only about Humphrey. That the issues—immigration, street safety, whatever—are not my issues. It's true this is what I've been thinking and feeling for weeks. But am I still saying this because I really feel it, or because this is what I'm used to feeling?

I do not know.

"Thanks, Becca," I finally say. "I know I can talk to you. That means a lot. I just—don't have the words right now."

She nods, hesitates, and then says, "That isn't a feeling I have a lot of personal experience with. . . ."

We both laugh at the reality that Becca *always* has the words.

"But I understand," she concludes.

"And when it comes to the issues," I say, "maybe I should be motivated by what happened. It's just—I'm not sure what I think about them."

"I get that. Although if you went to an US-2 meeting, it might help you figure out what you think."

"I think maybe I'm not an activist at heart."

She's looking at me skeptically again.

"What?"

"*Ma chérie*, of course you're an activist," she says. "You have it in you. Remember fifth grade? You wrote that letter to the Franklin Grove Board when they were talking about turning the community hall rec room into some kind of computer lab."

"They never answered that letter," I say. "And I can't believe you remember that."

Becca taps her head in a wizard-like way. "I remember every-thing," she says.

"They never answered the letter," I repeat. "So big deal."

"They may not have answered the letter—which was very

rude, but never mind—but, tell me, did they turn the Ping-Pong room into a computer lab?" Becca asks.

They did not.

"You are too an activist, Danielle," Becca says. "You just haven't decided what you're an activist for."

My bus comes, and this time I climb aboard.

38

JOIN US

COME TO OUR 2ND MEETING!!

We are . . .
Students like you.
They call us "illegal."
We have done nothing illegal.

Some of us were born in another country and brought to the US by our parents. The US is the only country we know and love, yet we live in constant fear of being sent back to a country we don't know.

Some of us were born in the US but our parents are undocumented immigrants. We are citizens. But some lawmakers want to take away our citizenship. Some people even want to kick us out of public schools.

Learn more about immigration law and policy and how it affects your peers. Join us in fighting for fair laws. Come to a meeting on:

FRIDAY, NOVEMBER 13 * 2:30 * ROOM 235-C

We are US, too!

US-2!   US, TOO!   US-2!

I'm not a joiner. I'm not an activist. I'm not speaking to Justin.

But I find myself, at 2:28 p.m. on November 13, walking down the hall to room 235-C.

39

BEING INVISIBLE

The doorbell rings. Mom and Dad aren't home from work yet. I'm not expecting anyone. I turn off the stove, where I've just boiled a kettle of water, and go to the door.

Justin.

Justin Folgar, fugitive from justice.

Stop it.

It's been fifteen days since I've seen him or talked to him, not that anybody's counting. He hasn't called or texted. And I certainly haven't reached out to him.

But hurt and angry and disappointed as I was—still I'm happy, or relieved, or something, to see him. When I went to the US-2 meeting at school, I thought about how Justin ended up in his precarious position through no fault of his own. I thought about how pained he looked when he told me about why he disappeared when the police and EMTs came to the ice rink. How sad he was when he told me about the blue minivan.

How dishonest he was with me for weeks and weeks, not telling me about the blue minivan.

Still. I'm not going to shut the door on him.

"Come in," I say, in what I hope is a chilly tone. He follows me to the kitchen. "I was just making some tea."

He doesn't want any, but I fix myself a mug. We sit at the kitchen table.

"They're not charging my father with anything. They said the accident wasn't his fault. It's official."

"Good," I say flatly. "That's great."

I can't help but think: If it's officially not Mr. Folgar's fault, is it now officially my fault? I mean, the police have told us that it's definitely not a police matter—I'm not going to be arrested or prosecuted or anything. But what about being sued by the Dankers?

I did finally talk to my parents about this. Turns out, they've been worrying about it from day one. They didn't mention it to me, though, because they didn't want me to worry. So we've all been in this cone of silence to avoid freaking each other out. They've actually consulted a lawyer and talked to their insurance company. What they haven't done is ask the Dankers, *So, are you going to sue our daughter?*

Justin continues. "The place my father works, though, this lab—they freaked out because of all the trouble they can get into for having an undocumented alien on the payroll. Even though they've always sort-of-kind-of known about it. But now, with all the publicity—they fired him."

"I'm sorry," I say, intending to sound sorry, only in a cold and indifferent way.

"And now ICE is all over them—"

"ICE?"

"The government. Immigration enforcement. You know—*La Migra*. As they say."

I have never heard Justin say a word of Spanish before.

"Can't your parents become legal now?" I ask. I think I remember Justin saying that they could have done this years ago but never got around to it. And I heard people talking about it at the US-2 meeting I went to—about going from illegal to legal by filing a bunch of papers.

Justin shakes his head. "It's not even close to that easy. For one thing, as of last week my dad doesn't have an employer anymore to sponsor him. You don't get to stay and get a green card just because you've lived here a long time. Just because you think it's your home."

"I'm sorry," I say again. It's hard for me to stay cold and indifferent. He looks like he's going to cry. "What will happen now?"

"We can leave voluntarily. Or we can go through a trial in immigration court, which we'll lose, and then be deported."

"How do you know you'll lose?"

"We will," Justin says. His voice is tight. "Trust me."

"But your little sisters are citizens!" I say. "That should help."

"Not really."

"And what about the police not knowing that you're here?" I ask. "Not knowing that you exist? Remember you told me— how the newspaper said your little sisters were the only kids, and you and your parents were glad about that?"

He half rolls his eyes. "I wouldn't say we're glad about anything. But yeah, I think so far the ICE doesn't know I exist. Or my big sister. But who knows how long that can last? And what am I going to do—live here by myself after my parents and the girls go back to Colombia?"

I don't know.

"So it looks like we're going to leave," he says. "In theory, we can come back."

"What's the theory?" I ask.

"Say, if my mom or dad finds some company in the U.S. to sponsor one of them," he says. "Or maybe I could come back for college, on a student visa."

"Like your parents did."

"Yeah. Look how well it turned out for them."

We sit in silence for a few minutes.

"I feel so bad," he says.

"Something could still work out," I say. "Listen, maybe you can live with your older sister in Philadelphia. The two of you can stay."

"No, I'm talking about us," he says. He sort of slumps in the kitchen chair. "I feel so bad about not being up front with you. It's like, once I didn't say anything when we first met in the park, I got trapped—in the half-truth of just being this random guy who met you in the park."

I squint at him. "The *half*-truth?"

I would call it a lie. I get up from the table to lean against the counter. A lie, not a half-truth. If that's what he's calling it, I can't even sit at the table with him.

"The untruth," Justin says. He reads my mind. "The *lie*. But it's not like everything was a lie, which is why I have a hard time using that word. I didn't know that you and Humphrey were going to turn out to be—who you turned out to be—when I saw you guys playing catch and dancing, and when I thought, *Hey, that's a cool girl.* And then later, after, when you and I first met, I didn't know for sure that you were the girl in the accident."

"Oh, come on!" I say.

"No—I wasn't sure. Not at first. There could have been other girls babysitting other little kids in your neighborhood."

"But you had to have figured it out pretty quickly," I say. "As in, as soon as we started talking."

He looks away from me for a second. "Yeah," he says. "I did."

"And you said nothing."

"You were cool. And funny. And pretty. I didn't want to ruin it."

There that is again. That—ruination thing.

And as quickly as I got angry, I get un-angry.

"And I ended up ruining it anyway," he says.

"Yup," I say.

"Is there anything I can say or do to make you not hate me?"

"Yup," I say, while I'm thinking, *You already called me cool and funny and pretty.*

"Are you going to tell me?"

"Yup."

"And?"

"Don't give up so easily. Don't just surrender and decide you're leaving, that you have no choices. Maybe you should go to one of those immigration law groups where they take cases for free. I heard about them at the US-2 meeting. And in the meantime, keep on being invisible to the ICE."

"This is what will make you not hate me?" Justin asks.

"Yup," I say.

"That's what my parents want me to do, too."

"I guess they're smarter than your average parents, then," I say.

"I hate being this scaredy-cat 'illegal' keeping my head down. I hate being too scared even to feel good about helping that referee on the ice. I hate having to be invisible."

"The idea is to be *selectively* invisible," I say. "Invisible to the government, at least for now. But not invisible to everyone."

A small—tiny, tiny, but I see it—smile starts to play around Justin's mouth.

"Kind of like a superhero," he says.

"Let's not get carried away," I say.

"And it's okay if I lie to the government by pretending I'm

not here, but not okay to lie to you about being a random guy from the park?"

"Because a lie of *o*mission is less bad than a lie of *c*ommission?" I offer. I don't know. I can't make it come out all tidy and consistent, even if I try.

Justin gets up from the kitchen table and comes over to the counter where I'm standing. He leans into me. I lean into him. He is definitely not invisible to me. His presence feels so strong, I am a little concerned that he can't possibly be invisible to anyone.

"This is no lie," he says.

"Neither is this," I reply.

We kiss.

Pleasurably. Pleasingly. Un-platonically.

40

Q-&-A

I am sitting at a table in front of the esteemed and honorable members of the Meigs County Council.

When I called Jen, the council aide, to tell her that I would testify at the hearing, she sounded surprised.

"What made you change your mind?" she asked.

"Oh, you know," I said. "I wanted to do my civic duty."

She offered to e-mail me a list of questions the council members were likely to ask. I turned her down. If I had the questions in advance, I thought, I would feel compelled to compose answers to them in advance. Then I would rehearse them. It would be too much like giving a speech—or like being on the bimah with the Torah in front of me with specific words I was supposed to say.

It does help that the witness chair, where I'm sitting, faces the council members, who are sitting up on some sort of platform. So I can't see the people in the audience, which I hope will help me survive this. I can try to pretend I'm just talking to the seven council members.

The hearing is being held in the Franklin Grove Community Hall, rather than the Meigs County Council building. I think they held it here so that a lot of the neighbors would be sure to come. And the hall is filled—overflowing, even. Who knew this many people lived in Franklin Grove.

Which makes me realize that, no, actually, I really don't think I *can* pretend I'm just talking to the seven council members. And if I can't pretend that, how am I going to stop the panic from overtaking me?

Visualization. That's supposed to be my solution, according to Dr. Gilbert. She and I could spend months and years trying to get to the bottom of why exactly I became afflicted with this fear of public speaking. I'd really rather not. I like Dr. Gilbert, but, as I told her, I'd rather have some coping mechanisms up my sleeve than struggle to get to the bottom of my deep, dark psyche. The coping mechanism at the top of her list of suggestions is to visualize something soothing. Like the beach.

Now that I'm actually sitting by my lonesome self in front of the council members, knowing that there are maybe two hundred people at my back, I'm having serious doubts about visualization. I love the beach. Love the ocean. But when I bring up a picture of it now, what I see is a sea full of angry whitecaps, and then a giant tidal wave pushing toward me, and then crashing over me. This is not a helpful image.

What is soothing? Nothing. Nothing comes to mind. Okay, here's something soothing: sleep. I'll visualize my bed, sleeping in my bed. But that makes me think of my really unacceptable morning bed-head. And my very favorite sleep shirt, which is very comfortable but hideous and not for anyone's eyes but my own. Also not helpful.

"Ms. Snyder," Council Member A's voice, amplified by a microphone, brings me back. "May I call you Danielle?"

I nod.

"All of us here on the council share your pain at what was certainly a traumatic and heartbreaking experience. No one here wants to cause you, or the Danker family, any additional pain. No one here blames you for what happened."

Council Member B: "Our questions for you today are simply to assist us in determining whether certain improvements to Quarry Road would be appropriate in light of the accident that resulted in Humphrey Danker's death. We do not hold you, no one holds you, responsible for that tragedy."

I am not going to be able to keep the names of these people straight. To me, they are A, B, etc.

Council Member A: "Maybe it would be most helpful if we started by having you tell us, in your own words, the sequence of events that led to the accident."

I open my mouth to speak. Nothing comes out.

Council Member A: "Is your microphone not working, Danielle?"

The microphone is fine. I clear my throat. Imagine the beach—no, don't imagine the beach. Imagine the park. The crummy park, mine and Humphrey's and Justin's. The little jungle gym. Imagine the Bumble-Boos.

Humphrey. *Say something interesting*, he said to me. *Something highly interesting.*

I start talking.

I give them the big picture. How we were walking home from the park along Quarry Road. Eastbound, on the north side of the street. (I have mastered the points of the compass.) Facing the westbound traffic, not that there was much of that. Not walking in the street, but on the shoulder, way over where the pavement meets the brush and weeds and where the trees are.

I am holding a football. Humphrey is walking beside me, mostly. I am holding his hand, mostly. But at some point we drop hands. At some point, the football pops out from where I have it tucked between my right arm and hip. It goes bouncing into the street. Humphrey runs after it. I see a silver car heading westbound, and a pickup truck and white car heading eastbound. I don't notice the blue minivan until later.

Council Member A: "I understand it was around seven thirty at night when the accident happened. How much visibility would you say you had, walking along Quarry Road?"

287

Me: "Uh—I had enough visibility. I mean, I could see."

Council Member C: "But the question really is, how well drivers can see pedestrians."

Council Member D: "How safe and secure did you feel walking along the shoulder on Quarry Road?"

Me: "I felt okay walking on the shoulder. It's where I've always walked. Everyone walks there. There's a lot of room, so you're away from the traffic. And, anyway, there weren't many cars on that side of the road, at least not that time of day."

Council Member A: "Yes, the westbound lane of Quarry Road is fairly quiet in the evening rush hour. It's the eastbound lane that carries most of the traffic that time of day."

Council Member D: "If there had been a sidewalk there, though, would you have still walked in the street?"

What a stupid question.

Now here is something highly interesting: I had begun to see, kind of out of the corner of my eye, the evil wave of panic edging toward me. I saw it, and I felt it in my throat. Then came the stupid question. It pushed the scary fear right back to wherever it comes from. Like Moses pushing back the Red Sea just by stretching out his hand.

Me: "I'd walk on the sidewalk if there was a sidewalk."

Council Member D: "You would have walked on the sidewalk, and not on the side of the busy road."

Me: "Yes. Yes, of course I would have."

Council Member D: "You understand, young lady, no one

blames you. You had nowhere else to walk. But if a sidewalk were built alongside Quarry Road, it seems to me future trage-dies might be avoided."

He's not really talking to me, but rather to the audience.

Council Member E: "I'd like to get back to the question of visibility. There are no streetlights on Quarry Road. You said you had 'enough visibility.' Now of course, you're not an expert, but can you tell us what makes you say there was enough light?"

Me: "I could see. I saw the cars. I saw Humphrey. I could—I don't know, I could see everything."

Council Member B: "The sun didn't set that day until eight fifteen p.m."

Me: "And the moon rose at six forty-eight p.m. And it was almost full."

At least three sets of eyebrows go up among the council people.

Me: "Humphrey liked knowing that sort of thing, about when the moon rose and the stars came out."

Council Member E: "So you're saying, in your opinion, there was *plenty* of light for a young woman, and a child, walking along the street that night. The street lined with tall shade trees."

From the way he says "plenty"—lots of emphasis—I think he thinks there couldn't possibly have been plenty of light.

Me: "It wasn't dark. I could see everything. I think the cars could see us. But everything happened so fast. Sometimes accidents just happen."

As I continue talking, I can see the possibility for everything to work out okay: Humphrey, in the street, but still in the lane on our side, sees that the ball is *BOING*-ing its way to the other lane, the one with all the cars. He may be only five, young enough to forget, momentarily, while under the spell of a bouncing football, that you don't run into the street. But he's smart enough to know not to run after a ball into a lane of traffic. He turns back and looks at me for guidance.

I'm about to scream at him to run back to me. I'm about to run into the street to grab him. But I do neither, because suddenly I see the silver car zooming down Quarry Road toward us—toward Humphrey, to be precise.

When I say "zooming"—do I even know if it's speeding? I don't. The cars in the other lane, heading east, are moving slowly because there are so many more of them. "Zoom" is a relative term.

So as the silver car approaches, I am paralyzed. Can Humphrey make it back to me before the silver car? If I were better at math, I could calculate this: the distance between the silver car and Humphrey, divided by the car's estimated rate of speed, equals how long before the car will arrive at the point where Humphrey is standing. Is this greater or less than the number that equals the distance between Humphrey and me, divided by Humphrey's rate of speed?

Or maybe the silver car will notice Humphrey in the street, and stop.

When Humphrey sees the silver car, at first he is paralyzed, too. What he really needs to do is just inch over to the center of the roadway. He needs to get over there and stand just on the bright double yellow line, not in the way of the eastbound traffic, and out of the path of the westbound silver car, which will soon be past him. That is all he has to do. Make himself small for a few seconds. There's no car behind the silver one, so once it's passed by, I'll dash out and grab him and drag him back to safety.

But Humphrey takes matters into his own hands. Runs away from the silver car. Away from me. And into the traffic in the eastbound lane.

There are a few seconds of what I would call respectful silence; respectful, since I've just replayed Humphrey's death in front of two hundred people. And then:

Council Member C: "The silver car is mentioned in the police report."

Council Member B: "There is no suggestion that Humphrey was struck by that automobile."

Council Member F: "Perhaps we should be thinking about

the speed limit on Quarry Road, since it is downhill going west. . . ."

Council Member G: "The police report does not indicate that the car was speeding down the hill—"

Council Member C: "And yet we are not limited here to the police report. The point of having our own hearing is to elicit facts that may not be in the report."

Council Member G: "Yes, but I don't wish for us to be distracted by, for want of a better term, facts not in evidence. I know we're not held to legal standards here, but Ms. Snyder is not saying that the silver car was speeding, is she? Are you?"

Me: "No. I'm not. I don't know what the speed limit even is. Maybe I shouldn't have said 'zoom.' All I'm saying is the silver car was heading down the hill in our direction. And I think Humphrey ran to get away from it."

Council Member E: "As you say, Ms. Snyder, in a situation such as the one you faced, everything happens so fast. In view of this, I'm of the opinion that it would be beneficial to pedestrians and to drivers to improve the lighting on Quarry Road, and it would also behoove us to take a serious, serious look at sidewalks, as well as crosswalks and crossing signals at appropriate intervals on this thoroughfare."

Right. We are talking about road improvements. On another note, wouldn't Humphrey love the word "behoove"?

I hear murmurings in the audience. *Mm-hmm.* A couple of people applaud, and then a lot of people applaud. These people want their road improvements.

I have to admit, although my heart goes out to the Littleleaf Linden trees that may lose their lives if sidewalks and stuff are put in, I don't care much one way or another about streetlights and sidewalks and crosswalks and crossing signals. If people want to "improve" Quarry Road, whatever; I'm not going to live here forever. I can just see them naming a lamppost after Humphrey and feeling all warm and righteous about that.

Council Member F: "But you're correct, Ms. Snyder, when you remind us that sometimes accidents just happen. This was one of those accidents where no one is to blame, least of all you."

I've now been told by a majority of the county council that I am blameless. It's like they passed a law about it. This should make me feel good, right? But instead, this vote of confidence punctures something inside of me, something that feels like a balloon between my ears. It's the audio blackout my brain has imposed on the accident from the moment I dropped that football; it's dissolving. The white noise that has been the sound track of the accident suddenly lifts, and the sounds and words take shape.

Me: "Actually—I *am* to blame. Or, at least, I'm the cause. It's not the street's fault. It's not some driver's fault. It's me."

Council Members A–G: "No, no, no. Unfortunate-blah-blah. Circumstances-blah-blah. Safety-issues-blah-blah."

Me: "No, really. I was there. I take back what I said. Yes, sometimes accidents just happen. But this wasn't one of them."

41

Fumble

Humphrey and I walked along Quarry Road, holding hands, as we had so many times before.

"Oh!" Humphrey said suddenly. He stopped and dropped my hand. "Look!"

It was a huge moon, orange above the trees.

"Whoa," I said.

"Whoa," he said.

"Okay," I said after we were done admiring the moon, "now we really have to get going. I think when we get home it'll be time for—"

"Second Dessert!" Humphrey said.

He started to run ahead of me.

"Humphrey!" I called.

He came back. We walked together, talking about what there was in the house for Second Dessert besides juice pops.

"You're too slow!" Humphrey said. "Let's run!"

"You have to stay right next to me," I said, but I did break into a slow jog. At first, he ran right by my side. Humphrey was a good listener and followed directions. But soon he fell behind— even jogging slowly, with my long legs, I easily pulled ahead of Humphrey—so I turned around. When he saw me stopped and facing him, he put on some speed.

"Tackle!" he said.

Maybe six feet separated us, that was all. Humphrey ran into me. It didn't hurt, but the football popped loose.

And then I said it.

"Fumble!"

I wasn't thinking. I wasn't thinking about what a good listener and direction-follower Humphrey was.

"Fumble!" he echoed, pleased as could be.

Fumble and pounce. Fumble and pounce.

Humphrey pounced, just like I had taught him.

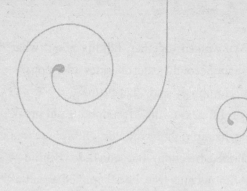

42

I Need to Tell You

When I've finished narrating the worst forty-five seconds of my life, no one says anything. Not at first. Then they all start talking at the same time, again.

Council Members A–C: "Admirable assumption of responsibility." "Certainly no cause and effect." "Can't blame yourself."

Me: "It is about cause and effect. There isn't a sidewalk or streetlight or crosswalk or anything that could have kept Humphrey from running into Quarry Road to try to get that football. Just me."

Council Members D–E: "Unpredictable young boy." "Understandable feelings of guilt."

Me: "I think that people are using the accident just because they want to go ahead with their pet projects, and you'll be cutting down trees and putting up streetlights and chasing away wildlife for no good reason."

Council Member E: "Well, now, young lady. Well, now. There are people who are experts in safety and road engineering, Ms. Snyder. We here on the council are going to be looking to these experts for their informed opinions and proposals about such matters, and about what can be done to prevent future tragedies from happening. We'll be relying on studies and experts and not, with all due respect, Ms. Snyder, on your emotional and subjective view—which is understandable, and is not your fault—of what might or might not keep a child safe on Quarry Road."

So then why did you people pressure me to testify in the first place?

I don't actually say that. Instead, I say:

"And then there are the people who are using the accident to go after immigrants, just because immigrants happened to be in the car that Humphrey ran into—"

"*Illegal* immigrants!" someone behind me yells.

"Not just immigrants! *Illegal* immigrants!"

I turn around and face the audience for the first time. My parents, Adrian, Becca, Justin, and other people I know are out there (no doubt including Doris Raskin), but I can't see a single one of them. All I see are unfamiliar faces.

"Illegal immigrant drivers kill more people than secondhand smoke!" a voice calls out. "They're hazardous to our health!"

"They had nothing to do with it!" someone replies. Loudly. "You may want to pretend that this accident and your—your *cause* are connected, but they're not. Don't use the accident as a pretext for targeting undocumented immigrants!"

Oh. That was me. Facing two hundred people.

Isn't that a good word that Humphrey would appreciate? *Pretext.*

"Unlicensed to kill!" another person yells.

Council Member A bangs a gavel and the shout-outs die down. He hurriedly thanks me and calls me brave and says that the council will, in fact, take into consideration all the testimony and information they gather, including—take *that*, Council Member E—mine. I am dismissed. I could leave the hearing, but I don't. I sit in one of the empty chairs reserved in the front row for people who are testifying.

As Council Member E promised, experts are called after me, and they say things about all the improvements needed to make Quarry Road a safer street. Then Mrs. Joseph goes up and talks about the character of the Franklin Grove neighborhood. Then there's the tree history lady. Someone from a local environmental group talks about toads and frogs and how road improvements will "adversely impact" the "fragile ecosystem," which will mean good-bye, toads and frogs. Council Member E wants to know if the toads and frogs are endangered species. No, the environmental expert says. They're mostly wood frogs and American toads.

So just ordinary toads and frogs, Council Member E says.

The way he says it makes me feel much more protective of them than I ever have before.

"We have one more witness," Council Member A says. "Mrs. Gloria Padilla Folgar." His eyes search the first couple of rows. "Do you still wish to make your statement, ma'am?"

A small woman approaches the witness table. A circuit of energy bounces around the room. Becca would call it a *frisson*—like a collective shiver. To me, it feels like a long chain of falling dominoes.

"Mr. Chairman, yes, I wish to address the council and the community," the woman begins. "I am Gloria Padilla Folgar. My husband, Eugene Folgar Guzman, was driving our car the night of the accident that took Humphrey Danker's life. It was our car that struck Humphrey. Although the police have absolved us of legal responsibility for this tragedy, we want to apologize to the Danker family and the community. My husband was driving on an expired license. I, too, have an expired license. It is no secret anymore that we are undocumented immigrants. As such, we were unable to obtain valid new licenses when our old ones expired. We should not have been driving. We know that. We would do anything to undo the tragedy. We know that is impossible, but at the very least, I wanted to express our sympathy and our apology publicly."

"Not good enough!" someone says loudly.

Council Member A bangs his gavel again.

"Go back to Colombia!" someone yells.

"Don't apologize! Leave!"

The gavel again. This time Council Member A loudly thanks Mrs. Padilla Folgar, thanks everyone who spoke, thanks everyone for coming. But the outbursts don't stop.

"When will you schedule a hearing on Councilman Foster's bill?" someone says.

"Illegals off the roads—that's the best safety program!"

"No need to spend millions on streetlights—just enforce our immigration laws!"

"Let's take back our community!"

Council Member A is trying to gavel these people into silence, but it's not working. A man stands up.

"Will the chair permit me to speak?" he asks.

Council Member A looks like he'd rather hit himself in the head with his gavel, but he nods.

"Order, please!" He bangs the gavel. The people who were calling out seem to recognize the man who is standing, and they shut up.

"We want to know when the Meigs County Council will take up Councilman Foster's bill to direct our law enforcement officers to refer undocumented aliens they encounter to federal authorities," the man says.

Council Member A looks sideways, over at Council Member E, who, I gather, is Councilman Foster.

"We will take up calendaring in executive session," Council Member A says. "But perhaps Councilman Foster wishes to address your . . . concerns."

"Well, now," Councilman Foster says. "I introduced that

bill and I plan to pursue it. Safe streets and communities are not only a matter of infrastructure, as you say. I will see to it that the council holds hearings and gives full consideration—"

"Not good enough!"

"It's time for action!"

Council Member A is banging his gavel like crazy, but it can barely be heard. People are on their feet.

"Take back our communities!"

"Unlicensed to kill! Unlicensed to kill! Unlicensed to kill!"

I would say this hearing is officially adjourned.

A woman I don't recognize is yelling into Mrs. Padilla Folgar's face. And then I see Justin, slowly coming into focus behind the yelling woman. He puts himself between this woman and Mrs. Padilla Folgar—his mother. Then I see him steer her away from the angry woman and toward the exit. They disappear into the crowd. I look after them, and I see another familiar face. Marissa.

Why is she here? We've been texting lately, since the drama at the hockey rink. Not every single day, but frequently. It's been nice. Back to normal, for us, which is real friends but not best friends. I didn't tell her that I was speaking here tonight; I didn't exactly spread the news far and wide about this. It's possible that Marissa found out I was on the agenda and she came to lend me moral support. But if she's not here to support me—what, she's interested in the subject of Quarry Road improvements?

Now Marissa sees me. Our eyes meet. She lifts her eyebrows

in some kind of indecipherable greeting, and then she's jostled and I lose sight of her.

Meanwhile, Adrian finds me.

"How are you feeling?" he asks.

I don't really have an answer. "I'm feeling like . . . myself," I say slowly. "My real self. I'm also feeling like someone else, but it's someone else who I'm supposed to be." I pause. "I'm not sure how much sense that makes."

"It makes enough sense," Adrian says.

"I also feel like I had water in my ears," I say, "and now I don't."

"That's got to be a relief," he says.

"Yeah," I say. "I'm feeling better."

"I'm glad," he says.

We hug and he doesn't say anything more. Then we start looking for an exit. The room is crowded and noisy and feels almost dangerous. As we approach the door we see the blue-and-red flash of police car lights. No sirens, just lights. Six cops jump out of three cruisers, bound up the stairs to the community hall, and rush past us into the room.

It doesn't take long for things to quiet down after that. There is something about men in uniform—yes, all six cops are men—with guns on their hips. Suddenly everyone in the room is a law-abiding citizen. This wasn't a riot, after all. Not quite. Just concerned citizens exercising their rights of political expression.

The room is emptying out around Adrian and me. My parents find us and say they're proud of me.

"Danielle!" Becca falls on me with one of her big hugs. "I'm so proud of you for taking a stand!"

"It wasn't much of a stand," I say.

"*Tu es formidable!*" she says. "You spoke truth to power!"

I have to smile at Becca. Sure I did. I'm a regular rabble-rouser at the barricades. I am *Les Mis*.

"Plus, you did it," she says. "You conquered your fear."

I did, didn't I. At least for today. At least to say what I had to say.

"I knew you could do it," Becca says. "And another thing: Remember how you said you're not an activist?"

"Right."

"And I said you are too; you just needed to figure out what you're an activist for? Well, you're an activist for Humphrey. Don't you think?"

An activist for Humphrey? I just want to keep Humphrey out of the whole debate. I don't want Humphrey to belong to people who never even met him.

"I don't know," I say. "Something just clicked inside, and I got tired of hearing everyone blame all the wrong things. And the wrong people."

"That works, too," Becca agrees. "You're an anti-hypocrisy activist."

I smile. I'm tired of talking. "That's it."

"But, Danielle."

"But, Becca."

"I hope, really hope, you won't keep blaming yourself."

That may take a while. "I'll work on it, Becca," I say.

"You know, those anti-immigrant people—most of them were plants," she says.

"I don't understand."

"As in, infiltrators," she says.

Now I have to laugh. "As in, spies, right?"

"Really—they're not from Franklin Grove. They don't care about the hearing on the Quarry Road improvements. A lot of them aren't even from Meigs County. They're part of the Alliance for Lawful Immigration. They come to community events like this to stir things up."

"And you know this how?" I ask.

"I have my sources," Becca says. "You know I know all."

Adrian, Mom, and Dad leave after I tell them that Becca will walk most of the way home with me. Mom and Dad offered to drive Adrian out to his place, since his car is in the shop—and he accepted, rather than take two buses.

"Quality time," he whispers to me.

I feel Justin next to me. He takes my hand.

"Where's your mom?" I ask.

"She came with a friend," he says. "They're driving home together."

Soon Justin needs to go, too; he has a bus to catch, and the buses run less frequently at night. "You're not walking home by yourself, are you?" he asks.

"I'm walking with Danielle," Becca offers.

Justin hugs me. "You were stupendous," he whispers. "You are my superhero."

As Becca and I start out the door, it occurs to me that if she walks me to the corner of Quarry and Franklin, as planned, then she'll have to keep hiking down Quarry Road to the bus stop near our house. Too much walking. So much easier for her to leave from here; she should really go to the community hall bus stop, where Justin went. I can make it home alone just fine. It's a ten-minute walk, and it's a mild night.

"But I promised your boyfriend!" she says.

I give her a look; I guess he is my boyfriend. But I tell Becca that I think I can decide for myself if I want to walk home.

We say good night. She goes out one door, and I walk in the opposite direction to a different exit, and down some steps toward the street. It's a cool, clear night. I look forward to airing out my head.

"Danielle."

Whoa. Jeez.

It's Marissa. I wasn't expecting anybody to be here at the bottom of the stairs, and her voice startles me.

"Marissa. Hi. You surprised me."

"Sorry. I didn't mean to."

She congratulates me on my testimony. "You handled all the questions so well. I was proud of you."

Another person proud of me.

"I can give you a ride home," Marissa says.

"I thought I'd walk," I say. "It's not too far."

"Let me drive you, Danielle."

I really was looking forward to the walk. But Marissa has sort of an ache about her. Like she really wants to drive me home. So okay. She points down the street to where she's parked and we walk in that direction.

"I was surprised to see you here," Marissa says. "I didn't realize you'd be speaking."

That answers the question of whether she came to lend moral support: no.

"I guess I'm surprised to see you, too," I say.

"It's . . . not like you, is it, to speak in front of people like that? At least not like the you that I know."

"Hard to know how to take that," I say. I suddenly realize that I haven't even thought about the wave of panic since Humphrey's image appeared to me, like Mom's cardinal, and suggested that I say something highly interesting.

"You did well," she says. "Actually, outstanding. That's how you should take it."

"Thanks. But, Marissa, why were you there?"

"There's this group," Marissa says. "It's involved in promoting legal immigration. I'm starting to get a little bit involved in it."

"Huh," I say. "There were people yelling about *illegal* immigration in the meeting. I didn't hear anything about *legal* immigration. And anyway, the hearing was supposed to be about road safety."

I'm being a little bit of a hypocrite here. After all, I'm the one who brought up the immigration issue toward the end of my testimony. But I'm going to let myself be that much of a hypocrite.

"It wasn't supposed to be so rowdy," Marissa says. "Actually, it wasn't supposed to be rowdy at all." She explains that the man who asked to speak at the end of the evening was supposed to say something like, "These are the people of your community who support legal immigration and are concerned about unlawful immigration." Members of their group—organized by the Alliance for Legal Immigration, just as Becca said—were then supposed to stand up. Quietly.

"I don't know why people starting yelling things out," she says. "It's like, once they did, they acted like they had permission to do and say whatever they wanted."

"It was pretty ugly," I say.

"I want you to know that I wasn't there to yell and stomp around," Marissa says. "If I'd known you were testifying, I probably wouldn't have come at all. Or I would have come for a different reason: to support you."

"Okay," I say. "But why do you say you might not have come at all? Because you're embarrassed by what you stand for?" I don't mean for that to sound as harsh as it probably does.

"Because I respect what you were trying to do," she corrects me. "You were speaking from the heart. Other than you, everyone else was just repeating the same canned speeches we've all heard before. So it seemed fine to raise the issue that the council always wants to duck—immigration. But as soon as you spoke, it wasn't fine to do it anymore. Except—it was too late to change the plan."

"Well," I say. "It's too bad you weren't in charge."

"It is too bad," she says, and we both smile. I think we both know that one of these days, Marissa will be in charge. Of something.

Marissa presses a button on her key, and a car twinkles.

Here I am, it says. This one.

A silver Volkswagen Jetta.

A shiny silver car.

We get in. In the darkness Marissa turns to me.

"I need to tell you something," she says.

43

MORE TO BLAME

Matt and Martin had been arguing over the car. According to the infamous "car wheel" posted on the Martinezes' refrigerator, that Friday was Martin's turn to have the car. As a new driver, Martin wasn't allowed to have his friends as passengers in the car, because they're all under eighteen years old. That's one of the state's rookie driver rules.

"But—you drive Marco places," I say. Marissa is not a rule-breaker.

"Yes. You can have family members as passengers. Immediate family members, but no one else, not until you get your full license."

So Matt had heard Martin talking to one of his friends, James, making plans to pick him up to go to a movie with a group of their friends. Earlier, Matt had tried to get Martin to change car days with him; Matt had his own plans downtown and didn't want to take buses and the subway to get there.

"He offered to drop Martin and James off at the movie on his way downtown," Marissa says. "Mom or Dad could pick them up later. Martin said forget it. It was his turn to have the car, period. He also said Matt was wrong about him planning to drive James. But I knew he'd made plans to do that, too; he wasn't telling the truth."

"Martin, not telling the truth?" I don't know him that well, but I've always thought of him as pretty much of a Boy Scout.

"He's changed this year—so much. My parents are blind to it because he's always been such a star. They'll be in for a shock when we get second-quarter grades. I don't think he'll qualify to play lacrosse next spring."

"Wow." A Martinez not on a school sports team.

"So this becomes a huge argument. Martin needs to leave if he's going to be on time for the movie, so he goes to get the keys off the hook in the pantry. They're not there. Matt has taken them. Martin goes ballistic and jumps on Matt."

"Where are your parents?"

"Out to dinner. So the guys are fighting over the car keys. Hitting each other. It's ridiculous."

It's also hard for me to picture. The brothers were always so buddy-buddy.

"Martin gets the keys away from Matt. He runs out the door, yelling about how he's late. You'd think he was going to miss a plane or something. He was so mad."

"Sounds like a bit of an overreaction," I say.

"A *bit*? He was crazy," Marissa says. "But this is how he's been lately. Something weird is going on with him and, so far, like I said, my parents are blind."

"I'm sorry, Marissa," I say. "This sounds upsetting."

"It is upsetting. But I'm telling you about it because he runs out the door, gets into the car—this car, this silver car—and heads over to James's house. Which he has to get to by going down Quarry Road. And I'm also telling you, the way he left the house, I would not have wanted to be in the car with him. Or walking alongside any street he was driving on."

Is she saying what I think she's saying?

"When I heard about the accident," Marissa says, "I didn't even think about the timing. I had no reason to. I mean, I didn't read anything about what time you and Humphrey were there. On Quarry Road. I had no idea it was—when it was. I guess I assumed the accident happened earlier in the afternoon."

Until tonight. And she heard me talk about the silver car.

Silver cars are not unusual, are they? It seems to me there's a good chance that more than one silver car drove down Quarry Road in the westbound lane sometime between seven and seven thirty that night.

"Marissa, it wasn't Martin," I say. "Why should you assume it was him? I mean, what are the chances? I'm sure it was some other silver car. There are tons of silver cars."

"Tons of silver cars driven by stark raving teenage lunatics?"

No. Probably not tons of those.

"I was there, Marissa," I remind her. "I'm the one person who was there for sure. And I can't say that it was a silver Jetta, or a stark raving teenage lunatic."

"The odds seem good, though, don't they?"

Do they? I am suddenly very tired of trying to understand what happened that night, when it happened, and where everyone and everything was when it happened. Meanwhile, Marissa's got her hands over her face. She's usually so cool and collected.

"First of all, the silver car didn't hit Humphrey," I point out.

She moves her hands to her lap. "No. It only scared him into running into another car. I think that makes whoever was driving the silver car more to blame than the driver of the minivan."

"Second of all, we don't know who was driving the silver car. Martin went to his movie, right?"

"I guess so," Marissa says.

"I bet he would have said something if he thought he was anywhere close to the accident."

She snorts, which is a very un-Marissa thing to do.

"I don't know about that," she says.

"This was a tragedy without a villain," I say. "I'm quoting Adrian here." When he says it, of course, Adrian is usually trying to help me forgive myself.

"Maybe," Marissa says. "But that family would be quietly living their lives if it wasn't for . . . whoever was driving. This isn't the way I would want them to be found out. Because of something some speeding driver did, and got away with. Some speeding legal citizen who just could be Martin."

The way she says "that family" and nothing more specific, I know that she doesn't realize that it's Justin's family. Did she not see Justin with his mother tonight? I guess not. She doesn't know. I decide that she doesn't need to know. I make comforting noises.

"I know you love your brother," Marissa says.

Huh. Where does this come from? I wait for the "but."

"You are about the most loyal sister I know," she continues.

"Okay," I say.

"And I love my brothers, too. All of them. And I'm a loyal sister, too. But Martin—"

She has to stop to steady her voice.

"Martin," she resumes, "is really testing my loyalty. The stuff I could tell you that he's up to. The stuff I could tell my parents. I don't want to. I want to be loyal. But—dang."

That is as close as Marissa gets to a swear word.

"It's like he's trying to become another person," Marissa says. "And not a better one. He's got these new, dodgy people he's hanging out with. I don't like them and I don't like him these days. And I really don't like feeling there's nothing I can do about any of this."

"I'm sorry," I say.

"I'm sorry, too."

"Are you talking to him?" I ask. "He always listened to you, I thought."

"All of our 'always' are changing," Marissa says. "He doesn't want to talk to me."

"Well—you can talk to me about Martin anytime," I say. "I really do understand how you're feeling."

I know how important family is to Marissa. For Martin to be wandering off the straight and narrow path—that has got to be painful to her. So much for the picture-perfect Martinez family; I guess every family has its wrinkles, even though it looks perfectly smooth from the outside.

We've been sitting in the car for a while by now. She never did turn it on. I put on my seat belt.

"Danielle . . . about the other thing. The ALI group tonight."

"ALI?"

"Alliance for Lawful Immigration."

"Right."

"I'm not a hater," she says. "It's important to me that you know that, that I'm not a hater."

"I do know that," I say. "I just don't entirely get why you've chosen this as your cause."

Marissa was about to turn the car on, but my question distracts her. "First of all," she says, "it won't be my so-called cause for long if the people involved act like they did tonight."

I believe it. Marissa is not one for rowdy, rude behavior.

"But second of all," she says, "you know how I feel about following the rules, like my family did when they came to the U.S. And third of all, you know how I feel about how people lump together everyone who has a name like Martinez. To them, we're all Mexicans, or, more likely, just generic Hispanics. They read about undocumented immigrants with Hispanic names, and we're all the same."

"I know it bothers you," I say. "You could take a different approach. You could make it your mission to educate the ignorant people who are doing all that lumping together. To let them know that you can't just assume that everyone with a Hispanic name is the same."

Marissa seems to think about this.

"But—" she begins.

"So," I continue at the same moment, "your problem would be about the people who are doing the lumping together, rather than about the people you're being lumped with."

About the lump*ers*, not the lump*ees*.

"You have a point," Marissa says. "But I'm not sure I can give up my resentment so easily. What if I'm not that generous?"

"Well," I say. "Actually, you are generous. You've got a big heart. But I guess you're talking about a different kind of generous."

"It's complicated," we both say at the same time.

I've been tired of talking ever since I finished speaking at the council meeting. Now I'm completely and totally done for.

"Marissa," I say. I hear my voice; it's practically croaking with burnout. "Can you please take me home?"

She does.

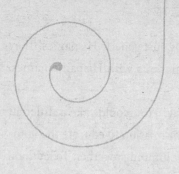

44

THE BENEFITS

IMPROVEMENTS VOTED FOR QUARRY ROAD

by Diana Tang

Observer reporter

Responding to a deadly accident that occurred after years of concern over pedestrian safety on Quarry Road, the Meigs County Council has approved the expenditure of $1.4 million on a stretch of that thoroughfare that runs through the Franklin Grove neighborhood. The vote, taken last week on December 2, was 5–2 in favor of improvements recommended by safety experts, including sidewalks, streetlights, crosswalks, and a crossing signal. The projects will be undertaken in cooperation with the State Highway Administration.

Last July, five-year-old Humphrey T. Danker was struck and killed by a minivan when he ran into the street while walking home with his teenage baby-sitter. Since then, residents of the leafy neighborhood have ramped up efforts to convince the county and the State Highway Administration to take action on a package of road improvements.

Construction is expected to start next March.

Let there be light. Light and sidewalks and all the rest.

I hear my cell phone vibrating, rattling on the kitchen counter. I'm at the kitchen table, reading the *Observer* and waiting for Adrian. He's picking me up, and then we're getting Becca and Justin and driving to the capital, about an hour away. We'll be part of a group of US-2 members and friends delivering a petition and demonstrating against anti-immigration proposals the state legislature is considering. On the way home, we're going to swing by Adrian's restaurant—where they're not quite done with the renovations—to see what a hot-spot-in-the-making looks like. We might even help with a little painting.

And yes, Justin is coming to the demonstration at the state assembly. He's showing his face.

"It's not like you'll be wearing a sign saying 'Hi, I'm an undocumented immigrant,'" I said when we talked about it.

"True," he said.

"Like when you helped your mother at the hearing. Nothing happened to you because of that."

"True."

We talked after the meeting, though, about how exposed he felt there. He didn't like that feeling. Justin didn't want me to tell Becca about his status; I told him there was no way Becca wouldn't connect the dots after his mother introduced herself as Gloria Padilla Folgar at the county council hearing. She knew him as Justin Folgar, and she just wouldn't miss the connection. So he told Becca. Becca told Justin that although silence did not come to her naturally, she was capable of it and promised not to breathe a word to anybody. She swore on her future Pulitzer Prize, a vow she does not take lightly. Justin also said I could tell Adrian. I'm sure Adrian, with his great intuition, has figured out the link already as well. I'll talk to him about it after today.

Justin still doesn't know what he'll be doing—leaving when his parents leave, staying behind and below the radar, staying behind and appealing to the immigration authorities. He went to an immigration law clinic, like I suggested, and they were nice—but super-busy. He doesn't think they'll have time for him anytime soon. He's afraid he'll just fall through the cracks there. Funny how when you want to be visible, that's exactly when you become invisible.

The number on my phone's display: it's the Dankers'.

Oh, no.

"Hello, Danielle. This is Tom Danker."

I don't say anything.

"Danielle?"

"Yes—um, hi. Hi, Mr. Danker."

This can't be anything good.

"I heard you at the county council hearing," he says.

Oh.

"You said some interesting things there," he says.

Yes.

"Yes, you made some highly interesting comments," he says.

This would be a little bit funny and little bit cute, hearing shades of Humphrey in Mr. Danker's voice, only it isn't because, after all, it's Mr. Danker.

And if he heard me speak at the council hearing, then he now knows for sure what he always suspected: that I really am to blame for what happened to Humphrey. Excuse me; I'm trying to get away from the blame game. That I really am the *cause* of what happened to Humphrey.

"I'm sure you've heard about the vote on the safety improvements to Quarry Road," Mr. Danker says.

I tell him I have.

"So now they have that out of their system—the neighbors. The Franklin Grove Board. The council."

"Yes," I say. "I guess that's a good thing."

"It's what happens in these situations," Mr. Danker says. "I don't know if it's good or bad."

"No. I guess I don't really know, either."

"I wanted to tell you, though, that I was impressed by your testimony, Danielle. It took guts to accept responsibility."

I'm waiting for him to tell me that thanks to my guts, thanks to my confession in front of two hundred people, I should look for a lawsuit against me in the mail. Only I don't know—do you get a lawsuit in the mail? No, you get served with a lawsuit, right? Someone comes to your door, hands you a bunch of papers, and says something like, "You've been served!"

Mr. Danker has paused and seems to be waiting for me to say something.

"Oh—well—uh—"

"A 'thank you' will suffice," he says. "I am paying you a compliment."

"But I'm just so sorry, Mr. Danker. I feel—I just feel—"

"I know," he says. "I know. But, Danielle, there's one thing on which I don't agree with you, and that is when you said that sometimes accidents just happen but Humphrey's wasn't one of them. In fact, it was indeed such an accident. You're linking the terrible outcome to a chain of events for which you acknowledge responsibility—but still, you didn't cause the accident. There were too many elements of causation for you to consider yourself truly at fault."

He speaks like such a lawyer. It's actually a little bit hard for me to follow him. But I do catch his drift.

"Well," I say.

"But what also impressed me about your testimony last month was your effort to call out attempts by others to turn our tragedy into something that they can use—especially the anti-immigration forces."

Our tragedy. He called it our tragedy. Because he recognizes that it was mine, too, that I loved Humphrey, too? Or because he's making clear that it's his and Mrs. Danker's only, and not mine to claim?

"Well—thank you," I say.

We're both quiet. This goes on for what feels like a long time.

"I know you cared for Humphrey very, very much," Mr. Danker says finally.

"I loved Humphrey," I say. "I really did."

More silence.

"I also know that during your summer of babysitting for Humphrey, I may have occasionally been less than—gracious."

I nod, as if nodding makes sense over the phone. He doesn't continue right away. This man is not afraid of a pause.

"I was—distracted, to say the least. Of course you know about Clarice's cancer."

"Yes," I say quietly.

"She contracted cancer at a young age—she was thirty-four the first time."

"I didn't know," I say. "I didn't know there were first and second times."

"Yes. And a third time, this recent bout."

"I'm so sorry."

"Thank you. She's doing well. My point is, this was a diffi-cult summer. I was distracted, and I fear I was not as kind as I could have been to you—"

"No, Mr. Danker, you were—"

"—or to my boy. Or to Humphrey."

When Mrs. Danker became pregnant with Humphrey, he tells me, she was so happy. Mr. Danker had children from his previous marriage, but Mrs. Danker had no other children. She was just so happy. She'd already had cancer once. Getting preg-nant was such a happy thing. Such a bonus.

They learned, though, that pregnancy would increase the risk of Mrs. Danker's cancer coming back. Apparently, being pregnant can give you breast cancer. That's overstating it. It's more like, some types of cancers can be made worse, or trig-gered, by the tons of hormones you produce when you're preg-nant. According to Mr. Danker, Mrs. Danker's doctors warned them of this. According to Mr. Danker, Mrs. Danker didn't care. She wanted to have Humphrey. I suppose it's more accu-rate to say she wanted to have a baby, and Humphrey turned out to be her baby. And then, during her pregnancy, they found that Mrs. Danker had breast cancer again.

"We could have had—we could have done something about the pregnancy. It was early enough. But my wife wanted this baby. She couldn't have treatments for the cancer during the pregnancy; they're too harmful to the baby. She knew the risks to herself, and she decided that the benefits outweighed them."

And now the benefits are dead.

Mr. Danker doesn't say that. But it's true.

"After Humphrey was born, Clarice went through a whole battery of treatments, tough treatments. Then she was clear for five years. This latest cancer occurrence—her third—wasn't shocking, because she had such a serious case. Still, we were surprised. And I felt very—very angry, for want of a better word."

I think of the times that nosy old Doris Raskin hinted at all that Mr. and Mrs. Danker lost, risked, suffered, or otherwise went through relating to Humphrey. I didn't get it. Now I do. But I still hate the way Mrs. Raskin made it sound like Humphrey was some terrible burden the Dankers took on.

"So, Danielle, this is all by way of background to say that I'm sure you were a fine babysitter to Humphrey, even if I wasn't in any sort of condition to acknowledge it at the time. Moreover, as I said, you impressed me at the council meeting with your insistence on speaking truthfully and, I might even say, your passion for justice. I couldn't help but notice that the young man who helped Mrs. Padilla Folgar out appeared to be a friend of yours."

I don't say anything.

"I saw him come up and hug you afterward. From the

family resemblance, I would venture a guess that he is Mrs. Padilla Folgar's son."

I still don't say anything. It is my turn to be comfortable with pauses.

"Perhaps you might communicate to him that I would like to offer my assistance, in terms of legal services. This would be on a pro bono basis, of course."

Pro bono?

Before I can show my ignorance and ask what he means, Mr. Danker explains. "At no charge. Immigration law isn't exactly my bread and butter, but I did argue a significant asylum case before the Supreme Court a couple of years ago. I think I could help."

"Danny-girl? You in the kitchen?" It's Adrian.

"Yeah," I call out.

Adrian pokes his head in the kitchen and points at the watch on his wrist. "Sorry I'm late," he mouths.

"*Yeah*?" Mr. Danker repeats.

"Oh, no, not 'yeah' to you!" I say. I would never express the affirmative that way to Thomas R. Danker.

"Danielle?" Mr. Danker says. "If I'm wrong about your friendship with this young man, or if you're not comfortable getting involved, then forgive—"

"No, no, no. You're not wrong. I'm comfortable. This is—I really appreciate—my brother just came, though, and we have to go if we want to be on time—"

I stammer for a few more half sentences. Somehow Mr. Danker deciphers what I'm saying, I agree that I'll happily talk to Justin about his offer, I click off the call, I dance my brother around the kitchen, and we fly out the door.

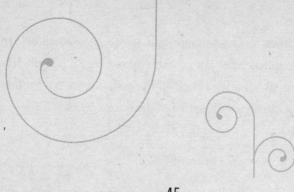

45

The Question

"Hello, young man," Mr. Danker says. He reaches out to shake Justin's hand. "And hello, Danielle."

It feels good to have my days as "Young Lady" behind me.

"We'll go into my office, Justin," Mr. Danker says.

I have never seen the inside of Mr. Danker's office.

"And Danielle, Clarice is in the kitchen."

It looks like I won't be seeing the inside of his office today, either.

Mrs. Danker doesn't even say hello, or my name; she just reaches for my hands, and brings me to the living room.

"I'm glad you came," she says finally, once we're seated.

Whereupon I burst into tears, which is not what I had in mind at all. Mrs. Danker moves over to where I am on the sofa and puts her arm around me. That she should be comforting me is more than pathetic.

"I'm sorry," I say.

Whereupon she bursts into tears, and we cry together for a while.

"Tissues," she says, getting up to run to the kitchen. She brings back a box of them. We blow our noses in unison.

It's December 14. In three days, Humphrey would have had his sixth birthday. I can feel that fact pressing down on us as Mrs. Danker and I sit there in the grown-up room.

"We practiced," I say.

She gives me a questioning look.

"We practiced five months ahead of time for December seventeenth, so that if he got disappointing presents, he would still be able to say a nice thank-you. He was so funny about it. But serious at the same time."

"He did love his presents," Mrs. Danker says. "He did love his birthday."

"I wondered whether he felt shortchanged because his birthday was so near Christmas and he didn't get a whole month just for himself."

Mrs. Danker shakes her head. "I think he considered Christmas really just a continuation of his birthday." She laughs. "Just the whole world celebrating him."

I can see that. I can see Humphrey enjoying the extravagance of that thought, but also knowing, in his heart and mind, that it was fantasy.

"I'm so sorry," I say.

"I know," Mrs. Danker says.

"I'm so sorry about Humphrey. And I'm so sorry about you, and the cancer, and Humphrey."

She tilts her head in an inquiring way.

"You had to have cancer for nothing," I blurt out. I hear how stupid that sounds, so I try to fix it. "I don't mean that people have cancer for *something*. Just . . ."

I'm in some kind of verbal corner.

"Where did you—? Oh. That Doris Raskin," Mrs. Danker says. She rolls her eyes. "I know she means well." I find some people use this expression when they're holding their noses about someone. I don't correct Mrs. Danker's impression that it was Mrs. Raskin who told me about her cancer history.

"It wasn't for nothing," Mrs. Danker says. "Having Humphrey for five and a half years was not for nothing."

Yeah, no.

"Tell me, Danielle," Mrs. Danker says. "Tell me about Humphrey and you."

She sits across from me in a chair.

"I hope you know he loved having you in his life."

Her hazel eyes are softly inviting.

"What was his last day like?"

Finally. The question I've been waiting for. From the person I've been wanting to hear it from, although I didn't know that until just this second.

46

I'M FOR HUMPHREY

"'S up, Humpty?" I asked.

Humphrey looked up at the ceiling. "The lightbulbs," he said.

"Ha!"

"A spiderweb," he added.

"Really?" I said.

Humphrey pointed to a corner of the kitchen.

"Hmm," I said. "A cobweb."

"A spiderweb," Humphrey said.

"Whatever." I rolled a newspaper into a baton and took a swipe. The ceiling was higher than I thought. "Be my spotter, Humphrey," I said, moving a chair from the kitchen table to a point beneath the cobweb.

"Huh?"

"'Huh?'" I mimicked him, but not in a mean way. "Make sure the chair stays put while I'm standing on it," I said. "So I don't fall. That's being my spotter."

Standing on the chair, I swatted down the cobweb.

"Mission accomplished," I said. "Now what?"

"Dinner?" said Humphrey.

It was only four thirty, and Humphrey usually ate at six. But he was hungry, so why not?

"This way," Humphrey said twenty minutes later as he dug his spoon into SpaghettiOs, "we won't have to come in for dinner. We'll be able to play and play and play and play. We'll play until . . . until . . . we'll play until . . ."

"The first star?" I prompted.

"Until the first star and also . . . until . . ."

"You throw a perfect spiral?" I said.

"Until the first star and a perfect spiral and . . ."

"Until you want dessert?" I tried.

"Until the first star and a spiral and I want dessert and until . . ."

"It's almost bedtime?"

"Until the first star and a spiral and dessert and bedtime and until . . . we explode!"

"Until we explode!" I said. "Now that's really something to look forward to."

After finishing his SpaghettiOs and chicken tenders, Humphrey decided he preferred to have dessert immediately—one less reason to come in from playing a single second earlier than absolutely necessary.

"Berry or orange?" I asked, peering into the freezer at the juice pops.

"Borange," Humphrey said.

I chose berry for Humphrey, and took orange for myself. A Popsicle-chewer, rather than a Popsicle-sucker, Humphrey was done in three minutes.

"Can I have an orange one now?" he asked.

"One Popsicle," I said.

"But I didn't really want the berry one," he said. "I wanted borange, remember? You only gave me the berry part. Now I need the orange part."

"You just ate dessert, Humphrey," I said.

"Sometimes I get Second Dessert," Humphrey reminded me.

"Right. When First Dessert is a piece of fruit. You just ate a whole Popsicle."

"A fruit juice pop," Humphrey corrected me. "It's healthy."

I sucked on my own orange fruit juice pop. "This discussion is over."

"Maybe later," Humphrey said.

By five thirty we were heading out the door. "To the park, right?" I confirmed.

"Yup."

"Then what're you waiting for? Come on, slowpoke!" I ran to the end of the driveway.

"You're the slowpoke!" cried Humphrey, catching up to me and passing me. He made it to the front yard of the next-door neighbor, when I called to him.

"Hold on, Humphrey," I said. "I forgot something. It's kind of important to our mission tonight." I keyed in the code to the garage and ducked in as the door was opening. "Now we can go," I said.

"Throw it!" Humphrey said, seeing the football I had retrieved.

I looked up and down the street before I let it fly.

"Kind of wobbly!" I called out.

"Perfect!" Humphrey yelled at the same time, because he caught it.

Humphrey kept sprinting ahead as we walked along Franklin Avenue.

"I told you you're the slowpoke!" he called over his shoulder.

"You need to wait for me," I said. "When we make the turn on Quarry Road, we have to walk together."

"I know," said Humphrey. He waited.

Some kids passed us on Franklin, walking in the opposite direction.

"Hey," they said.

"Hello," I said.

"Hey," said Humphrey in that special not-little-boy voice he reserved for interactions like this one, with older kids.

They looked familiar to me, although I didn't really know them. They were a few years younger than me. Probably going to the pool, farther back in the neighborhood, to one of the Friday night cookouts they had to attract kids.

"Hay is for horses," Humphrey said when the kids were out of earshot. "That's what my father says when I say 'hey.'"

"Hay is for haystacks," I said. "Haystacks are for needles. Needles are for sewing."

"What?" Humphrey said, delight at this new game breaking out all over his face.

"Sewing is for buttons. Buttons are for—"

"Clickers!" Humphrey said.

"Good one, Humphrey," I said. "I wouldn't have thought of that."

"More!" Humphrey said.

"Clickers are for televisions. Televisions are for—"

"Cartoons!" Humphrey said. "Cartoons are for kids. Kids are for playing. Playing is for fun. Fun is for Humphrey. Humphrey is for Danielle. Danielle is for—"

He had run out of steam. "What are you for, Danielle?"

"I'm for you, Humphrey," I said.

I hadn't played the game in ages. Adrian made it up; at least, I thought he did. One day, as we sat at the kitchen table working on homework, he started tapping the eraser end of his pencil on the table. He picked up another pencil and got a rhythm going. This was before he actually took up drums. Mom was making dinner—so it must have been a Sunday. Adrian was in fifth grade. "Pencils are for writing," she said.

He kept tapping. "I know," he said. "Pencils are for writing.

Writing is for letters. Letters are for alphabets. Alphabets are for languages. Languages are for words. Words are for songs. Songs are for singing. Singing is for listening. Listening is for music. Music is for rhythm. Rhythm is for drums. Drums are for tapping. Tapping is for pencils. And pencils are for writing."

"Now go ahead and put that kind of genius into your homework, Adrian," Mom said. "And I'll be thrilled."

But homework didn't really call for that kind of genius. So it just remained Adrian's game, which he and I played to pass time on car trips, as we sat in the backseat, or just to fend off boredom. The idea was to get back to the original statement, whatever it was. Pencils are for writing. Hay is for haystacks. Or not. It was fine just to blab on for a while.

"Now why don't you give me the ball while we're walking on this street. I don't want it to accidentally pop out of your hands."

"I won't drop it, Danielle," Humphrey said. "I can carry it."

When we reached the park, Humphrey made a break for the playground.

"Hurry to the spaceship!" he called. "It's about to take off!"

I ran the rest of the way up the hill to the scrubby little playground. I mean, I wouldn't want to miss takeoff. I didn't remind Humphrey that since I was the spaceship's rocket fuel—I'm the one who always sent the roundabout spinning before jumping on—it wasn't taking off until I got there.

And . . . we were there. Humphrey waited until the round-about came to a complete stop before carefully stepping off.

"I always have to get used to the zero-gravity conditions on Thrumble-Boo," he said.

Today Thrumble-Boo had zero-gravity conditions? Okay. He picked up and put down his feet in big, exaggerated steps, and I followed his lead.

"We're back, Bumble-Boos," he said. He climbed on top of the faded blue bumblebee. He really was almost too big for these springy ride-on critters, something that I hadn't noticed before.

"We come in peace," I said, copying Humphrey's usual greeting.

"They know that by now," he said, and bounced around on the bumblebee for a while.

"I just realized something," Humphrey said.

"What's that?"

"You know how we always say they're aliens?"

"Friendly aliens," I said.

"Yeah. But we're on their planet. We're on Thrumble-Boo. On Thrumble-Boo, *we're* the aliens, not them. We're aliens!"

"*Baah*, we're aliens!" I clowned. "With our weird . . . what's this?" I touched my head. "Hair! *Aagh*! Alien hair! And our scary—look at this!" I held out my hand. "Long bony things. *Aah*! Fingers!"

"But we're not invading their planet," Humphrey said. "So we're friendly aliens, too."

I agreed. After we climbed around on the mountain—also known as the jungle gym—we went back to the spaceship and spun our way back to Earth.

"Football?" I asked.

In answer, Humphrey grabbed the football off the ground and ran as if going out for a pass.

"Look, I caught it!" he said once he was about twenty-five feet away.

Ha. Ha.

He threw the ball back to me, a wobbly, sideways effort that fell a few feet short. We played catch—our version of catch, in which I threw a variety of types of passes and he tried to catch them and run them back to me. At this point in the summer, he caught a lot more than he missed. And after weeks of throwing, my passes were nearly all perfect tight spirals.

"Okay." He panted, running a long pass back to me. "Time to practice throwing."

I don't know why it was so hard for him. He was a little guy, but his hands were like puppy paws: big for his age. He tried, throw after throw. You've never seen such a wobbly football. Earlier in the summer, I actually thought maybe it was the ball, so I brought one from home, one of Adrian's. Nope. Wobble wobble, no matter which ball we used.

I adjusted his fingers on the ball, first one way, then another. Wobble wobble. I suggested pretending different things: Pretend you're launching a rocket. Pretend there's nothing in your hand. Pretend there's a hot potato in your hand.

I really didn't know what I was doing.

"Humphrey," I said, "I am not a football expert. We are going to have to get your instruction from someone who knows what they're talking about."

He plopped down on the grass. "A little more," he said, and stood up. "I'm going to throw—to throw *myself* in the air." He attempted another throw.

Less wobbly. A lot less wobbly.

"What'd you do there, Humphrey?" I asked.

"I threw *myself* into the ball," he said.

He did. All this time, he'd been throwing only with his arm. Now he put his whole self behind it, and the throw was much stronger. This must be Throwing 101, but football is not my subject.

"Do that again," I said. "Really put your body into it. Make your shoulders part of your arms. And step into it, like you're walking toward me."

He threw a spiral. Not real tight, not perfect, but a spiral.

"I did it!" Humphrey yelled.

"Do it again!"

A spiral. And another. One imperfect but very nice spiral after another.

"I did it!" He was practically dancing. No, he was totally dancing. I joined him.

"Congratulations, Humphrey!" I said.

"This is the greatest day of my life!"

We threw some more, and he didn't lose his newly discovered

touch. Then we played our Marco Polo–like Thrumble-Bumble game.

"Oh! Humphrey!" I said. "I need to check the time."

It was 7:10. The first star that night, I had found out from some star-tracking website, was going to be Venus—low in the western sky, even before the sun set.

"Okay, now don't look at the sun," I said.

"It could burn your eyes out of your head," Humphrey said.

"Something like that."

We stood and stared at the sky.

"A UFO!" Humphrey exclaimed. "I see a UFO!"

No. That UFO was Venus. And only Venus. The first star tonight.

"Yes!" Humphrey shrieked. He looked at Venus steadily, wanting to make sure, I think, that it was actually hanging still in the sky and wasn't a UFO. Then he surveyed the skies; there were no other stars out.

"Now I've seen the very first star," Humphrey said. "This is the greatest day of my life."

"I thought it already was," I reminded him. "Or are you already all ho-hum about throwing spirals?"

"No. It's double-great now."

We needed to start walking home.

Right before the path into the park meets the shoulder of Quarry Road, Humphrey squealed.

"Look!" He pointed.

A frog.

"I love them," Humphrey said.

He approached the frog carefully and knelt down. He was completely entranced.

I didn't get what there was to love about a frog.

"Did you ever touch a frog's belly?" he asked me.

"Um. Not recently."

His hand darted out, and he was holding the frog.

"Touch," he said. "Underneath."

It was soft. Soft and smooth and vulnerable. It made me think of Humphrey's chest when he got run over by the bicycle.

"Isn't it so, so, so soft?" he whispered. "It almost gives me tears."

"Almost," I said.

"Now it's the *triple*-greatest day of my life," he said.

"A trifecta," I said.

"Yup," he said. "It's a trifecta."

I can't imagine that he knew that word, but he didn't really need to. He caught my drift.

"A try-my-pie-die-why-bye-bye-*fecta*!" he said.

He pretty much always did catch my drift.

"Yup, it's the greatest trifecta of my life," he said.

Humphrey gently set the frog down. Then we set out for home, and Second Dessert.

A Note from the Author

Imperfect Spiral is woven mostly around themes concerning friendship, fear, courage, connection, and heartbreak. There's also a thread relating to immigration—a topic that claims a special place in my heart and life, probably because I'm the daughter of a refugee whose family struggled to gain entry to the United States in the face of restrictive immigration rules.

Meigs County, the setting of this book, is a fictional place. Fictional, too, are the proposed county and state laws targeting undocumented (or "illegal") immigrants that the story mentions. However, some states and communities have adopted laws like these in an effort to push out undocumented immigrants. Such laws might order local police to check the immigration status of people they stop, or deny driver's licenses to undocumented immigrants. The U.S. Supreme Court has weighed in on the question of what actions states are allowed to take, but the answer to this question continues to evolve.

At the broader national level, policies on illegal immigration are also always evolving. The usual tools for addressing the issue include control of the nation's borders, arresting and deporting undocumented immigrants, and punishing U.S. companies that hire them. On a few extraordinary occasions, the national government has also taken a very different approach, offering some undocumented immigrants a reprieve from the threat of deportation and a chance at citizenship. The favored groups have included farm workers, immigrants who were in the United States for a certain period of time or as of a certain date, and young adults who had been brought to the United States as children. This happened during the administration of President Ronald Reagan and also during President Barack Obama's administration. *Imperfect Spiral*, however, reflects the far more typical situation for undocumented immigrants, in which there is no special program to help them.

Illegal immigration is a topic that often incites heated discussion. Reasonable people can disagree about the issues. I'm always hopeful that those who formulate immigration policy, as well as those who simply debate it, are mindful that it's *people* we're talking about here—even if the immigration laws insist on referring to anyone who isn't a citizen or a national of the United States as an "alien."

Please visit my website, www.debbielevybooks.com, for links to places where you can read more about immigration issues.

ACKNOWLEDGMENTS

Writing is a solitary endeavor, but making a book takes collaborators, and I'm grateful for mine. Many thanks to Caryn Wiseman for loving Danielle and Humphrey and launching them into the publishing world; Stacy Cantor Abrams for receiving this story so warmly; and Mary Kate Castellani for fearless yet sensitive editing. Pam Bachorz, Adam Meyer, Deborah Schaumberg, and Jon Skovron gave me writerly encouragement in the important early stages, for which I thank them. Finally, loving thanks to Rick Hoffman and Ben Hoffman for reading many drafts of this book—but, if they are to be believed, and I choose to believe them, never too many for them.